THE SOUL'S AGENT

by

WENDY KNIGHT

The Soul's Agent
by Wendy Knight

THE SOUL'S AGENT

ISBN 13: 978-1517240813
ISBN: 1517240816
Cover Art Designed by P.S. Cover Design

CHAPTER ONE

Navi

NO GHOSTS. NO ATTACKS. NOTHING AT all. So what was up with my heart?

"Bad heart." I blotted my sweaty hands on my jeans. "Don't explode out of my chest and I'll buy you Cheerios for lunch. Deal?"

This was a regular thing—having conversations with my heart.

Did that make me crazy?

Probably.

But it was necessary. For one thing, I have important work to do, work that requires a strong heart, so I have to tell it to keep beating and keep fighting because I kind of need it. For another, I'm still in love with a guy that I haven't seen or talked to in years. I spend half my time telling my heart to forget about him, and the other half trying to convince my heart that we are in love with whatever guy we're dating at the time.

My heart doesn't listen. If it pounded any harder, it would break a rib. That would be hard to explain.

It had been four years. Four years since we broke up. "Seriously, heart? Pounding just because his truck is in the parking lot across from ours is ridiculous. I would like it to stop. Yes. He's close." I pressed a hand to my chest. "Now quit, already!"

Realizing my potentially fatal mistake, I quickly corrected myself. "Calm down. Please don't quit." Good *grief,* that was a close one.

I sat in the parking lot of the veterinary office, waiting for my roommate to get off work so we could go home. I could just see Alec's truck parked in front of the electrical company he'd worked for since we'd been together. Right there. So close, yet unreachable. "Why oh why did you have to work in the same business center as he does, Konstanz?"

She tapped on my window just then and I jumped guiltily, almost throwing myself through the roof. "Hey Navi." I could see the smirk she tried to hide, but she politely refrained from commenting. Instead she slid into the car. "Did you have to wait long?"

"Nope. Just a minute or so. How was work?" I turned the car on, backed up, and drove slowly through the parking lot, trying really hard not to look toward the electrical company's building.

I should have tried really hard to watch who I was about to cut off.

I saw the big truck out of my peripheral vision and slammed on my brakes, squealing nearly as loud as my tires. "Sorry! Sorry!" I squeaked, waving my hands around like that would convey my message better.

"Um, Navi?" Konstanz asked quietly.

I blinked at her and looked at the truck. Alec's truck. He stared at me with his mouth hanging open, probably wondering how the girl he'd taught to drive had nearly killed him in a parking lot. *Karma, buddy.*

Ever so grateful that he couldn't see my fierce blush through the glare of the windshield, I forced a cheerful wave and slammed my foot down on the gas pedal. My jeep rocketed forward and we escaped onto the road.

"Well. That was awkward," Konstanz said with no trace of hysterical laughter at all. I glanced at her out of the corner of my eye. Clearly, it was a fight for her to keep that solemn look on her face.

Konstanz and I shared a room in our two-bedroom apartment. There were two other girls who shared with us, which seemed to be the life of a college student. I hadn't been there long, since I'd only returned to Oregon a few months ago.

Her phone buzzed, and already frazzled I nearly drove us off the road. This time she lost her battle and started giggling. I glanced in the rearview mirror, wondering if whoever was behind me might report me for drunk driving.

Alec's truck followed several car lengths behind. "Holy Hannah. Could this get any less fun?" I moaned as Konstanz answered her phone.

"Reese wants to know if we want to go to open mic night tonight. You up to singing?"

Why was he following me? What if he followed me home? What would I say? We hadn't parted on the best of terms. In fact, we had been bitter enemies for the rest of high school. Ironic, wasn't it, that I was still in love with him?

Yes. Yes it was.

It took me several seconds to realize she was talking, and several more to figure out what she was saying. "Umm. Yeah." I shook my head, trying to get Alec *out* of it. "Yeah, I can sing. I have homework but I'll work really hard so I can go." I flashed her an apologetic smile, because she'd known me long enough to know why she only had half my attention. And she loved me anyway.

I turned at the light, flying through the yellow when I realized that he would pull right up next to me in the outside lane if I didn't. Crisis averted.

"You should just talk to him. Realize he isn't the Greek god you remember him to be and he'll be out of your system." Konstanz watched him in her side mirror as I sped away.

"I don't want to talk to him. Or see him every time I turn around, or anything. I just want to forget him completely. Why don't they make a potion for that?"

"Did you think about him when you were in Alaska or is it just because he's so close now?"

Every day. "Sometimes," I lied.

"OKAY LADIES! LET'S SEE what you're wearing. If you're gonna dress like grandmas, you don't get to go," Reese yelled from the living room, clapping her hands like some twisted, diabolical gym coach.

"Your grandma dresses better than I do," I muttered, twisting my scarf around my neck. I grabbed my stiletto boots – five inch heels and all black, and scuttled out to the living room, plopping myself on the couch to tug my boots over my jeans.

"Navi passes, no surprise there. You gonna pull that long hair of yours up or leave it down?"

I had planned on leaving my dark hair down, so I could hide behind it if I did something embarrassing—which was entirely possible. Apparently, though, that wasn't what Reese had in mind. With a sigh, I pulled it up into a ponytail.

"Konstanz! Where are you?" One day, Reese would be the highly successful CEO of a huge company, of that I was sure. Right now, she put her organizational skills to use keeping us in line. "Terrie! Konstanz! You girls in or out?" Reese bellowed like an infuriated gorilla.

Konstanz brushed by her. "Seriously Reese, we're two steps away. Could you not scream like a banshee?"

Reese opened and closed her mouth but no matter how long she'd known Konstanz, she never got used to the back talk. It was an endless source of entertainment for me.

Terrie didn't even make it all the way into the living room before Reese caught her. "No, Terrie. Go change." Reese spun away from Konstanz, facing the hall, and pointed sternly. I tried not to giggle, zipping up my boots. To be fair, getting four girls ready to go in a reasonable amount of time was a daunting task for anyone. Reese had my respect.

Terrie came in, glaring at Reese. "Will this do, your highness?"

Reese eyed her outfit, all bright colors and clashing prints. "At least it leaves something to the imagination." She whirled on the rest of us. "Let's move it."

We obediently filed out. Terrie had the big SUV, but Reese drove it. Konstanz and I piled in the back. "How come you got to leave your hair down?" I whispered.

Her brown waves fell around her face, and her light brown eyes crinkled when she winked at me. "Reese has given up telling me what to do." With a grin, she reached up and pulled my elastic out, fluffing my dark hair around my face. "That's better."

I quirked an eyebrow at her but said nothing.

The karaoke club was on the coast, about ten minutes from home. By the time we got there, Konstanz was bouncing nervously in her seat, and I was grateful the seat belt kept her securely fastened or there was a chance she'd bounce herself right out the window. I'd grown up on stages, singing since I was little. This was no big deal to me, but Konstanz had stage fright big time. Which explained why she was so determined to do it every chance she got. My best friend was big on facing her fears.

"We'll be fine, girl. Don't stress," I murmured as we climbed out of the back seat. I didn't want the others to hear. Terrie would make fun of her, because Terrie fed off other people's fears, and Reese would just order her to get over it and that would be that.

"I'm not feeling particularly brave tonight. Maybe you guys should go on without me." Konstanz's face was pale except for the two bright pink spots on her cheeks.

I put my arm around her shoulder and led her inside. "You got this. Ain't no thing!"

She rolled her eyes but couldn't help but chuckle. I'm adorable that way. "Tell you what. I'll make you a deal."

I paused, frowning suspiciously. "What is this deal you speak of?"

Sliding out from under my arm so I wasn't as aware of her shaking like a small dog in a hurricane, she said, "I'll go on stage tonight with the rest of you, if—"

"If. There's always an *if* with you," I muttered, crossing my arms over my chest and waiting. I thought about tapping my foot but it's hard to do in stilettos.

A wicked smile broke across her pretty features. "*If* you give your number to at least three guys tonight."

I heaved a monumental sigh. "Seriously, K? Haven't we realized how bad guys are for me? I don't get over them, remember?"

Since we were standing outside in the parking lot by ourselves and it was dark and cold, Konstanz grabbed my wrist and led (or dragged, depending on who you asked) me inside. I let her, but I did lean back just a bit, so she'd know I wasn't cooperating completely.

"I signed us up to sing the next set," Reese yelled over the music. She'd found us a table, and I wasn't surprised that it happened to be right next to a group of hot guys. Nice. Maybe my new boots would finally get the attention they deserved. I walked past them, slowly. I wasn't Konstanz. Or Reese. I didn't turn heads or stop guys in their tracks. But the boots?

They did.

Konstanz snickered as I settled next to her, letting my feet dangle because even with five inch stilettos, I couldn't reach the floor. What exactly was the point of these raised tables that bars and clubs seemed to be so fond of? I'm not a drinker, but I've hung out with enough of them to know that tall chairs and alcohol do not mix. Although it is pretty good entertainment for those of us not intoxicated.

"Whatcha thinking, beautiful?" a cool male voice said next to my ear.

"I'm thinking it's pretty blasted creepy when someone whispers into my hair and I've never even been introduced," I snapped as I spun on him, nearly knocking him over.

He had a nice smile. His eyes were pretty —sort of an ice blue. If I weren't still head over heels in love with my stupid ex, I might be interested. But… eh. I wasn't. Dang heart.

Apparently he couldn't read my thoughts. His grin widened and he held out a hand. "Bryson."

I frowned, considering him. Konstanz nudged me, none to gently, in the back. "You want me on stage tonight?" she hissed through what I could only imagine were clenched teeth.

I shook his hand. "Navi."

He glanced down at my off-the-shoulder blouse. "Fitting."

"My name is fitting because I wore a navy blue shirt? I don't dress to coordinate with my name."

Instead of being insulted like I'd attempted, he leaned back and laughed, holding up his hands in surrender. "Can I buy you a drink?"

"She doesn't drink. But I do. Hendricks Ellison." Terrie somehow managed to fit herself between us, and I leaned back, watching in amusement.

Bryson handled it easily, nodding at a passing waiter like it'd been his intent all along. "Hendricks Ellison for the blonde, and…" he paused, raising an eyebrow at me.

"Pepsi. No ice," I finished. "And my gorgeous friend Konstanz will have water *with* ice, please."

Bryson leaned around me. "Just water? Not even caffeine?" he teased.

"Trust me, I'm jittery enough without the added sugar."

On cue, Reese bellowed from the stage.

"That's our fearless leader." I stood up, grabbing Konstanz' hand. "Watch our table for us?" I batted my eyelashes. It was a good table. I didn't want to lose it.

"Of course." He settled into my seat, leaning back and planting a foot on the one next to him. There were low cheers from his friends at the next table; like we were playing football and he'd just had a good run. *Trust me boys, he doesn't have a snowball's chance.* Cocky and arrogant were definitely not my type.

I marched up the stage steps, holding tight to Konstanz so she wouldn't attempt to flee. I prayed, quickly and fervently, that Reese had picked anything other than songs spelling out words about demanding high regard from one's mate. Because *that* hadn't been overdone at all. Luckily, she hadn't. It was a popular, new song that I knew the words to. It was suddenly clear to me why Reese had been blasting this song non-stop all week long. She'd been practicing and subliminally implanting the words into our brains so we'd be ready for tonight.

I'd grown up singing in front of people. I felt safe on stage; confident. Here, I knew what I was doing. The music started and I closed my eyes, feeling the song pour into my blood and swirl through my veins, waking me from the inside.

The first note was my favorite. I was small. Pretty ordinary. People didn't fall in love with me and never get over me for years and years. But my voice, it was something people didn't forget.

And when I opened my mouth, it shocked the crowd into silence. *That* was why I agreed to come to karaoke nights.

The song ended and the crowd applauded. They yelled for more and Konstanz fled the stage, cheeks red but *proud* of herself for facing her fears. Reese yelled that we were done for a while and we followed Konstanz.

"That was... incredible. I've never heard someone sing like that before." Ah, Bryson. He'd guarded our table so well.

"Thank you." I smiled, pulling him to his feet so I could steal his chair—which was rightfully mine. His hand held onto mine until I untangled my fingers, and I gritted my teeth. Definitely not my type. My type was tall, lanky. Gorgeous. Bryson had blue eyes but they were too light. And his face was too open, too friendly. He looked like he worked in an office. I liked... *electricians*. Sighing, I realized what I was doing. I was comparing him to Alec. I compared everyone to Alec. Was Alec here, wanting to talk to me? No. Had Alec wanted anything to do with me in the last four years? No. Angry at myself, I turned the force of my smile on Bryson. "Thanks for saving our table. You guys should come on over." I waved at his friends. Bryson's face lit up like I'd just given him a pony, and he spun away, dragging their table over to ours.

"Good girl," Konstanz whispered with a wink.

I pulled a face.

Bryson slid his chair right up next to mine and introduced me to his four friends, whose names I would never remember because I'm completely awful with names unless they're stapled to someone's forehead. I was pondering whether or not anyone would let me do just that when Bryson leaned closer. "You're the most gorgeous girl in this entire place. You know that, right?"

I raised an eyebrow. "How much have you had to drink tonight?"

He laughed, leaning back. "Nothing. I'm driving tonight."

I twitched my lips to the side, considering him. "Are you sure?"

"Positive." His grin widened. "So. Pretty thing like you must have a boyfriend, right?" He watched me with those ice-blue eyes and I looked, panicked, to Konstanz for help. She was talking to one of Bryson's friends and completely missing my drama. I swallowed hard, looking back into the light blue eyes and easy, too-white smile.

"I work a lot. That's my focus right now. Not finding male attention."

"Oh yeah?" He smiled but his eyes said he didn't believe me. "What do you do?" He reached for his drink, which apparently contained no alcohol but sure looked like it did, and raised it to his lips.

Hmmm. How to answer that one. "It's… complicated. I'm sort of in the probation officer line of work."

His eyebrows shot up as he sputtered and coughed. "You? You're…"

More powerful than you'll ever know, buddy. Yeah, okay I was five foot two and barely weighed a hundred pounds. I didn't look tough at all. But all I needed was my voice and some very desperate souls to do my bidding. Trust me on this one.

"What do you do?" I asked sweetly, steering the conversation away from his assumption that small girls were helpless, and back toward him.

He coughed once more, for effect mostly, I'm sure. "I'm a loan officer."

"Sounds fascinating." I tried to look interested. "Do you

like it?"

"Yeah. I get to help a lot of people achieve their dreams and I don't have to be out in the elements. One of my roommates is in construction and he's outside, rain or shine or snow or wind. He comes home either freezing or sunburned."

Yeah. That was the kind of guy I liked. Stupid Alec, finding his way into my thoughts again. "That must… suck."

"Hey, do you wanna dance? I happen to be an amazing dancer." He grinned again. He *did* have a nice smile. I could see that Terrie was swooning from across the table. I'm sure there were lots of girls who thought he was hot. But I just… didn't. Stupid Alec. Again.

"I'm sorry. I can't dance."

"C'mon. I'll lead. All you have to do is follow me and move your hips." He winked and I felt my cheeks go bright pink. Holy snowballs was I an adult or a giggling teenager?

He raised an eyebrow suggestively and I'm sure my cheeks went pinker. Clearly, I was still a teenager despite my birth certificate saying I was twenty-two. I cleared my throat. "No, seriously. I dance like a wounded goose. But Terrie!" I grabbed my roommate and practically shoved her in Bryson's lap. "Terrie would love to dance with you!" Clearly unsure what to do with this startling new predicament, Bryson led Terrie out to the dance floor. I sat back in my chair with a sigh of relief.

And felt the hair stand up on the back of my neck. My hair is super thick. So the tiny little hairs? I feel them when they rise to attention. It could only mean one thing.

I scanned the room, biting my lip when at first I didn't find what I was looking for. It took me sweeping the entire club twice before I saw her, standing by the door. One of my parolees, Elizabeth, stood nervously, alternatively wringing her hands and motioning me frantically. Every so often, someone would come in the door and walk right through her.

Good thing she wasn't paying attention.

I glanced at Konstanz. "Work is calling. I gotta go." I slid to my feet, wondering how fun it was going to be fighting in my favorite boots.

Konstanz frowned. "You work too much. When are you gonna sleep, girl?"

I grinned as I backed away. "I'll sleep when I'm dead!" Hopefully. Hopefully I'll sleep when I'm dead. Unless I screw up and spend the afterlife in prison. Or, unless I don't screw up so bad, but just bad enough, and I spend the next several years of my unlivingness being someone's parolee.

I hurried past Elizabeth, meeting her translucent eyes once, before escaping out the door and into the fresh air. "What's wrong?" I asked.

I hid in the shadows, blending like I'd been trained to do and speaking low so no one could see me talking to myself. Because they wouldn't see Elizabeth. No, the only one who could see Elizabeth was me.

Because Elizabeth is a ghost.

CHAPTER TWO

Navi

"THERE ARE REPORTS OF ACTIVITY ON the coast. I think the asuwangs are hungry." Elizabeth spoke with an accent I had never been able to place. I had no idea when she'd died, only that she'd joined my army several years ago. Apparently, she'd gotten a good look at hell and decided it wasn't where she wanted to spend the rest of her life. Funny how a glimpse of fire and brimstone will do that to a ghost. She'd made some bad decisions while still alive. Not enough to send her straight to hell, but enough that she was eligible for my probation program.

"Okay. Can you gather the others? I'll meet you there." I could already feel it pulling me—the call to protect. It was in my blood, tugging me toward danger when others ran away from it. Frustratingly, I could only fight at night. My ghosts could only come out at night. Luckily, demons only liked to play at night, too. On the bright side, it left me daytimes to have a real life.

"I will." Elizabeth nodded and faded into the shadows.

I started to follow, when a voice caught me from behind. Resisting the urge to swear, I dragged myself back and turned, plastering on a fake smile. "Bryson."

"Hey. You didn't say goodbye." Was that a flirtatious smile he was giving me? Did he not realize how dangerous the situation could become if I didn't get to the coast and stop the asuwangs before they escaped into town? No, of course he didn't. Because I was *very* good at my job. No one here had ever heard of asuwangs. Or believed demons were real.

"Sorry. Work calling. I gotta go." I hiked my jacket collar up like I was cold, and hoped he didn't notice that I'd come in a car with other girls who were all still inside.

"I didn't get your number."

I stopped, staring at him in confusion. "I didn't give you my number."

His smile broadened.

"Oh. Right. Konstanz? My friend inside? She's got it. You can get it from her if you'd like. I really, really have to go now." I may or may not have been bouncing like a five-year-old at Christmas.

"Okay. Expect a text from me tomorrow."

"Will do. See ya!" I turned, unable to resist the call any longer, and raced through the parking lot. I let the layers fall away as I ran, so fast that to anyone watching I would be a shadow, a blur in the night.

A ghost.

My swords, which had long, ancient names, unfolded against my back like wings. One, a golok, I had nicknamed Golly, and the other, a kalis, I'd named Kali. It was easier that way, to name them and pretend they were pets and not deadly weapons. I wished so much that I could somehow shed my clothes and have different attire replace them as I ran. My swords appeared out of nowhere, so why couldn't I have battle armor that was resistant to stains also appear out of nowhere?

It was a bit ridiculous to fight in five-inch stiletto boots and an off-the-shoulder navy top. Just sayin'.

The asuwangs could only enter through a rock formation that acted as some sort of gate or doorway between their sea witch's lair and my world. She and her sisters—there are nine of them, could only open the doorways at certain latitudes and longitudes throughout the world, and this was one of those places. It was under water and rose up through the sand of the beach, causing the surf to be wild and dangerous. Thankfully, it also kept most regular, non-fighting-demons-at-night people away from the area and it was hard to get to if you didn't have super speed and mega-high jumping abilities. Unfortunately, it didn't keep the asuwangs *in*. They could climb the rock like creepy giant spiders. Fittingly, the locals had named this place Devil's Gate, because it divided the beach and inside was hollow—that's where I made my first stand. Some say the angels, who are Death's good friends, created the gate when the doorway was first opened, calling up the mountains to help protect the humans. But the rock wasn't enough, so everywhere that a sea witch had a doorway, Death placed an Agent. That's me.

I hit the sand but didn't slow, even when my blasted heels sank and wobbled. Totally rocked the mighty warrior thing—if by rock I meant I looked like a wounded goose. I raced past late-night yoga classes and couples on moonlight strolls and old men walking their dogs. A few of them sensed me, I could tell by the way they would tense or look up. Luckily I was a blur of the imagination or I'd have some weird questions to answer. The closer to Devil's Gate I got, the fewer people I encountered, as if they somehow sensed the danger in the area and stayed away. The huge formation loomed in the distance, stretching bigger and bigger the harder I ran. When I got within leaping distance, I jumped, felt my heels not catch like they were supposed to *because they are stilettos*, and had to scrabble for my grip. I flung myself onto the rocky plateau and tumbled over the other side, landing in a crouch.

My ghosts, all thirty-three, hadn't even waited for me to get there and sing for them—my way of calling them to battle. They also hadn't waited for me to yell, "Fight!" with my swords raised. They were already locked in deadly battle with the asuwangs, which at the moment were in the form of giant, hideous beasts that looked a lot like a cross between dogs and spiders. I stuck my hands on my hips and glared, feeling left out. During the day, asuwangs could be anything. A kitty, a baby, the sweet little old lady neighbor who smiled and waved when I raced off to school. Asuwangs were shape-shifters, but at night, they were forced to return to their roots.

And then I could hunt them.

Many of them didn't change at all. They lived in the ocean and came out at night to feed or capture souls for their sea witch. They especially liked children. As I was also fond of children but in a completely different, not creepy way, I killed them all. The asuwangs, not the children. The children, I protected. And I—

"Navi? Where you planning on fighting with us tonight?" I blinked, watching as Elizabeth materialized in front of me.

Death allowed souls like Elizabeth's, and a million gazillion others, one last chance. Fight with the Agents against demons and darkness and evil, and they won't spend an eternity roasting on a spit. It seems like an easy enough choice, but apparently roasting is easy and requires little effort, and fighting, well…

I looked out across the beach. Fighting is hard.

Fighting is hard, and if the demons escape, I have to submit a report saying my ghosts didn't fight hard *enough*. Sometimes, they get pulled from the project and sent… away.

More often, they work and fight so hard that they save

their own souls.

Then, there is Elizabeth, who was granted freedom to move on, and she didn't. She stays with me and fights, even when she doesn't have to. Actually, I wasn't sure I'd ever heard of it happening before. Elizabeth is a rarity. I'm not allowed to have favorites, but I do anyway. And Elizabeth is definitely one of my favorites.

"Navi?" she prompted.

"Yeah. Yeah, I'm coming. Sorry."

I unsheathed Golly and Kali and sprinted across the sand. I dived after the first creature I came into contact with, swinging my blades together like giant scissors around its neck. I winced, just a little, as the tarry black blood splashed on my favorite navy shirt.

Jesse, one of the newer ghosts, and one I had very little hope for, appeared next to me, pulling the body away to a pile with other rotting asuwang corpses. We would burn them all, when we were done. She didn't fight, but she was really good at dragging dead bodies away. It made me wonder what had gotten her in this situation in the first place.

"Navi!" Elizabeth yelled, flinging her sword end over end through the air. I spun, ducking, as it flew over my head and pierced the dog-thing reaching for my throat. Right in the eye.

"Nice shot!" I yelled. She rolled her eyes and turned back to the fight, her sword materializing back into her hand. These magic swords, they were nice like that.

I whirled, slicing first with Golly and following with Kali, pulling my hands apart and cutting the creature in two. Before it fell, I moved on to the next, and then the next. My ghosts surrounded me, protecting me even though, as a flesh and blood creature, I was more powerful than all of them. I don't know if they did it to make themselves look good or because they're honestly worried about my well-being, but I liked them a lot more if I assumed the latter.

My ghosts all had weapons of their own, similar to mine, and just as deadly despite the semi-transparency of them. Most souls don't have a clue how to fight with these things when they sign up.

By the time they leave, they're unstoppable.

With a scream of defeat, the asuwangs retreated, back into the ocean. Several ghosts followed, but I didn't. I don't like water and I knew how dangerous it would be. Asuwangs easily grab humans and drag them beneath the waves. They've been mistaken for sirens throughout history. They can even take the form of a beautiful woman during the day.

"Did any get by us?" I asked, panting, bent over with my hands on my knees, swords crossed awkwardly in front of me with the ends sticking in the sand. Like I said, I'm an uber-warrior.

"I don't believe so. They are becoming easier to control," Elizabeth said, sheathing her own swords.

"That worries me." I finally stood, sucking in air. Yes, I had more ghosts than I'd ever had before, more willing to fight for their eternal destiny, but seven years ago, battles like this would have lasted hours, not minutes.

"Do you think these are merely a distraction? That they are perhaps planning a bigger attack?" Elizabeth asked, staring off into the ocean.

"Well I do *now.*" I stood up, kicking the sand as I stuck my swords back in their sheath.

"It could also be because the sun will come up soon." Elizabeth nodded toward the horizon in the distance. The first rays breaking over the mountains were lighting the sky.

"Yeah. Let's go with that." I nodded. "Thank you, all, for tonight."" The others joined around us, nodding and murmuring their thanks as well.

For as long as there have been people, there has been a fear of the dark. I've heard mothers tell their children there isn't anything in the dark that isn't there in the light.

They are wrong.

The reason humanity is afraid of the dark is because that's when demons are allowed to play. They can't walk in daylight. No, that's left to the evil humans—or demons who have shifted into evil humans. Luckily, human-shaped or cute-pet-shaped or worm-shaped demons are pretty helpless. Their forms are temporary and they have a hard time using the unfamiliar bodies. Still dangerous, but they tend to hide out until sundown when they can shift back to their lethal/ugly normal forms. Unless they're hunting someone who has seen them. Then? Well then they're just possessed and it's super creepy.

Especially because I can't kill them without my swords.

Ghosts can't come out until the sun goes down, either. And Soul's Agents, like me? We're just normal, boring people until the shadows claim the sky.

And then we aren't.

During the day, I can't run fast. I mean, I run fast, yes. But not so fast I blur the light. I did track for six years. I run *that kind* of fast. But at night, well... I'm nothing but a shadow, as previously mentioned. Even in stilettos. Also, I don't have Golly and Kali during the day. I am pretty good with a regular old gun, and my dad, for my sixteenth birthday, gave me some regular old swords. In a pinch, they'll do, although I haven't had to use them before except for training.

"You should go home before you can't run." Elizabeth moved to touch my shoulder. It felt like an icy breeze as her hand went right through me. I have no idea how long she'd been dead, but by the way she winced, she still wasn't used to the whole ghost thing. My only clue was her clothing—it was colonial, if I had to guess. But she didn't offer information and I didn't ask.

Sometimes, I wished I knew why these souls were on the

brink of eternal damnation.

Most times, not so much.

I nodded, stretching. My shirt was ruined. My jeans might be salvageable. I swore when I saw the black, icky blood spattered all over my boots. There was no saving them. "It's admirable how you fight in such high heels." Elizabeth tried to hide a grin, and I had absolutely no defense, because she was right to laugh. I bet my mama never wore five-inch heels to fight demons.

"Okay then. You guys have a good day. I'll see you soon?" I backed away, waving at the others. Elizabeth gave me a sad smile as she faded into the darkness. Before I could even turn away, the rest were gone. And the sun was up.

I guess I would be walking home.

CHAPTER THREE

Alec

NAVI STOOD ON THE SAND, STARING out at the water. As always, I couldn't take my eyes off her—long dark waves tangled recklessly down her back, her perfect, so-gorgeous-it-hurt profile turned toward me just enough that I could see the shadow of her eyelashes against her cheek. She wore a long black dress with a low back, and my fingers ached to run themselves across the exposed skin. But I didn't. I stayed where I was, several feet away, watching her. Waiting.

I heard the sound before she did. Long before she did. The roar of hooves, pounding across the sand, splashing through the surf. The waves, in response, became wilder, more angry. I turned, slowly, too slowly, toward the horse and rider. Both of them black, like Navi's dress. It took several more seconds before I realized the rider was carrying a broadsword of some sort, the hilt bumping against his horse as they raced down the beach.

Straight at Navi.

"Navi!" I screamed, but she didn't hear me. She still

stared at the ocean, so serene, so content. I tried to race toward her, but there was something in the way, holding me back. Blocking me from her. I could see her, I could hear her breathe, but I didn't exist to her. I screamed anyway.

It did no good. The rider came closer, raised his broadsword. She finally saw him and turned, horror crossing her beautiful face. She tried to run, and I pounded on the invisible wall, keeping me from her. I threw myself against it, felt my shoulder break, my ribs crack. But the wall held firm.

She was fast, but no match for the horse. They caught up to her and the rider grabbed her hair, yanking her off her feet. Her hands struggled to grab his hands, to free herself, but there wasn't time. He swung his broadsword down and it sliced across her stomach. Then he released her hair and she dropped to the ground, curling in on herself, facing toward me. The horse reared once, and they were gone, racing back the way they came.

"Navi!" I screamed again, throwing myself at the barrier between us. She sobbed, clutching her stomach, and I could see the blood staining the sand.

"Help me," she whispered, reaching, seeming to reach for me, and I redoubled my efforts, but I couldn't get through. No matter what I did, I couldn't get to her.

She died before my eyes.

I swore, flinging myself out of the dream and out of my bed. The blasted blankets tangled around my legs and I collapsed on the floor, swearing more. I *hated* that dream. I'd had it so many times I could play it on repeat forward and backward, start from any given point and watch it clear through, and the ending never changed. I always watched her die.

It had started the night I met her. Years before we were together, long before I started realizing she was going out every single night, even longer before I'd realized she was going out every night to see other guys. It had stopped, briefly, when she'd gone away to college. But my subconscious knew she was back before I did. The dream had started again a few months ago.

And after I'd seen her yesterday, I'd been expecting her in my dreams last night. Hell, she'd been in my head all day long, why leave when I tried to sleep?

Although it would have been nice if she hadn't tortured me with the nightmare. "Just once, Angel, can't we have a dream that isn't bloody and involving your death?" I muttered. And then I was glad no one was around to hear me talk to the girl who had broken my heart four years ago. And who also, coincidentally, wasn't there to answer me.

I blinked at the clock, its red face trying to fry my eyeballs, and groaned. Five a.m., and I had to get up at six. No point trying to sleep now. Heaving myself to my feet, I stumbled to the kitchen, focusing solely on my need for coffee and trying desperately to shove the images from that stupid dream out of my head.

It never worked, but I could try.

I was leaning against the counter, drinking my coffee black and glaring out the window at the rising sun when my roommate stumbled in. "Hey."

He blinked at me. "What are you doing up so late?"

"It's morning, dude."

"Oh." He collapsed on the barstool like being on his feet was a monumental achievement. "You should have come with us last night. I met the hottest girl *ever.*"

I raised my eyebrow at him. "You say that every time you come home. Usually, though, you bring her with you."

He scowled at the counter top. "She left early. Had to work. I got her number though."

"Good for you."

"We're having a party tonight, by the way." Bryson

winced, because he knew how I'd react to that. But I was too tired to yell.

"Fine. Why?"

"So I have a reason to invite her over." I couldn't tell if he was exhausted or drunk, but I glared at him anyway.

"Why don't you just ask her out instead of messing up my apartment?"

"So she came with these girls. She lives with them. Her friend—I forget her name—her friend gave me her number and said she doesn't do the whole dating thing but she does go wherever her friends go. So I invited them all to a party here." He spread his arms wide and grinned like I should congratulate him.

I drank my coffee and went back to glaring out the window.

"You should see this chick, Alec. Dark, dark hair. Her eyes are huge. She's like a tiny doll in six inch heels, and her voice—"

I nearly choked on my coffee. My hand jerked so violently I spilled half the crap in my cup down the front of my bare chest as I swung toward him. "What about her voice?" I growled, ignoring the pain.

"She sings like an angel."

I swore. Again. "Hang on." I shoved past him, slamming my cup down on the counter as I went. I snatched a towel off the oven and wiped scalding coffee off my chest before I dropped it into the hamper in my room. I wished I didn't know exactly where that picture was. I wished I hadn't looked at it just yesterday. But I did, and now I snatched it out of the bedside table drawer and stormed back in to Bryson. "Is this her?"

He took the picture, looking at me before he turned his attention to it. "Yeah. This is her." He handed it back to me. "Why do you have a picture of the love of my life?"

I snarled, jerking it out of his hands. "Because she was the love of my life, once. When I was young and stupid."

"No way. Are you serious? Are you gonna have a problem with this? Because I can find a new apartment…"

I sighed, rubbing the back of my neck and searching for inner peace. "No. I don't care about her anymore. Go ahead."

He peered at me and I decided he must definitely be drunk. "You sure?"

No. "Yeah."

He gave me a lopsided grin. I'd seen girls swoon over that smile, but it just made him look half-paralyzed to me—I didn't have a clue what girls saw in it. "So, you knew who she was from her singing? Does that mean she used to sing when you were together?"

His words hit me hard and pulled me back to when I'd drive her anywhere or everywhere because she absolutely did not want to learn to drive, and she would sing to every song on the radio. It pulled me back to all the times I'd gone with her to competitions and performances and watched her rock the stage like she owned the world. But my favorite, the memories that hurt the most, where of her sitting on my bed, rubbing my shoulders after football practice, singing nursery rhymes under her breath. "Yeah. She sang when I knew her." *She was my own personal angel.*

Unable to take his love-drunk expression anymore, I left to take a shower. This day was going to be just stellar. I could already tell.

But you'll see her tonight. And I hated the fact that my stupid heart leapt at the thought.

BRYSON WASN'T A HORRIBLE roommate. He had weird friends, and I'm not exactly sure he had a job at all because he came and went whenever he felt like it, but he paid the rent and his half of utilities on time. The fact that he was trying to date the one girl in the entire world that I would sell my soul to forget was sort of a mar on his record, though.

That being said, he could pull a party together faster than anyone I'd ever met. By the time I came home from work, the house was stocked with food and music was already blaring on my stereo. "Hey. Do you know what kind of music she listens to?" Bryson asked, his back to me as he thumbed through his CD collection. Most people put it on an iPod now. Not Bryson. He had ten thousand little disc things taking up space in my living room.

"She listens to everything," I mumbled, dropping my keys on the table. "And stop. I'm not your personal Navi consultant. If you want a chance at her, leave me the hell out of it." I opened the fridge, searching for something that would dull the nervous energy trying to swallow me whole, and surveyed his drink selection. "You don't have any Pepsi," I said, standing up. "Only a lot of alcohol. How many people are you inviting?"

"I don't know. About thirty, maybe? There are three of just her and her roommates." He glanced over his shoulder at me. "She was serious about the not drinking thing?"

I shrugged. How should I know? I hadn't talked to her in four years. Not since I'd told her she was a cheating, lying…word… that I don't need to repeat. She'd thrown Pepsi in my face then. I assumed it was still her drink of choice. She had a weird thing about alcohol and anything else that made her sluggish. Trying to get the girl to take cold meds had been a nightmare.

"Hey, maybe you can hook up with one of her friends. She hangs out with some hot girls… and some creepy ones. But whatever." He turned back to his music and I slammed the fridge a little too forcefully. Hanging out with her friends was the last thing I wanted to do. Yeah, let's get an up close and personal show of Navi's life and how she'd moved on with no problem whatsoever.

I was the one who'd been cheated on. Shouldn't she be the one still wallowing?

"I'm getting in the shower," I muttered. So what if this was the second one of the day? Being an electrician was dirty work. I'd spent that afternoon slithering through crawl spaces trying to find dead wires. I was positive there were still spiders crawling through my clothes. I made it halfway across the room before I decided I should definitely bring my drink with me. I jogged to the fridge, grabbed a beer, and went back to the bathroom.

"Party starts in an hour!" Bryson said cheerfully.

I swore as I slammed the door.

SHE WAS LATE. THERE were fifty other people in my small apartment by the time she showed up. I had to work in the morning and was trying to convince myself to go to bed, but my traitorous heart wouldn't give up hope that she would still show up. And for some unfathomable reason, I desperately wanted to see her. Like, I'd chew my foot out of a bear trap to see her.

I hated myself.

I was playing bartender, standing in my kitchen passing out drinks and laughing with Josh at drunk people. He'd been my roommate before Bryson, but decided to up and get married, and his new wife hadn't wanted to share an apartment. Go figure.

And then Konstanz walked through the door. Konstanz was gorgeous. She always had been, and after high school, she was even hotter. There was no mistaking her. And I knew, wherever Konstanz went, Navi would be right behind. My pulse leapt as three, four more girls—not Navi—walked in after Konstanz. Maybe she wasn't coming? I felt my shoulders sag with disappointment, more crushing than I'd been expecting.

And then Navi came through the door.

I'd seen her yesterday. But it was through two windshields and the glare of the afternoon sun. I'd seen her in the nightmares, too, but nothing compared to real life. Her hair was longer and thicker than it had been when I'd seen her last. And Bryson had been right. Her body... made my mouth dry.

She wore boots with heels at least six inches high, putting the top of her head to just above my chin. I watched as she scanned the room and her hand tugged nervously on the end of her red scarf. And then those big, dark eyes settled on me and I watched her suck in a breath through her teeth as pink stained her cheeks.

Oh yeah. She hadn't forgotten me.

I nodded, all cool, and went back to pouring drinks. "Damn. I haven't seen Navi since high school," Josh said, keeping his voice low even though there wasn't a chance she could hear us over the music and the ten thousand people shoved into my living room. "She looks good."

"She went to Alaska after we graduated. I don't know how long she's been back. Bryson's after her now."

"Ouch, dude. That's awkward."

I nodded.

"Alec. It's been a while." Konstanz sidled up to the kitchen counter with a smile, shoving Josh lightly with a bump of her hip.

I smiled. Even after Navi and I had broken up, Konstanz had played mediator. Until she'd suddenly hated me. I still wasn't sure why, but it was nice that she'd forgotten the animosity. That, or she just wanted a drink. "It has. How are ya? What can I get you?"

"Water, no ice. I'm good. How are you?"

"Hi, Konstanz. I'm here, too." Josh waved.

"Oh my gosh, you totally are. I didn't see you there." She grinned and he scowled at her. I turned my back for thirty seconds to grab her a glass, and when I came back, Navi stood next to her, looking immensely uncomfortable.

That made me feel better. A little.

"Navi. I heard you were back from Alaska." I tried to keep my voice cold. Instead, I was forced to wince when it jumped like a kid right before puberty.

"Yeah." Her voice was soft and sweet. It didn't jump at all. She peered up at me through those thick lashes and I couldn't swallow. Or breathe. "Sorry I almost ran into you yesterday."

I meant to be cold and distant. I really did. But I couldn't help the grin because she looked so damn apologetic. "It never has been safe to be on the same road as you." I nodded as her cheeks flamed. "What can I get you?"

"Pepsi?" she asked hopefully. "And I'm a much better driver now. Honest, I am."

Good thing I'd run out last minute to get her a twelve pack. "Yeah… I'm sure you are." I was trying to make her smile. This was not okay. Not okay at all. Why did I want to see her smile?

She opened her mouth to respond but Bryson showed up and I would never get to hear what she was about to say. If he had been any closer to my fist, he'd be missing teeth. Or something less violent. "Navi, right?" he said like he hadn't been running this conversation through his head—and out loud—all day long. "I'm so glad you could make it." He slid his arm around her shoulders, taking the Pepsi I pushed across the counter and handing it to her. Like she couldn't pick it up herself.

"Yeah." She smirked, just a bit, and Bryson wouldn't catch it because he didn't know her well enough but I did and I caught it.

She didn't like him.

Suddenly, I didn't have quite the overwhelming urge to hit him.

"Let me introduce you to everyone. I take it you've met Alec." At my name, she raised those eyes again, and my heart stopped again, and I wanted to kick myself for feeling anything again, and I wanted to kick Bryson for taking her away from me—even if it was just across the room.

"Yeah. We've met," she said with a hint of sarcasm. "Josh, it's good to see you again, too."

"Finally. Someone acknowledges my presence." Josh threw up his hands. Navi grinned at him over her shoulder as Bryson led her away.

"So, you know Bryson?" Konstanz asked. Navi's eyes were dark, almost black. Konstanz had light, friendly brown eyes, but they were trying to read my soul right then, judging by the look she was giving me.

"He's my roommate."

"And…?" She propped her chin on her hand and kept watching me.

"And…" I shook my head, trying not to laugh. "He's a Pisces? What are you looking for here, K?"

She glanced over her shoulder to where Navi was now surrounded by people, looking awesomely uncomfortable. "I don't want her to get hurt again. What's he like? Is he a player? Is he a nice guy?"

"Again?" Josh asked innocently. "Who else has hurt her?" He was my best friend. And the second guy I'd wanted to punch in one day.

Konstanz gave him a Look, so we all clearly knew it was

me. "She cheated on me, K. I didn't hurt her."

She rolled her eyes. "I've known Navi since we were three, Alec. She would never do something like that. And yes. You did hurt her. She left the entire state to try to get away from you."

I felt like someone had poured ice in my veins. "She went to Alaska to get away from *me*? Why? What'd I ever do to her?"

Konstanz sighed. Josh whistled low through his teeth and got off his stool. "This just got way more fun than I wanted to deal with tonight."

"You trashed her reputation. You have no idea what kind of comments she got after you were through with her." Konstanz's eyes narrowed. "Or maybe you do."

I tipped my head back, staring at the ceiling. "This is why you stopped talking to me." Holy shit. Could this be true? How could what Konstanz said have any truth if I had absolutely no idea it had happened? We went to the same school, right?

She crossed her arms over her chest and glared at me and suddenly, those light brown eyes weren't so friendly. From across the room, I felt Navi watching us. Somehow, I always knew when I had her attention. It was like some inner alarm woke up and started screaming the minute those eyes landed on me.

"Konstanz." I leaned over the counter so I was eye level with her, and lowered my voice. "I told one person why we broke up. Just one. I was hurt. I thought Navi was the love of my life. To find out she was spending every freaking night with who knows how many guys—it killed me. But I only told one person."

She couldn't argue with me about the cheating. She'd been with me the few times I'd followed Navi out at night. Because she didn't believe me, otherwise. So I dragged her on night stakeouts for over a week, and we saw Navi go to several different houses. No, Konstanz could hate me for ruining Navi's reputation, but she couldn't say Navi didn't deserve it.

She studied me for several long seconds, until someone who smelled like he'd had way too much to drink already broke between us, slurring while he tried to ask for another beer. I passed him his drink and shooed him on his way, trying to find Navi in the crowd again. Bryson I could see because he was loud and always the center of attention. But not Navi.

"I believe you." She shrugged. "Your breakup was pretty… public… though. But you were an ass for thinking for one second she would do that." I opened my mouth to defend myself, but she cut me off, this five foot nothing girl who looked like she spent her afternoons volunteering for who-knew-what local charity. ""Who'd you tell? Because I'm going to hunt him down and kill him."

"Who are we hunting down?" I jumped when Navi appeared at my shoulder. The smell of her lilac lotion hit me like some big sledgehammer. It was the same lotion she'd worn when we were together. Because I'd given it to her. Lilacs were her favorite flower.

I nearly drowned in memories. That smell. Her hands on my face, running through my hair. Pulling me closer.

"No one," Konstanz said, plastering a sweet smile across her scowl while I struggled for air. "How's the party?"

"Fine." Navi eyed us before holding out her empty Pepsi can. "Recycle bin?"

How could one girl be so damn adorable? I motioned with my head. "Under the sink." Yeah, I'd purposely not taken it from her so she had to slide past me to throw it away herself. So I could feel her skin brushing mine. And so I could protect her from Bryson.

He showed up seconds later. "Damn, Navi, I'm so sorry. I didn't realize you needed a refill." He rubbed the back of his neck like he'd made some huge mistake that she would never get over.

She shook her head, big eyes wide. "No, you're fine. I just needed a breather. Too many people over there."

"Right. You need somewhere quieter? We can head to my room." He grinned, like a cat. I looked, panicked, from Bryson to Navi and back again.

"No. Thanks though. I'm fine." She leaned back against the sink and crossed her arms, planting those six inch heels in my laminate flooring. Feisty little thing. That, I hadn't forgotten, and I fought to hide a grin.

Bryson looked crushed.

"I think they're ready for a genre change." I motioned toward his stereo and the eight gazillion CDs that were currently on display. People were touching them. Touching his precious music. Josh, actually, led them. Which didn't surprise me and made me forgive him for his earlier attempt to cause me problems. As Bryson yelped and hurried across the room, Josh met my eye and I nodded my thanks.

"So my roommate has a thing for you." I turned on her, wanting to see her reaction.

"Your roommate is a player. He has a thing for a lot of girls."

I shook my head, "No he doesn't. It's an act." *There ya go, Bryson. Don't say I never gave you anything.*

Navi watched Bryson wander through the room, being a good little host, and I wanted her to watch me. I wanted those dark eyes on me, not him. She raised a hand to tuck her silky hair behind her ear and for the first time, I noticed the tattoo on her wrist. I caught her arm, tugging her toward me. Her eyes widened and she sucked in a breath, but she took baby steps closer. "This is new," I said.

Her smile shook. "If by new, you mean two years old, then yes. Yes it is."

I twisted her hand around, trying to see it clearly and pretended that the mere touch of her skin didn't send hot waves of electricity pounding through my blood. Some things never change. "What is it?"

She pulled her hand out of my grasp, studying her own tattoo like she'd never seen it before. "It's a phoenix."

I nodded. "Fitting."

She smiled faintly but didn't answer.

"Navi, we can't decide on our next playlist. We need your opinion," Bryson reappeared and I resisted the urge to hit him. Again. *I hate her. Remember what she did. Remember how bad she hurt me.* But as Navi slid past me, peeking at me through her lashes, I knew I didn't hate her. Not even close. Despite what she'd done to me, it didn't matter now. Maybe it never had. And watching her walk away, even if it was just across the room, felt like someone had punched me in the stomach with a unicorn.

"K? Need your help here." She grabbed Konstanz's wrist with grip of iron Konstanz apparently couldn't escape from. They both disappeared into the crowd.

Josh reappeared at the bar, settling onto a stool. "You're watching her like we don't want her to die anymore."

I grimaced. "We don't."

"She cheated. Remember?"

"She never admitted it." In fact, she adamantly denied it. But she would never tell me what she *had* been doing. That little seed of doubt was what had sent me up to Alaska to find her. Doubt and hope. Hope that I had been wrong and hope that she would forgive me if I had.

He rolled his eyes. "You saw her, bro. Her best friend saw her. Konstanz couldn't even defend her." He smacked his fist onto the counter like he was karate chopping it. "She went into that house. And ten thousand other houses. In the middle of the night." He gave me a pointed look.

"Yeah… but even when I met her at the back door as she snuck out, she still denied it. Maybe I was wrong. Maybe…" I scrubbed my hand over my face and watched her trying to escape as Bryson urged her to dance with him. She smiled, laughed, and tugged her hand away, hugging herself. And then she looked away from him, and her eyes found me. She flushed and ducked her head, the dark waves falling across her face. "I just want to talk to her. People change, you know. There's no reason we can't be friends."

"There is too a reason. It's the way you're looking at her right now." Josh leaned back on the barstool and nearly fell off. He righted himself as he looked around to see who noticed. "That is not how one friend looks at another friend."

"I don't know what you're talking about. But that girl needs saving." I refilled one last drink and slipped out of the kitchen, working my way through the crowd. To Navi. To the girl who broke my heart and haunted my dreams.

CHAPTER FOUR

Navi

"BRYSON, REALLY, I DON'T DANCE!" I laughed as I backed away, bumping into other sweaty, pulsing bodies.

"You can't sing like you do and not dance." He grabbed my hand and pulled me back to him, into his arms, against his chest, and I wanted to like it. I knew other girls watched him and practically drooled. But I hadn't gotten over the shock of seeing Alec. Of Alec's hand on my wrist. His eyes watching me across the room.

If I was anything except vulnerable, I would have played it up. I would have thrown myself all over Bryson and tried my best to make Alec jealous. That's what I was supposed to do in situations such as these, right? But I couldn't do it. All I wanted to do was leave, to run all the way back to Alaska, or failing that, at least to the coast with my swords so I could kill things.

Actually, if we're being honest, all I really wanted to do was throw myself all over Alec.

He hates you. He hates you. He ruined your reputation. I tried really hard to remember all the guys who followed me around school, thinking I was easy because of Alec's rumors. I tried to remember how I wanted to hit him with my truck or tear him apart with Kali and Golly. Of all the nights I cried while my mom stroked my head and told me it would get better. Of the strict rules I made with myself not to look at him, not to even think his name.

"Hey. I think one of your roommates is passed out in the corner."

I jumped, knowing the second he touched my arm that it was Alec and not anyone else in the room. There was heat there, something that made me instantly want to curl myself against his chest and stay there. I looked up, got caught in his blue eyes. Swallowing hard, I tried to tear myself out of his gaze as his lips curved in a slow smile.

"She's over there." He motioned with a slight tilt of his head and I nodded quickly, finally free.

"Terrie. Of course she's already passed out in the corner." I stumbled past him, my hand brushing his hand, and I was assaulted by ten thousand memories of my fingers twined through his. I yelped and escaped into the crowd, grabbing Konstanz as I went by.

"Seriously, what are we gonna do with her? She can't hold her liquor and she passes out every time we take her anywhere." Konstanz groaned as we knelt next to Terrie.

I tugged her skirt down so she wasn't showing the whole party way too much skin. "We'll just take her home."

Konstanz looked disappointed and I realized that maybe I was the only one who desperately wanted to escape. Where was an asuwang attack when I needed one? I sent all kinds of internal, desperate vibes to Elizabeth, hoping she'd show up and tell me it was time to go. "I'll just take her—"

"No, you can't lift her by yourself. I'll help you."

"Or," Alec said, kneeling next to me, "I can carry her to

my room and she can sleep it off until you guys are ready to go." The entire side of my body seemed to vibrate with an electrical energy at his nearness. I swallowed hard and tried to hide my suddenly shaking fingers.

Konstanz beamed at him like he'd just saved the world. I wanted to bury my head in my hands and cry. But I refrained. Because I'm super tough like that. "That works, too."

"Navi, there you are. Is there a problem?" Bryson asked, his shadow looming over us.

I looked up and plastered on my best apologetic smile. "Just a passed out friend. Sorry to desert you."

He opened his mouth to respond, already holding out a hand to help me up or point at Terrie or something else my poor, frazzled mind couldn't process with Alec so close, those dark blue eyes watching me, and I couldn't breathe, couldn't think—

"Bryson, we're out of beer!"

Bryson turned away and Alec blew out a breath. "I got this. You just make sure she's not showing… anything… she might regret later." He scooped Terrie up like she weighed as much as a bag of cotton balls. I scurried around him, tugging her clothes into place and cursing the fact that she liked her skirts so short. People barely noticed as he carried her across the room. "Can you get the door?" he grunted.

I nodded. "This one?" I reached for the first door but he shook his head, motioning to the next one over.

I got the door open, and there was no one inside, thankfully. I hurried to the bed and pulled the covers back, then got myself out of the way. He laid her down and I helped pull the comforter back over her. And then I realized I was in his bedroom. With him. My cheeks flamed and I was infinitely grateful I hadn't turned the light on. At least he couldn't see me blush like I was some hormone-driven teenager.

"There. Now let's hope she doesn't puke in my bed. That

would suck." He stood back and watched her suspiciously.

"She doesn't usually do that 'til the next day." I started to leave but he grabbed my wrist, and my blood pressure rocketed through the roof.

"You okay? You seem… nervous."

I could lie. I could tell him I was fine. Or I could half-lie and tell him that I was uncomfortable in crowds. But I hung my head in defeat, staring at the floor and our feet so close together. "Honestly? It's nerve-wracking being here with you."

He chuckled, low in his throat. I'd forgotten how completely, devastatingly sexy he was. "I'm right there with you, Navi."

Ouch. I brushed my hair out of my face and nodded, too quickly, like a rag doll with a loose neck. "I'll leave. I don't want to—"

"Don't go."

My heart stopped.

"But I thought—"

He ran a hand over his face and peered at me through his fingers. "Stay. Talk to me. Tell me what you've been doing since graduation. I don't know anything about you anymore." He dropped his hand and he looked so vulnerable, like asking me to stay was baring his soul.

And I nodded. "Okay."

He sat down on the carpet I'd just been staring at, leaning his back against the bed, and I sank to the floor next to him. He took my hand, his finger idly tracing the tattoo on my wrist, and I thought this couldn't possibly be happening. This boy, this boy I had hated and loved, whose memory had absolutely driven me insane for the past four years, was holding my hand like we hadn't had the most infamous breakup in our entire high school.

"What do you do now?" he asked, glancing up briefly to

meet my eyes before he went back to the tattoo.

"I'm… a probation officer. Sort of."

That caught his attention and he looked up again, eyebrow raised. "You're a probation officer."

"Sort of." I changed the subject. "Still doing the electrician thing?" Like I didn't already know.

He smiled, acknowledging my subject change and raising me another. "Yes. Is this the only one you have?" He held up my wrist, and I shook my head.

"No. Three more. One on my back and one on my rib cage. One on my foot."

His eyes skimmed from my wrist to my rib cage and I sucked in a breath. He wasn't actually touching me but it was so intimate. Like he could see through my soft pink sweater to my very soul… or at least to the tattoos underneath.

And I was blushing again.

"You've changed." It was a statement, not a question, and I didn't know how to answer that.

"I had to. Life changes us."

He inclined his head. "How's your family?"

It was such a different path than I'd been expecting that I could only blink at him for several seconds. "That good, huh?" He winked.

The world stopped moving.

Catch up, brain! "Yeah." I smiled, struggling to keep my thoughts from racing all over the room. "They're good. My mom is… retired." Yes, she'd hung up her swords and bid her army goodbye a few years ago. "My dad is still taking over the world, one tactical training center at a time." It had been a few weeks since I'd seen them. Too long. When I could die on an almost nightly basis, I really should make more of an effort to see them regularly.

"What made you follow your mom's line of work? She was always so stressed out she wouldn't even talk about it. I figured you'd go into something more low key."

Ah. I'd forgotten my mom had fed him the probation officer line, too. But this one, at least, I could answer honestly. "It *is* hard to talk about it. People don't understand. It's scary. But the way it changes lives, the way it *saves* souls… there's nothing like it."

He tipped his head to the side, studying me. His eyes were dark, dark blue, the irises rimmed with black. They looked like colored contacts, but I knew they weren't. And those eyelashes—so thick and so long and so black I was jealous. He kept his hair much shorter than he had when we were together. I used to love to tangle my fingers in the blond streaks, but now it was close cropped. Not finger-tangling material. "How are your parents?" I asked, trying to tug my thoughts away from the way I'd catch my hands in his hair and pull his head down toward me—

"They're good. They still don't regret adopting me, so there's that." He grinned.

"That's always a bonus." I nodded wisely. He'd been adopted as a baby. His parents had always been very open about it, telling him when he was ready they'd help him find his biological parents if he'd like. As far as I knew, he'd never been interested.

"When we were together, I thought you were the most gorgeous girl in the world." His voice was soft, so low I could barely hear him over the throb of the music making the walls shake. He stared hard at the tattoo on my wrist. "But you—somehow you managed to get even more beautiful. Alaska was good to you."

I almost sobbed. He had no idea how many times I'd imagined him saying something like that to me. Or anything even remotely sweet, actually. In all my fantasies, though, I'd never formulated a response because we'd always been kissing by now. But that wasn't happening so a response was necessary. What, exactly, did a girl say to that? "Thank you."

He smiled—not a grin, but slow and sexy so my heart melted and my blood roared in my ears and I wanted to crawl into his lap. "You—you look good, too."" I sounded strangled. His grin broadened and he leaned forward, tugging on my wrist, pulling me closer.

I panicked.

"When I walked in and saw you standing there, I almost turned around and left." Not what I'd meant to say, but he stopped leaning toward me. His smile died and he frowned. "I mean—I didn't think you'd want me here... And I didn't know–" I stopped, blew out a frustrated breath.

"That was my fault. I'm sure nearly running you over yesterday probably wasn't the welcome back you deserved."

I nodded, laughing. "Yeah, let's go with you almost ran over me and not the other way around."

"So you saw me then?" His eyes lit, teasing.

"In that big ole truck? Pretty hard to miss." I twisted my fingers together, peering up at him through my bangs. "Are we—do we not hate each other anymore?" He sat up, studying me, and I hurried on, in case we did and I just hadn't realized it. "Or do we still, but we're in a temporary truce for the sake of the party. Or—"

"I never hated you, Navi. Not ever."

"But high school—"

"We were young and stupid. We made mistakes."

Well, he'd made mistakes. He'd told everyone I'd cheated on him. I'd actually been killing demons, not sleeping around, but I suppose it was an honest misinterpretation on his part.

And I couldn't even explain.

"I saw you." There were tears in his eyes and his hand was shaking. "I saw you go in. In the middle of the night." He pointed in the general direction that he must have thought the house was I'd gone to the night before. I could correct him, tell him the house was

actually *the other direction, but I sensed this wasn't the time.*

"Alec, it isn't what you think."

He ignored me. "And then I asked Konstanz, and she said there's no way, so she went with me and we followed you." He looked at me with so much betrayal, so much pain in his face. I would have sold my soul right then to take that pain away. But I couldn't. It wasn't my soul that was at stake here. It was so many others.

"We followed you to one house. And then another house. Four, Navi. Four guys in one night. All this time—" His voice broke and he ran a hand over his face, staring up at the ceiling. "We've been together for three years. Did you just get bored? Am I not enough?"

"Alec, it isn't like that."

He lowered his head, staring at me now instead of the ceiling, his dark blue eyes pleading through the tears. "Then what is it, Navi? Please tell me what it is."

And I couldn't. Because if I'd told him I was an agent for lost souls, that I had an army to kill demons but I'd failed and the demons had made it into the city and blended with society… it would open his eyes, and then the demons I hunted would hunt him. And I'd be breaking an oath. I'd sworn to protect those souls, and his. No matter what.

"I'm sorry, Alec. I can't. Please." Now it was my voice breaking because he'd started to shake his head and back away, "Please just believe me. Just… I would never do that, Alec. Please," I sobbed, but he turned around and shoved his way through the crowd that had gathered around us. And I never spoke to him again.

"Where'd you go?" he asked, jerking me out of that awful memory.

I swallowed, trying to settle back against the mattress we leaned against, but I was just a tad too short, so it dug into my neck. "I was lost," I said quietly. His hand came up, his knuckles brushing against my cheekbone as his eyes devoured mine.

He opened his mouth and I was hanging on his every

word—except he didn't get to say them. "Navi! I've been looking everywhere for you!" Bryson's spiked head popped through the crack in the door, obliterating what little light there was. So he pushed the door wide open and nearly blinded us both.

"Terrie passed out. We didn't want to leave her alone in case she was sick." I pointed to the bed, feeling ridiculously guilty even though all we'd done was talk. Bryson looked hurt, too, like I *should* feel guilty.

"Well everyone's been asking for you. I've been bragging about that voice of yours so much we're thinking a little impromptu karaoke is in order." He raised his eyebrow.

All I really wanted to do was spend the rest of the night, in the dark, talking to Alec. But I shoved myself to my feet and held out my hand, tugging him up with me. He glowered at Bryson like he was thinking the same thing I was, but I hopefully I hid it better. As I passed, I grabbed Bryson's wrist. "You're gonna sing with me this time, right?"

If I was gonna be put on the spot, I was taking him down with me.

CHAPTER FIVE

Alec

IF I HAD TO WATCH BRYSON pull Navi against his chest and slide his arms around her waist one more time, and lean so close his breath made her hair move, I might kill him. That was all. Apparently the girl who haunted my nightmares brought out the violent side in me because I'd never wanted to hurt someone so many times in one single night.

Especially someone that, until today, I had considered a tolerable friend.

Bryson and I never really hung out. He was… not my type. At all. There were times I wondered if he was really even straight. But now, with his hands all over the girl I found myself desperately wanting, that question was answered. Not the way I'd hoped to have my doubts laid to rest, though.

And Navi. She was still my Angel. She still sang so sweetly it brought peace to my soul. Watching her with Bryson *hurt.* It was almost unbearable, which might explain the violence. Except when she sang, I forgot the pain. I knew the line between love and hate was a thin one. I knew that I hated her so much because I'd been so completely in love with her before she'd hurt me. Apparently, the hate had faded but…

There was a chance love hadn't.

I wasn't sure what had happened.

I watched her laugh, pushing the hair away from her face and behind her ear, and I wondered how in the hell it was even remotely possible that I was still in love with her. Yeah, I'd gone up to Alaska to try to find her. That hadn't been cheap. Or easy. But I'd had questions I needed answers to. Not because I was still…

Yeah. I'd gone to Alaska because I was still in love with her.

I sat back and blew out a breath like I was being deflated. I was still in love with her. After all this damn time.

"So." Josh sat on the couch next to me. "You sang one. I'm impressed."

I grimaced. "I had to. It was a duet. I didn't want her to sing with Bryson."

"But he sang anyway." Josh frowned, as confused as I was about why Bryson had felt the need to join us.

"I know," I growled. Violent side, yet again.

He looked from me to Navi and then raised an eyebrow. "You're… watching her like a hawk. Ya know, for a guy who isn't dating her. Like at all."

I swore. "He's all over her. Why the hell doesn't she stop him?"

Josh shrugged. "Maybe she likes it. Girls like Bryson, Alec."

Again with the ice through my veins. "But she—she doesn't."

Josh smirked—apparently he could hear the blind desperation in my voice as well as I could. We both turned toward her, me with panicked eyes that I wanted to hate myself for but didn't, and Josh with critical, appraising eyes that had no trace of panic at all. Did he not realize what was on the line here?

"Well, she does seem like she moves away from him every chance she gets." Josh nodded. "Maybe she really doesn't like him. If that's the case, and you think you might want another shot with her, you should get her away from him, huh?"

Yeah. That would be nice. But I had no idea how to do that without starting some Navi tug-of-war in the middle of the party. And she, apparently, hadn't realized that she was still in love with me.

But she had to be, right? I couldn't feel like this alone. It had to be a two-way thing. Because otherwise, I was lost. Completely, devastatingly lost.

CHAPTER SIX

Navi

SINGING KARAOKE WITH A BUNCH OF drunk people usually ends up with rounds of "Row, Row, Row Your Boat", and this night wasn't any different. My abs got the best workout I'd had in weeks from laughing so hard. It was nearly three a.m. when everyone finally started heading out. Konstanz had left with some guy to get ice cream an hour ago, mostly to get out of singing, I think. Terrie was still passed out. "Reese, you ready? We gotta get Terrie back home in one piece." I yawned. I'd slept for three whole hours yesterday morning.

"Yep. At least there's two of us to carry her in. She's not exactly a light girl." Reese scanned the room hopefully, like a hand truck might pop out of the molding and offer to help us. Bryson had his hand on my waist, like I was his.

Alec sat on the couch by my leg, arms crossed over his chest. But when Reese spoke, he sat up. "I'll follow you home and carry her in for you."

"You don't need to do that, Alec. It's my party. I'll go home with them." Bryson tugged me closer, his arm circling my entire waist now, my back against his chest.

"You've been drinking. Sorry, bro. You're not driving." Alec stood, towering over both of us. I'd forgotten, in all my imaginings, how tall he was. I was strong enough to carry Reese in without either boy, at least until the sun came up, but not if there was anyone around to see me. And if we didn't wrap this up soon, I wouldn't be strong enough to carry even myself in.

"I can ride with them. Maybe Navi can drop me back home on her way to work in the morning." He looked at me hopefully but Alec shook his head.

"She works nights." I supposed Alec remembered that my mom had worked nights and that's where he got his information, but it still took me by surprise that he remembered.

"Well. While they fight it out, come help me drag her to the car." Reese stormed off, clearly annoyed. I hid a smile and went after her, Bryson and Alec arguing behind me.

"Navi, can you give me a ride home in the morning?" Bryson came in after us, flipping Alec's bedroom light on. I got my first real view of the room. It was plain, except for a few framed pictures on the window sill of a kid. My feet froze to the floor in confusion. Was it Alec's son? I knew he'd had several girlfriends since we'd broken up. We were both twenty-two. He could easily have a kid or even two. Still, the thought hurt. A lot.

"Yeah, sure Bryson. I can bring you back home." My voice sounded stiff in my own ears and Reese looked over at me, raising one perfectly arched eyebrow.

"She's tired, Bryson. There's no reason for her to have to drive you home. I'll just follow them and drive myself back." Alec sounded annoyed, but I couldn't tear my eyes off the kid in the picture.

Bryson started to argue, but Reese, thankfully, cut him

off. "Seriously, you're just making more work for her and she's exhausted. If you're trying to look good, you're failing miserably. Alec, get your keys."

Alec reached for the basket on his night stand and grabbed his keys. "Yes ma'am." He scooped Terrie up, and Reese threw her jacket over Terrie's legs, trying to give her some semblance of modesty. They both left and I went to follow them, but Bryson tugged me back, sliding his arms around my waist, turning me so I faced him and also, conveniently, had a perfect view of the two framed pictures. The kid was cute, there was no denying it. Bright eyes, big smile. "I had fun tonight."

I tore my eyes away from the pictures and tried to focus. "Yeah, me too. Thanks for inviting us. Karaoke is fun."

His hands twined with my fingers and he raised them to his lips as he peered at me over our hands with those ice blue eyes. "I really like you, Navi." I could smell the alcohol on his breath, which distracted me. I did not love alcohol. It slowed my responses. It could be a death sentence, not just for me but for the entire city. I was so caught up thinking about just how catastrophic that could be that I didn't see Bryson leaning in, eyes closed, until it was too late. His lips mashed awkwardly against mine as he pulled me tight against him. I squeaked and my eyes flew open. "Bryson—" Our teeth ground together, "Bryson, stop." I pushed against his chest.

"I'm sorry. I couldn't help myself. You're so pretty and I really like you." His hands were roving over my shoulders and down my back. I wriggled away, praying this was a drunken haze he wouldn't remember the next day because holy crap. Awkward. "I know I just met you, but I really think—"

"Navi. You comin'?" Alec literally growled from the front doorway. I leaped away from Bryson, and without my hands holding him up, he toppled forward.

"Oh!" I stooped, tried to catch him before he face-planted—without moving too fast because Alec still stood, arms crossed, in the doorway watching. "Are you okay?"

He mumbled around the carpet in his mouth. His eyes drifted closed and he promptly started snoring. I looked up at Alec in bewilderment. "Does he always get this plastered?"

"I think you make him nervous." Alec didn't move, glaring at his roommate from the door jamb he was apparently holding up.

"So… I'll just drag him to his room by myself then." I stood up, grabbed Bryson's arm and tugged. Hmm. How to do this without showing my freakish strength…

"Trust me, Navi. You go anywhere near his room and you're not coming out of there tonight."

I blew out a breath, pushing my bangs out of my face. "Well would you like to take him in or will you have the same problem with the never coming out again?"

He smirked but didn't move. "Leave him there. He'll find his way to his bed eventually."

I glared at him, reached down to grab Bryson's other arm and tugged, stumbling backward toward his room. Alec watched me for several steps before he left the doorway and came over to help me. "He doesn't deserve this, you know."

I peeked at him through my hair as I tugged. Alec lifted him from the arm pits. "You're not very happy with him, are you?"

"He just attacked you. I'm not thrilled." He didn't look at me as he said it.

My heart tried to climb out of my throat. "You—you care that he attacked me? I mean, he didn't attack me. It was just a kiss. Sort of."

"Did you ask for that kiss, Navi?" He dropped Bryson just inside his bedroom door, pushing his legs in with his foot. He straightened and looked at me. "Did you want Bryson to kiss you?"

"I didn't ask for it, no. But it's not unheard of for someone to want to kiss me, you know."

His eyes darkened as they dipped to my mouth. "No. It's not unheard of at all."

I sucked in a breath through my teeth and straightened my spine. I could not kiss him. And if I fell for him again…

Pain. So much pain.

I brushed past him. "Reese is gonna kill me. She's probably freezing out there."

"I sent Reese home. I told her you could ride with me."

I froze, my back to him. I had to be alone with him. In his truck. The memories in that truck alone would be my undoing. There wasn't enough willpower in the world.

"Navi." His voice, low, right behind me. I could feel his warmth he was so close. "I'm not going to attack you."

"I know." The problem was I wanted him to. So, so much.

"Just talk to me. That's all I ask. I missed you."

He missed me. He *missed* me? I went all the way to Alaska to try to forget him.

He told the entire school you cheated on him. With a bunch of different guys. Remember that, Navi, a strong, fierce voice growled in my head. It sounded like Elizabeth, and I grabbed it, holding tight. *Remember the guys that followed you into the bathroom because they thought you were easy. Remember the looks. Remember the whispers and the laughter.*

"Yeah. We can be friends. Of course. Ready?" I grabbed my purse and slung it over my shoulder, hurrying toward the door.

"Navi, what happened? Three hours ago you were happy to talk to me. Now you act like I'm no better than him." Alec flung his arm toward Bryson's room and I cringed.

"I'm just tired, Alec. I haven't slept much lately, and the sun is coming up soon."

He glanced out the window, a brief smile lighting his face. "You always hated the sun rise. Most people dread the night, and you dread the dawn." He headed out the door and I imagined the lecture Konstanz was going to give me when we finally made it home. To say she was prone to worry was an understatement. Hopefully, Reese hadn't thrown up in the SUV, or I'd never hear the end of it.

"I came on too strong. I'm sorry."

I glanced at him in surprise. "You don't need to apologize." The air outside bit at my cheeks, distracting me. It hadn't been even a fraction of this cold last night. Where had this chill come from?

"I didn't think it would be like this. When Bryson said you were coming over, I thought it would be awkward. But it felt like I was stepping back in time. Like you never left."

I nodded slowly as he came around to my side of the truck to open the door. "I did expect it to be more uncomfortable. Especially since you nearly ran me over yesterday."

His face lit up. Adorable. He was completely adorable.

I wanted to bury my head in my hands and cry. Or scream. I wasn't quite sure which.

He climbed in, started the truck, and backed out. "I have no idea where you live now."

"Oh. Right. So, not far from here, actually. If you just want to hop on the highway and head south, we're only about ten minutes away."

We rode in silence for one entire song. "I swear this station isn't usually all mushy. It's supposed to be rock." He glanced at me quickly and back at the road. I hadn't even noticed the music until then but yes, it was definitely a love song.

"Your tastes have changed," I teased.

His lip quirked but he didn't respond. I leaned my head

back against the seat rest and stared out the window. Luckily, I saw no demons and only a few wandering spirits. That was pretty normal.

"So… are you… are you thinking of going out with him again?"

I rolled my head slowly so I could watch him in the glow of the dashboard lights. A muscle worked in his jaw. I could play games. I should play games. Isn't that how this whole social thing worked? I should tell him that yes, I was going to go out with Bryson. Reese would tell me to make him jealous. But I couldn't figure out why he even cared. Why he'd spent four years pretending I didn't exist, but the first night we hang out… he says he missed me. I was confused. And I'd never been good at games. "I just spent the night talking to you. Not him."

The tense set of his shoulders relaxed. "You spent most of the night singing with him. With his arms around you. He kissed you. I didn't."

"It's different. He and I don't have the history that you and I have. Turn here."

He raised an eyebrow as he signaled to turn left. "You know me better so he gets to kiss you and I don't?"

"You didn't –I didn't know—" Words failed me. "Yes."

"But you don't know me anymore." He sounded positively triumphant. "So I get to kiss you now, right?"

"You're driving," I pointed out like my heart wasn't pounding hard enough to convince me I might need medical attention. "And I don't know. Maybe I do know you."

He pursed his lips. "You think so, huh. What's my favorite color?"

"Dark blue."

He winked, "Close. Navy. Navy blue has been my favorite color since I met you. How many brothers do I have?"

"None."

He grinned, thrilled at my apparently-wrong answer. "No. My mom and dad adopted a little boy right after we broke up. What else?"

I tipped my head to the side, considering him. "You're an electrician. You drive a big, black truck. You apparently like 90s love songs now instead of rock. You have one roommate named Bryson. You've lived in the same city your whole life. Our apartment is right up there."

"Wrong." He was ecstatic.

"What? What's wrong?"

"I moved to Denver for a year to help a friend." He parked by Reese's SUV.

"Took you long enough." Reese growled as I climbed out. "I thought I was gonna freeze to death waiting for you to show up. Konstanz isn't home yet. Big surprise. I always do the heavy lifting around here."

I kissed her temple. "Yes you do. And we love you for it."

Alec pulled Terrie out. At this point none of us even tried to muster enough energy to worry about her skirt. I dug my keys out of my purse and hurried to open the door so Alec didn't have to stand in the cold holding an unconscious girl who may or may not vomit on him at any given time. The blast of warm air felt wonderful after the chill of the night. I got out of the way as Alec came through the door and followed Reese to Terrie's room.

"Nice place." Alec said, smiling as he reemerged sans Reese.

"Thanks. Four girls. One house. Things get interesting." I twisted my hands awkwardly. Did I sit? Would he think I was asking him to stay and he wanted to go home? Or did I stand and hope he realized I wasn't hurrying him off?

"I have work in, like, two hours," he said, pulling his phone out to check the time. He ducked his head, peeking at me through his long lashes. "Can I have your number?"

My heart. It was going to quit on me if he didn't go soon. It was definitely not used to all this action.

"I mean, if it's okay. If it isn't pushing you—"

I didn't mention that he'd just been arguing about whether he could kiss me or not. Instead I took his phone from his hand and sent myself a text. Sneaky little ploy on my part to get his number, too. "There you go." I handed it back to him.

"Thanks." He tucked it in his back pocket. "I—I guess I should go. You need to sleep."

Don't go. Stay with me. "Yeah, and you should sleep while you can."

He pulled me closer, wrapping me in a hug. I could feel his heart through his jacket. It was beating as hard as mine. That made me feel ten thousand gazillion times better. "It was good to see you, Navi."

And he was gone. And our apartment was empty and sad and dark. And I felt like half my soul had gone with him. "Oh dear," I mumbled as I sank to the couch.

"Navi, bed. Now," Reese ordered as she half-stumbled past. I wasn't sure she was even still awake to be ordering me around.

I stood obediently and padded off to get ready for bed, tossing my purse onto my dresser. I was in the middle of spitting toothpaste when I heard my phone buzz. I rinsed my toothbrush and retrieved my phone.

"Glad you came tonight." I smiled as my fingers trembled over the keys. He couldn't be home yet, not unless he drove like a demon.

"Me too."

Seconds later, my phone buzzed again. *"You should come back."*

"I should?"

He took long enough to respond that I had time to change

into my pajamas. I climbed into my bed, pulling the covers up to my chin. When my phone buzzed again, I practically attacked it.

"Yes. Tonight. You should come back tonight."

He had no idea how much I wanted to do just that. *"I'm in my batman jammies. In bed. Not attractive."*

Five minutes passed and I was almost asleep when he finally wrote back. *"I want to see you in batman jammies."*

I sucked in a breath. How, exactly, did one respond to that?

"Navi. They come." My scratchy, exhausted eyes flew open to see Elizabeth, standing silently in the doorway. Konstanz was still gone and Reese and Terrie were in their own room, but even so it was dangerous for Elizabeth to be here. She could open Reese's eyes to the ghost world. To demons. I threw myself out of bed, leaving my phone in the heap of blankets. Yawning, I felt my swords humming to life on my back as I threw off my batman jammies and grabbed my fighting jeans and my crappy, holey sweatshirt. "I'll meet you outside," I whispered.

Elizabeth nodded and disappeared.

I assumed they would be already fighting at the beach, like last night, but my army waited impatiently outside my door. "They are slow this night," Elizabeth said by way of explanation.

I peered around at my ghosts, mentally trying to tug some energy from the rapidly dimming moon. "What do you mean?" I always felt super smart when I had to ask the dumb questions.

She raised an eyebrow. "We've been watching them fight their way from the doorway to the beach for hours. They have yet to make it, but they are close."

I blinked up at the moon. "If they don't hurry, the sun will rise and they won't get to fight." Get to fight. Like it was a privilege. Smiling to myself, maybe because I was exhausted-loopy-slightly-stupid, I realized that to me, fighting was a privilege. One I enjoyed very much when I wasn't in designer jeans and my favorite boots. "I'll meet you all there." I didn't wait to watch her disappear into the darkness. I took off running, realizing belatedly that I had forgotten to put shoes on. I felt many rocks dig into my feet, but the moon healed me faster than the blood could flow. By the time I reached Devil's Gate, I was fairly positive I had a whole new set of skin on the bottoms of my feet.

I leaped up the rock, much easier to do shoeless, and sat at the top, staring down at the water. Elizabeth joined me, watching silently. The asuwangs were just below the surface, barely visible in the wild waves. I checked the moon, but the sun wouldn't be up for at least three more hours. They had time. I grinned at Elizabeth, who heaved a long-suffering sigh. "Don't think I can't see the excitement under that scowl." I waved my finger in her face and the smile she'd been hiding found its way through. Yes, this was terrifying fighting demons on a regular basis. Yes, we could all die. Facing it with a sense of humor was the only way to not go completely mad. Plus, there's a teensy, tiny little chance that I got a rush from demon killing. *I wonder what Alec would think if he knew…* I banished the thought immediately. If Alec knew, he'd be in a ton of danger. It wasn't worth it. My secret had to stay my own.

We sat silently, watching while they sludged slowly to the surface. My army paced the sand below, some of them randomly swinging weapons. This was new. We'd never seen the asuwangs have so much trouble before. As the sky lightened, most of my army was practice fighting with each other, which amused me. I'd have to mention this to Death.

Elizabeth looked to the east, where the sun's first rays were penetrating the darkness. "We should go down there. I see their claws in the sand."

I nodded and jumped off the wall, landing in a crouch, my swords already in my hands. It was odd not sprinting across the beach to throw myself into battle. "I feel that they are testing us. Again." Elizabeth swung her swords nervously while we stood shoulder to shoulder, watching them come. The first wave of demons escaped the water and crawled toward us, but even then they didn't seem to be in a hurry—usually when they attacked, they moved slowly at first but faster and faster until their speed is almost blinding.

Luckily, my army and I are even faster still.

But this time, they just moseyed on up to us, almost falling on our swords. I swirled my blades through the hair, slicing the thick necks of two at once. Elizabeth shot into the horde of demons, her swords catching the moonlight and humming viciously. The ghosts were barely a mist they moved so quickly, falling on the demons and devouring them. Jesse and another ghost—he had a name and I couldn't remember it—were tugging dead bodies out of the way as fast as they could and still my army was leaving piles of dead asuwangs beneath them. I paused, panting, to brush black blood off my cheek, and realized that the second wave of demons was retreating.

"We scared them off!" one ghost squealed. I frowned, glanced at the sun—which wasn't even entirely up yet—and back to the water. I couldn't see them anymore. They'd retreated much faster than they'd come.

"They're definitely testing us. But for what?" I murmured as Elizabeth wafted to my side. Since they were ghosts, they never got icky black acidic blood on them. She was as clean as she had been before.

"I will ponder it while I am haunting today." Elizabeth smiled grimly as we clambered up the huge rock wall. By we, I of course mean me, and she politely floated next to me. The rest of my army were slowly sinking through the sand and back to their cages. If I didn't hurry, I'd have to walk all the way home instead of running.

"What do you do all day, anyway?" I asked as I jumped over the other side and landed in the sand.

"I wander. I visit relatives. I learn." She shrugged delicately. "Pretty much the same thing you do."

I opened my mouth to object, but I had no words. I *did* wander. And visit relatives. And learn. She laughed quietly, one ghostly finger brushing across my open jaw like she was trying to push my mouth closed. "Go home, Navi. We will fight another day."

CHAPTER SEVEN

Alec

"DUDE…" BRYSON STUMBLED OUT OF HIS bedroom, holding his head. I tried not to glare at him. He'd made a total ass of himself the night before and Navi didn't deserve that.

Like I know what Navi deserves.

Already, after one short conversation in the dark, one short car ride, and a few short text messages, I was protective of her. *She's mine.*

But she isn't.

Not yet.

But after last night, I was determined that she would be.

"What happened?" he mumbled, squinting at me. His hair stuck up all over his head and his eyes were bloodshot. If Navi could see him now, she'd never let him kiss her again. I thought briefly of taking a picture for her, but my hands were full of empty beer bottles and red plastic cups.

"Next time we have a party, you're cleaning up on your own. It wasn't even my stupid party and I've been cleaning up since I got home from work." Lucky me getting to work a half shift on a Saturday and then coming home to clean up the party I hadn't even wanted to have.

Except that now I was so grateful we'd had it, I would gladly clean up for the rest of the day.

"Did Navi kiss me?" Bryson completely ignored the mess and peered at me blearily.

I gritted my teeth and swore under my breath. "No. You attacked her and then passed out at her feet. I would have left you in a heap on the floor but she's more compassionate than I am. What's the matter with you? Do you have any idea how stupid you are? Do you know what you're pushing away?"

Navi. You're pushing away the one girl I'd give anything to have another chance with.

"She—oh shit." He turned and ran to the bathroom, worshiping the porcelain god as he deserved. I dug my phone out of my pocket, finally letting myself text her. I'd held off all morning, hoping she'd write me first.

She hadn't.

Bryson is sufficiently embarrassed about last night and he's paying for his idiocy.

There. That didn't sound desperate. Why hadn't she written me? I'd long since given up on trying to pretend I wasn't…in the light of day it was harder to admit to what I'd realized last night. But I definitely didn't hate her. I never had, which was clear by the fact that my resolve had melted the second she'd walked through my door last night and I'd pretty much thrown myself at her feet. At least I hadn't passed out at them like Bryson had.

My phone buzzed and my heart leapt. Glad that there was no one around to see my hands shaking, I dug my phone out of my pocket.

Good. Maybe he'll stop drinking so much. How are you?

An idiotic grin spread across my face as I re-read her message. "Does she hate me?" Bryson asked, staggering into the kitchen for coffee. He was in really bad shape. I almost felt bad for him, until I remembered that he'd kissed Navi last night.

And I hadn't.

"No, she doesn't hate you. But I told you she doesn't like alcohol," I answered, distracted because I was trying to think of something clever to respond with. *I'm good. How'd you sleep?*

Oh yeah, that was clever.

I ran a hand over my face and stared at the ceiling. What did this girl do to me? Four years later and she still made me a complete moron with one text message. I couldn't think straight. I couldn't sleep. It was like I was falling for her after just one night.

That, of course, was ridiculous. No one fell after one night. Unless they'd never unfallen…

Which I'm fairly positive I had determined last night was the case.

Yeah. You alternate between watching her die and watching her live in your dreams every night. That's perfectly normal for a guy who ever got over her. I shut up my inner critic as my phone buzzed again.

I just got up. Got called into work early this morning and didn't get back 'til about two hours ago. U?

I remembered how tired she'd been the night before. And she'd had to go to work. No wonder she hadn't written me yet. My heart thumped in my chest like it was celebrating.

Bryson slumped down on the barstool with his head in his hands, staring bleakly at the counter top. "I really like her," he mumbled. "I don't remember… I kept thinking she wanted someone else…"

Me.

I grinned again and stuffed the garbage in the recycle bin, but couldn't for the life of me figure out how to answer him.

Navi was mine. She might not know it yet, but I'd

convince her. *Sounds like you need someone to take you to breakfast. I'll be there in ten minutes.*

"You should try to sleep off that hangover, man. It looks pretty wicked." I smacked him on the shoulder, grabbed my jacket and shoved my wallet into my back pocket. He groaned as his head sank onto the counter, and I allowed myself a wicked grin.

I had my keys in my hand and was halfway out the door when she wrote me back but I ignored it. I knew what she'd say—she'd just got up and she looked like crap. But I couldn't wait. I'd waited all morning to see her again, and each second had seemed like an eternity. Even if I wanted to, I couldn't stay away from her.

I LEANED AGAINST HER door frame, waiting for someone to answer. I knew they'd heard my knock, because there'd been squealing and panicked footsteps on the other side. My lips quirked in a grin even as my heart tried to beat its way out of my chest. If she didn't open the door soon, I'd have to break it down.

I was that desperate to see her.

The door swung open and her dark, dark brown eyes slowly traveled up my chest to my face and finally met my gaze. She sucked in a breath and forced a shaky smile. "You ignored me, didn't you?"

I pretended to be wounded by her words, pretending too that I didn't feel my heart speed up and pretended that the blood roaring in my ears wasn't damn near deafening. I tried to take in every detail of her like I'd been drowning and she was my angel pulling me free.

Save me.

"Never," I said, my smile widening as she raised a

skeptical eyebrow. Her long, thick curls were piled on top of her head in a messy bun, and as adorable as she looked right then, I wanted to tug it loose and let the silky strands free so I could run my hands through them. Her hair had always been my undoing. We used to watch TV while she laid her head in my lap and I would wind the curls around my fingers.

She was in yoga pants and a tank top. My breath caught and held in my throat and I couldn't swallow. She had absolutely no business being so damn gorgeous when she'd only gotten two hours of sleep. "You're gonna freeze if you go out like that," I told her.

"I haven't even brushed my teeth yet," she objected. My eyes dipped to her lips. Bad move. All I wanted to do was pull her into the hallway and kiss her until she forgot we'd ever broken up. Until she forgot every guy she'd been with since me.

I forced myself back to her eyes, which I could drown in, but at least I could control myself. Had it been like this when we were together? This insane, overwhelming need to see her, hold her, touch her? I couldn't remember. I know I'd been obsessed with her, but I think it had been possible to have a conversation without wanting to devour her. I *do* know that no one had affected me the way she had since. Not even close.

A mischievous smile played around her lips as she stepped back and swung open the door. "Navi!" Terrie squealed as she leaped off the couch and raced into the hall, holding her head.

Navi snickered.

"She's doing about as well as Bryson," I said as I followed her inside. It felt so wrong to be this close and not touch her. Like the last four years hadn't happened and we'd never broken up.

"Yeah. It's entertaining." She grinned over her shoulder at me as she led the way over to the couch. I stopped next to her, closer than I should have but not close enough. It was near enough that I could feel the warmth of her skin against mine without actually touching her. And I really wanted to touch her. Just run my knuckles across her cheek bone. Or my thumb against the back of her hand. Or my fingers through her hair…

"Sit." She pushed me backward until the backs of my legs hit the couch and I sat. "I'll brush my teeth and we can go." My chest felt scalded where she'd put her hands and it took everything I had not to pull her down with me.

I was a mess.

She disappeared before I could, and Konstanz rounded the corner, yawning and rubbing her eyes. "You're here early," she mumbled. Her hair was a tangle of waves and her mascara was sleep-smeared under her eyes so she looked way more exhausted than she probably felt.

I glanced at my watch. "It's ten o'clock."

She gave me an impish smile. "Yeah. Like… six whole hours since you've seen her last."

I opened my mouth. And then closed it. Then opened it again. She sat next to me on the couch, completely delighted. "I can't help it," I said, my voice low. I'm pretty sure I sounded tortured. "Six hours was too long."

"Wow." Konstanz nodded slowly, eying me through rapidly brightening eyes. "You've got it bad."

I swallowed, staring at the coffee table, the floor, the blank TV screen. Apparently these girls were gamers—there were at least three different video game platforms on the entertainment center. "I've missed her."

"If I recall…" Konstanz tipped her head to the side, finger-combing her wild hair. "You said you hated her and you never wanted to see her again. I guess that only counted when you could actually still see her every day."

I thought back to those torturous months of high school.

We'd broken up right before we'd graduated, and every single day was a fight with myself to stay away from her. How could you hate someone so much and want them at the same time? We still had classes together. She started skipping school to get away from me. I started dating as many girls as I could to forget about her. And it had been hell. "She hurt me, Konstanz."

Konstanz shrugged. "You hurt her, too. A lot. You have no idea what she went through after you guys broke up." Her words were like a sword to the stomach—sharp, fierce, and sudden. Before I could respond, she leaned close, her eyes sparkling. "She was talking about you in her sleep last night."

The agonizing wound in my stomach healed as my heart sped up for the eight thousandth time in ten minutes. She leaped to her feet and danced away, laughing softly. If Navi was talking about me in her sleep, that meant she was dreaming about me. Before my heart could decide what to do with that new, exciting information, she came around the corner, tugging a hoodie over her head.

It was a good thing, because I think my blood pressure had already skyrocketed to dangerous levels and her in a tank top was more than I could handle for any extended period of time. "Teeth brushed. K, have you seen my wallet?"

She'd called Konstanz K when we'd been in high school. Hearing it again, so casually, sent a jolt through my system like I was being dragged back in time. Back to her. "You don't need your wallet." My voice sounded strangled, even to my own ears. She gave me an odd look. I cleared my throat several times before I trusted myself to speak. "I'm dragging you out of the house. The least I can do is pay."

She shook her head. "That's not fair. I can pay. I just gotta find..." Konstanz appeared next to her, holding the sparkling pink wallet with little skulls all over it. "Oh. Thank you."

"If you pay for yourself, it's not a date," I said as she

came toward me. She stumbled a little and her eyes widened, those perfect pink lips opening in a silent *O*.

"This—this is a date?"

I reached out, pried the wallet from her hand, and tossed it back to Konstanz, who stood grinning behind the couch. "I would like it to be."

She blinked, long lashes brushing her cheek as if in slow motion. "Oh—okay."

I had to summon a hell of a lot of courage to take her hand and wind her fingers through my own. In doing that, I knew she could feel me shaking, and she'd know in those first seconds that I was pretending to be way more calm than I really was. "Ready?" I asked quietly.

She nodded, a faint smile playing around her lips.

"Bye!" Konstanz called cheerfully as we left the apartment.

"She can't sleep when I'm gone at night," Navi said as I led her down the hall and out the door. It was raining steadily, but Navi, unlike any girl I've ever known, raised her head into the rain and spread her arms, smiling.

If I hadn't been consumed with thoughts of her before, that image of her in the rain would have taken over completely.

And then she dropped her arms, laughing, and ran to my truck. It was so *right* for her to be there, in the passenger seat. She belonged in my truck.

She belonged with me.

"So," I said, trying to sound like I wasn't falling so fast I didn't even have time to be scared, "Any requests?"

She leaned back, buckling her seat belt before she glanced at me, biting her lip. She shouldn't have done that.

My eyes dipped to her mouth and I couldn't look away. I wanted to tug her lip free with my mouth, smooth my tongue over the soft, pink skin.

She sucked in a breath and I finally, finally forced myself to look up at her. *I want to kiss you. I need to kiss you, Navi.*

"The Chicken Coop?" she asked softly, her cheeks coloring under my stare. I needed to chill out or she'd run screaming from my truck. "Do you feel like bacon and eggs?"

I nodded, starting the truck. "The Chicken Coop it is."

CHAPTER EIGHT

Navi

I COULDN'T BREATHE. IF HE LOOKED at my mouth one more time, I was going to launch myself across that truck seat at him. I wasn't sure exactly what would come after that, but I *was* sure it wasn't something that required advanced planning.

My hands twitched, like they were hoping desperately if they caused a commotion, Alec might notice and hold them again. They'd taken on a life of their own.

I watched him sneakily through my hair. He looked like a Greek god, all strong jaw and straight Roman nose and those eyes. It was insane how gorgeous his eyes were. I'd loved them before, but now, when they looked at me, they made me want to throw myself at his feet and beg for mercy.

Last night—in the middle of a battle with demons who wanted to sneak into society and eat us for a midnight snack—I kept finding myself thinking about him. It was a dangerous little habit that could probably get me killed.

And this morning. As soon as my eyes had opened, I'd reached for my phone. To write him. Because he was the first thing I thought of when coherency found me. Waking up to his text had sent butterflies into fits of chaos everywhere.

He reached over and snapped the radio on as he drove us easily through the light traffic. "You're awfully far away," he said softly, tugging gently on the edge of my hoodie. Holy crap, he wanted me closer to him? I could barely think straight as it was.

But my body had a will of its own. As soon as he stopped for the next stoplight, I undid my seat belt and slid over, buckling myself into the middle seat before the light changed again. "That's better," he said, glancing over, those eyes tracing my face, my throat, my mouth. Again. Did he have any idea what he was doing to me? My entire body felt like I'd had about eight thousand cups of coffee. It was buzzing. Positively buzzing.

"I remember in high school..." His voice trailed off as he looked over again, his hand leaving the steering wheel to find mine. His fingers shook just a little.

Ah. He did know what he was doing to me.

He cleared his throat, focusing on the road. "I remember in high school you used to sing to every song on the radio."

I smiled. "I knew you better then. It's just weird when a stranger starts bellowing in your car. Didn't you know?"

He frowned, his brows lowering as he risked a glance back over at me. "I'm a stranger?"

He didn't like that one bit. I hid a wicked smile and feigned innocence. "Well... I haven't seen you in four years. Maybe I don't know you at all."

He rolled his eyes. "We proved last night that you know me very well. I haven't changed, Navi. The only thing that's different is that now—" He froze, turning panicked eyes on me.

"Now... what?" I asked, reaching up to gently turn his chin back toward the road so we didn't both die in a fiery crash.

"Nothing." He flipped through his MP3 player and then focused on the road. The song came on, an old one. He started singing along, mostly, I think, to distract me from whatever he'd been about to say. It worked. I remembered how we used to sing together when he drove me to school every morning. And this song.

It was a duet.

I hesitated, because somehow singing in this car with him was way more terrifying than singing on a stage in front of a hundred people. But the girl started singing and Alec stopped, and the way his chin fell in defeat melted me. I started singing, quietly at first, but when he joined in again I gained courage and sang louder. His fingers tightened around mine. The sweet lyrics, his low, sexy voice, filled the car, filled my head until I felt like I was drugged and couldn't look away from him. I loved the way our voices flowed together, over and under and around.

And then the song ended and I crashed back to reality. He pulled into the restaurant parking lot and stopped the truck. Raising my hand, he kissed my knuckles softly, so softly, but the feel of his lips against my skin sent delicious shivers up and down my spine. The last thing in the world I wanted to do right then was get out of that truck.

Unfortunately, one must eat.

Alec let go of my fingers, but so slowly I hoped that maybe he was as reluctant to get out of the truck as I was. My eyes devoured him as he walked around the front to my door—with the tight black t-shirt under his jacket and his baseball hat on backward. The truck squeaked in protest as he swung open the door, like it felt the same way I did and we should just stay inside together. I twisted on the seat and slid out, but he caught me, his hands on my waist as he lowered me gently to the ground. Our bodies were close, so close I could feel his rapid breathing as he stared down at me, his hands sliding down to my hips, pulling me closer to him.

"Alec! Navi! What a surprise meeting you guys here!" Bryson yelled.

I jumped guiltily away from Alec, wondering what on earth was wrong with me. I didn't belong to Bryson. I had nothing to feel guilty about. Alec growled under his breath and turned slowly. "I thought you'd be in bed for the rest of the day."

"Nah. I'm just fine. Nothing a little coffee can't fix." He looked awful. His eyes were bloodshot and he was pale and shaking. Clearly, still in the throes of a hangover.

"Bryson?" I asked, leaving Alec's side. Bryson was tipping dangerously and I caught him just as he toppled over. "Are you sure you should be out of bed? You were pretty out of it last night."

He grimaced. "I know. I'm so sorry. I was hoping we could talk about that."

I felt so bad for him. He looked like he wanted to die. "Of course we can talk about that," I said quickly. Behind me, I heard Alec approaching, his shoes crunching on the gravel. I could feel him coming closer and everything in me hoped he would slide his arms around my waist and pull me back against him.

He wouldn't, of course, because we were… well, I wasn't sure exactly what we were. Obviously, more than friends. I mean, I thought we were more than friends. But we weren't together. But we weren't on some casual first date, either. There was too much tension. Too much need. Too much history. Alec stopped next to me, arms crossed over his broad chest. "You need to go home, Bryson. Go back to bed. You look like shit."

Bryson grinned at me. "I don't think that's possible."

Oh, it was possible. But I didn't want to be mean. "You

look like you're in pain," I said gently.

"I am." He nodded. "I'm in pain because I know I was terrible last night and it breaks my heart that you think I'm an idiot."

Alec sighed, shaking his head. "Dude, that was cheesy as hell."

Ignoring Alec, Bryson said as enthusiastically as seemed possible at the moment, "Let's go get some coffee, should we?" Bryson looped his arm through mine and started for the door.

Muttering, Alec followed along behind. This is not how I wanted things to be. I didn't want to be in the middle. I didn't want Alec to be angry today. I wanted to sit on his lap and drink hot chocolate and stare into his eyes all morning.

Now *that* was cheesy.

I reached back, summoning all my courage, and grabbed Alec's fingers. They were stiff with shock for about four seconds, and then he curled his hand around mine and squeezed gently.

The little bell above the door tinkled cheerfully as we walked in. "Table for three please," Bryson said, wincing as the dull roar from the very busy restaurant assaulted his tender head.

I leaned around him, clearing my throat. "Actually, we're getting our food to go, if that's okay. We're not staying."

Bryson's chin dropped in confusion and Alec chuckled. Now he did pull me back against him, tugging me away from Bryson's tight grip. His arms slid around my waist, holding me tight against his chest, so tight I could feel his heart pounding against my back. Like what he'd just done had taken a lot of courage.

I couldn't swallow.

The thought that his heart was pounding—that he was as nervous as I was—it was adorable.

Bryson turned slowly, his eyes widening. "Are you two—

are you here together?"

I blinked three times, trying to see how he couldn't already know that. I failed. "I—we—you saw me get out of his truck—"

Bryson waved a hand through the air. "I know but I mean—*together* together?"

I tried to figure out how to explain it without hurting his feelings. I opened my mouth twice, but couldn't make any sound come out.

"Yes," Alec said flatly. I twisted my head around to see his face. He looked down and smiled before he returned his glare to Bryson.

In my daydreams that he would come back, that I would find myself in his arms again, this was not at all what I had imagined. The hostess handed us menus and neither boy broke their cold staring contest to take them. I sighed, thanking the woman. "Guys?"

"Where are you going after this if you're not staying here?" Bryson asked. He sounded angry. Like I'd somehow betrayed him. Or Alec had. I frowned, wanting desperately to escape this place. Why were there never any demon attacks in the day? Although if there were demon attacks, I wouldn't be able to fight them. My powers didn't work when the sun was up and my ghosts couldn't come out of their prison. If there was ever an attack during the day, I'd be dead. Like, within two seconds, probably.

"I'm not sure how that has anything to do with you." Alec's arms tightened protectively around me, which was comforting given my train of thought.

"I saw her first, Alec."

He saw me what now? "Are you serious with this?" I asked incredulously. "You saw me first?"

"Actually, I saw her first. In seventh grade when we were thirteen. I've loved her ever since. So. Back. Off."

I froze. Everything in me froze—my blood, my breath, my heart, my brain. Alec had loved me ever since? What about the last four years when we were supposed to hate each other? What about now?

"You had your chance with her, Alec. You walked away."

"And it was the biggest mistake I ever made. I'm not going to make it again."

My head started to pound, whether from the extreme awkwardness of the situation or the extreme lack of food, I wasn't sure. I was suddenly very tired and very hungry and very confused. "Enough!" I yelled. The entire restaurant turned to stare at us. The hostess, who'd been watching with unabashed curiosity, hurried away. I slid out of Alec's arms. I needed space. I needed fresh air. And sleep. And food. "Bryson, I'm sorry you thought there was something between us when there wasn't. That was not Alec's fault." Before I could see the hurt in his face, I turned on Alec, shoving stray strands of my dark hair away from my face in frustration. "Alec, you owe me breakfast. So either you stop arguing with Bryson and decide what you want, or I'm walking home to make my own cereal." I crossed my arms and glared at them both.

Sure, I fought demons on an almost nightly basis with an army of lost souls. But confrontation in the daylight with people who weren't trying to destroy humanity? That was something entirely different and much, much harder.

Alec closed his eyes, briefly. "I'm so sorry, Navi. What do you want?"

"A bagel. Toasted with cream cheese. And hot chocolate," I muttered, still pouting. He nodded and strode off to find the hostess who seemed to be hiding behind her counter, probably ready to call the cops.

"Navi, please don't do this. Don't go with him. He's all wrong for you." Bryson took my hand, rubbing his thumb across my knuckles. "I know you don't know me well, but there's an undeniable connection between us. You can't tell me you don't feel it."

"Bryson," I said gently, disentangling my fingers. "I don't know you at all. And I don't feel a connection. I'm sorry. You're very nice." Yes. Add the nice bit. Because that always softened the blow.

He hung his head. "I never should have had that party. You'd never have found Alec again and it would be me taking you to breakfast, not him."

I bit my lip until the sharp little teeth threatened to tear through the skin. "No, Bryson. That isn't true. I'm sorry, but it isn't. Please. You guys are roommates. You have to let this go or you'll both be miserable."

Alec paid and reached for the two bags the woman handed him and I wanted to race back to the kitchens and kiss them all for being so quick with our food. But that would be weird, so I didn't.

Bryson shoved his hands in his pockets, staring at the floor. "He isn't right for you Navi." My breath caught in my throat as he looked up, his crystal blue eyes meeting mine, so full of pain. "One day you'll realize that."

"Ready?" Alec asked, his voice barely above a growl. I stared at Bryson in confusion for several seconds before I could manage to tear my eyes away from him and nod. Was that some kind of threat? It had sounded an awful lot like a threat.

But no. No way. He was a sweet guy, right?

"Yeah," I said slowly. "Yeah, I'm ready." To Bryson, I said, "I'm really sorry. I hope—I hope you feel better."

He didn't say anything, just watched us walk away.

The bell above the door didn't sound quite so cheerful as we left.

"WHAT WAS THAT?" I ASKED AS soon as we made it outside.

Alec hung his head, looking as dejected as Bryson had. "I'm sorry. I don't know what came over me."

"Alec—"

"No, wait." He opened the truck door and helped me in. I tried to remember I was angry so I shouldn't feel the heat spiral through my body where his hands touched my waist. "I do know what that was."

I thunked into my side and slid my seat belt on as he shut the door. He climbed in and jammed the key into the ignition but didn't start the truck. "Navi, you don't understand."

He had no idea how right he was. "So explain it to me."

He ran a hand over his face, leaning back against the headrest. "I don't—I don't know how."

Bryson had left the restaurant, coffee cup in hand. Alec must have seen him, because he started the truck and backed out, roaring onto the road like my demons were after him. "I have an idea. Can you wait to eat for about ten minutes?" He gave me the most vulnerable face ever. I was mad, but not mad enough to say no to that face.

"Yes," I said quietly.

We drove in silence. No singing, no talking. I stared out the window and wished I could cry. I hadn't cried in three and a half years. Now, I wasn't sure if I even could.

Alec turned off the main road and onto a dirt path barely wide enough for his great big truck. It was overgrown with tall grasses and low hanging trees, but I recognized it instantly. His parents had a piece of land in the middle of the forest. There wasn't much out there—they mostly used it for camping, but Alec and I had hung out there a lot in high school.

He backed up so the bed of the truck overlooked the

river. The leaves were starting to change, and we were surrounded by reds and golds and greens and the blue, blue sky. I was glad he'd parked in the shade. The sun and I didn't get along so well.

He got out and came around to my side. Again, he lifted me out. Heat seared me as I slid down his body. Trapped between him and the truck, I could only stare up at him helplessly, praying he would kiss me, praying he wouldn't.

I was a very confused girl.

He finally backed away, reaching around me to grab our breakfast. I felt equal measures of disappointment and relief, which made absolutely no sense.

Food. I needed food. And sleep. Then the world would be right again.

He opened the second set of doors without looking at me and pulled out a thick quilt. I wandered away to the river, absently sliding off my flip-flops so I could stick my toes in the icy water. We lived minutes from the ocean, and I knew Alec loved it, but he had never once taken me there. I didn't mind because I spent enough time at the beach fighting demons and knowing what comes out of the water at night makes me less likely to think it's beautiful in the day.

But rivers. Rivers are a different thing entirely. I had never seen a demon come out of a river. They bubbled and roared and were cheerful and beautiful. They were my weakness. This river, especially, because along with it being a river that was cheerful and beautiful and bubbly and roar-y, there were a ton of memories here. Good memories.

I glanced over my shoulder at Alec, who was spreading the blanket into the back of his truck.

Very good memories.

"I screwed up," he said, jumping down from the truck and coming over to me.

I raised an eyebrow and waited for him to continue.

"I know—look, I know we aren't together."

Ouch.

But he continued before I had a chance to register that my pain made no sense because we'd only just re-met.

"I know until yesterday you probably hadn't even thought about me for years—"

Right. Not even close.

"—but dammit, Navi! I haven't stopped thinking about you. You walked in last night and it felt like time hadn't passed and you were still mine and you still belonged in my arms. And those six hours without you felt like six more years."

"I—I thought you hated me," I whispered. "All those years—I went all the way to Alaska to get away from you!" Pain lanced across his face and I instantly regretted my words. "I didn't mean—"

"No." He shook his head. "No, I deserved it. But Navi, you have to know, what happened in high school—I didn't mean for it to get out."

I sighed. I didn't want to talk about high school. High school hurt.

"Letting you go was the stupidest thing I've ever done," he whispered, his voice hoarse.

The world stopped. Everything froze. Time shattered. "It was?"

He ran a hand over his face, peering at me through his fingers. "By far. Do you know how many times I called you after we broke up? To beg you to come back. But the way you glared at me in the hall—I always chickened out and hung up before it started to ring."

I'd done the same thing. A thousand times. Maybe two thousand. I still remembered my carefully rehearsed speech, in which I begged him to believe me and if he didn't, I told him the whole truth.

But yeah... even in my daydreams I knew how that conversation would go. Then the whole school wouldn't have just thought I was a cheating slut, they would think I was crazy, too. And Alec would die because I'd opened his eyes to the demons. They liked to kill the ones who could see them coming.

I frowned, remembering. Remembering the snickers and the guys following me around thinking I was easy.

"No. Don't you start thinking about it, Navi. Don't you dare. I finally got you to talk to me again." He tipped his head, catching me so that I was trapped in that dark blue gaze. "I *know* we just re-met, but I—I don't want you to date Bryson."

I blinked. That wasn't on the list of things I'd been expecting him to say. Trying to hide my smirk, I said, "What's wrong with Bryson?"

"Nothing's wrong with Bryson," Alec growled, scowling. "Everything. He's not right for you."

I leaned back, crossing my arms while I dug my toes into the mud. It was cold and squishy and reminded me of being a little kid when my parents used to take me to the river. Never, ever the beach, but the river, yes. "And who is it you think is right for me?" I asked innocently.

"Me, Navi. I think I'm right for you."

Now I couldn't help but grin. I raised an eyebrow, dancing away. "You do, do you?"

He swore under his breath as a rueful smile creased his gorgeous face. "Yes. I do. I don't want you to date anyone else. Just me."

"I don't know... you're practically a stranger. A stranger who hasn't fed me yet."

"Oh crap." He grabbed my hand and pulled me over to the truck, lifting me into the back as if I weighed less than a small dog. "You have all day to get to know me."

I laughed as I settled against the front of the bed and dug

out my breakfast. Holy Hannah, I was starving. One thing about fighting at night, it used a ton of calories and I had to eat like an elephant the next day.

So far, there had been no eating at all, elephant or otherwise.

"All day, huh?" I asked between bites. "I thought this was just breakfast."

"That was before you raised the stakes. If I'm gonna talk you into being with me and no one else, it's going to take more than breakfast."

CHAPTER NINE

Alec

I WATCHED HER. I'D PRETTY MUCH just bared my soul, and she hadn't run screaming. Instead, she ate like I'd starved her half to death. There was hope. Maybe, just maybe, she felt the same way I did.

For those fifteen minutes it'd taken to get from the Chicken Coop to here, I'd thought I had lost her. I didn't even have her yet and I thought I'd lost her. The panic in those minutes had nearly driven me over the edge. How could I be so afraid of losing something I hadn't even realized I desperately wanted until less than twenty-four hours ago?

"Whatcha thinkin', stranger?" she asked, looking up at me with those dark, dark eyes. I was caught and falling, drowning in her gaze—it was becoming a habit every time I looked at her. Her lips quirked in that teasing grin I wanted to kiss right off her mouth.

"I'm thinking..." *I'm thinking I'm falling hard and fast and it scares the hell out of me. But letting you go scares me worse.*

She raised an eyebrow when I didn't continue. "If I didn't

know better, I'd say you were as tired as I am." And she yawned.

She was the only person I knew who was adorable when she yawned. She sort of squeaked at the end, like a little mouse.

"You need to rest." I tried not to be disappointed. She had, after all, only gotten two hours of sleep but I'd been hoping I was entertaining enough that she'd forget how exhausted she was.

She shrugged. "Work takes a lot out of me."

"What happened last night?" I asked. I knew her mom had been a probation officer, but Navi was tiny and sweet. I couldn't picture her ordering around reformed criminals any more than I could picture Bryson actually working a real job.

"There was just a minor… skirmish. Nothing major but it took quite a while." She traced the seam on her yoga pants with her finger, shaking her head. "I'm worried about some of my charges. I think they're losing interest in saving their souls." She flushed and jerked her head up, like she'd said something wrong. I hadn't really ever thought about parolees as being in danger of losing their souls, but then I hadn't met a lot of them, either.

"I'm sorry." It sounded lame, but I honestly couldn't think of anything else to say.

She smiled and shook her head, scooting closer to me. My heart tried to claw its way right out of my throat. "I'm sorry I'm so tired for our first date in four years."

"Hey. Come here." I slid my arm around her shoulders and pulled her into me, sliding down and bunching up the quilt until it made a nice little pillow behind me. I hadn't gotten a whole lot of sleep the night before, either. I could nap.

She curled against me, her leg sliding up to lay across my thigh and she put her head on my chest. Yeah. There was not a chance in hell I was going to sleep at all. "Are you sure you don't mind?" she asked, tipping her head back to look up at me.

I kissed her forehead. "No. I definitely do not mind."

She sighed contentedly and burrowed against me, and I was absolutely positive my blood was humming. With her head against my chest, I knew she could hear my heart pounding. Any chance of playing it cool was completely gone. Instead I tangled my fingers in the silk of her hair, sliding it against my skin. I watched the sky above us through the thick leaves and stroked my other hand up and down her back until her breathing evened out and she relaxed against me.

This. This was heaven.

I COULD TELL THE SECOND SHE woke up because in the two hours that she'd been sleeping on my chest, I'd memorized her heartbeat. I could feel it against my side, and when she woke, it sped up. Quite a bit.

I grinned triumphantly. I wasn't the only one having trouble playing it cool.

She stretched, and in those few delicious seconds I could feel every curve of her against me. "How long have I been keeping you trapped here?" she asked, pushing herself up. The absence of her warmth felt like someone attacking my soul with shards of ice. I wanted her back.

"Not long enough," "I said. I crossed my arms behind my head and raised an eyebrow at her. She flushed and bit her lip. If she had any idea just how insane I went when she did that, she'd stop doing it. Or maybe she knew already and she was tempting me.

One could only hope.

"I forgot how beautiful it is here." Clearly, an attempt to change the subject. I didn't fight it, instead following her gaze to the river. She'd always loved the water. I shoved myself up and climbed out of the back of the truck, a little stiff because lying on the rough bed for two hours, even with the comforter, was uncomfortable.

But it had been worth it.

She started after me, her shoes still in the truck. "Hop on," I said. She didn't hesitate, sliding from the truck onto my back. I carried her over to the water and slowly let her down in the soft mud. She rolled her pants up to her knees and I drank up the sight of her tan, slender legs like they alone could save me. Did the girl have no flaws?

"I like the water," she murmured, almost as if she'd forgotten I was there. She waded deeper, dancing lightly over rocks worn smooth from countless years in this current. She'd always played sports when I knew her, especially football, but she moved with the grace of a ballerina. My mom had thought she was some sort of fairy princess in another life.

"Can I ask you a question?" She paused and looked over her shoulder at me through thick lashes. Her cheeks were flushed and I could tell that whatever was coming made her uncomfortable.

"Yep." Because honestly, what else could I say?

She turned to face me, twisting her hands in front of her and nibbling on her lip. Apparently she wanted to drive me straight to the brink of insanity. "In your room last night—"

I grinned and her cheeks went even brighter. "That's not what I meant..."

"Sorry." I tried to rearrange my face into a solemn expression, but must have failed, judging by the look she gave me.

"There was a picture..."

Holy crap. She'd seen her picture? I thought—I was sure I'd put it back in the drawer. Well this was awkward. Telling her I'd never gotten over her was one thing. Having her picture in my nightstand after all these years bordered on obsessed. "I can explain."

"Is he—is he yours?"

"It's just that—what?" *He*? Suddenly I had no idea what we were talking about.

"The picture of the little boy in your room. Is he yours?"

Finally, it all clicked into place and I burst out laughing. "No, Angel. No."

"Oh. I just wondered. Not that I have anything against kids, but, you know, if I agree to this girlfriend stuff I need to know—" She stopped, biting her lip.

In two short strides I crossed the river to her stride. I couldn't handle it anymore, her nibbling on that pink lip, pouting, tempting me beyond all sense of reason. I slid my hand up to cup her cheek and lowered my head to hers.

It was like coming home. The soft sweetness of her mouth against mine, the gasp against my lips as her entire body tensed. Then she sighed against me and slid her arms around my neck, twining her hands behind my head and pulling me closer.

I was only too happy to do her bidding.

"You have no idea how long I've been waiting for this," I said against her mouth.

"I might." Navi sighed as I slid my tongue across her bottom lip, reveling in the feel of her against me. She sucked in a breath.

I wanted her. More than I'd ever wanted anyone. But I couldn't let that happen, not yet. I didn't want to ruin this—I needed her too bad. Instead I scooped her into my arms and carried her back to my truck. I laid her down and stretched out next to her, leaning up on one arm so I could brush her dark hair back away from her face while she watched me.

"Who is he?" she asked suddenly, her voice breathy and shaking just a little.

"He?" For the life of me, I could not figure out who we were talking about.

"The boy in the picture. In your room."

I reached out and traced her lips with my finger, then trailed across her jaw line and down her throat, memorizing every detail, every freckle, every scar. There were a lot of them, I realized with a frown. Lots of little scars across her face, and a bigger one on her neck, usually hidden in her hair.

"Alec?" she asked, searching my eyes. Belatedly, I realized she was worried about this picture. Seriously, I needed to focus.

"He's my little brother, Jack. Remember, I told you about him last night?"

"Your brother." She let her breath out in a relieved whoosh, her eyes fluttering closed. "Of course."

"My parents were lonely. I grew up too fast or something." I leaned forward and kissed her again, gently, my fingers tangling in her hair. I could do this for the rest of the day. For the rest of my life. Just stay here with this girl under this sky.

CHAPTER TEN

Navi

THE SUN HAD SET OVER AN hour ago, and I had no desire to move out of Alec's arms. We'd covered four years worth of memories in one afternoon, and it still didn't feel like enough. I needed more, even as the little buzzing voice in the back of my head kept saying, *don't let him hurt you. Don't let him hurt you.*

He wouldn't hurt me. He'd said losing me was the worst mistake he'd ever made. You didn't say something like that and then turn around and break someone's heart.

Right?

I lay on his chest, listening to his heart beat while his hand slowly stroked up and down my spine, sending delicious shivers racing across my skin. "You know, I went to Alaska once. Looking for you. But I got there and had no idea where to even start searching. I came back empty handed."

My eyebrows shot up. "Seriously? You came all the way up there looking for me?"

He chuckled softly. "I told you I never got over you.

Sometimes I'd miss you so much I did crazy things."

Yeah. That I understood.

I still love you. After all this time. I could tell him…

"I only had a couple of weeks, though. I had to get back home. Responsibilities." His voice dropped so I had to strain to hear him. "It killed me leaving there without you."

"When?" I asked, leaning up so I could see him. "When did you come?"

He watched his hand as it trailed over the tattoo on my wrist. "Two years ago."

Two years ago. If he'd actually found me two years ago, that would have been two years less of the torture I'd been going through trying so desperately to forget him. The waste of time made me feel a little sick. "What did you do after that?"

His smile turned rueful. "Don't hate me."

"I couldn't possibly."

"I dated. A lot. Went through a lot of girls trying to forget you." His fingers stilled against my wrist and I wondered if he could feel the way he made my pulse jump. "Jealous?" His dark blue eyes danced as a grin played around his lips. He pulled me back down onto his chest, so our faces were only an inch apart.

"Maybe a little," I whispered.

"I'm yours now, Navi. Just say the word."

Behind me, beyond the bed of the truck, someone cleared her throat.

With a strangled screech, I sat up and whirled around. "Elizabeth," I gasped.

"Who?" Alec frowned, also sitting up, but more slowly, which was wise on his part. I was still slightly light-headed from moving so quickly.

"They come, Navi."

As much as I was loathe to leave Alec, I had a job to do.

People to protect. Souls to save. I nodded and dug my phone out of my pocket, pretending to check a text message. "I have to go to work."

"Now?" Alec asked, squinting up at the sky.

Yes, it was probably close to midnight. It couldn't be helped.

I nodded. I could run faster than his truck could drive, but leaping out and taking off would be a little hard to explain. Instead, I pulled him out of the bed, wadding up the quilt and tossing it in the back before he could even get his bearings. "I'll be there as soon as I can," I said to Elizabeth when he went to open my door. She nodded, regret in her eyes. Elizabeth, more than anyone, knew how hard I'd fought to get over Alec. And so she would understand how much I wanted to stay with him. Her regret was for me, and I loved her for it.

"If you could just drop me off at Vine and Center Street, that would be great." I clambered up into the truck and gave him my sweetest smile.

"Drop you off alone on the edge of town? Are you serious? What about when you want to get home?"

Oh shoot. I hadn't thought of that. Life would be so much easier if I could just tell him—except for, you know, the mortal danger I'd be putting him in and everything. I really didn't like to lie, but desperate times and all that. "I'll catch a ride home with one of my friends. It's fine."

He gave me an odd look before shutting my door and going around to his side. He swung smoothly into the cab. "You're sure about this? Do you even have a weapon?"

Oh yes. I couldn't tell him that, though. "It will be fine, I promise." I danced around the truth. "I do this all the time."

He sighed. "Is it going to get any easier having a probation officer for a girlfriend?" The lopsided grin he gave me sent my heart spiraling through my rib cage.

"Hey now," I teased as I slid closer to him. "I don't think you even asked me. What's with the assuming, Alec?"

He turned wide innocent eyes on me before reaching across with his free hand to buckle my seat belt. "We have to keep you safe." He looked back to the road and cleared his throat and if I didn't know better, I'd say he was nervous. "Navi, about that girlfriend thing... what do you think? Just me? No other guys?"

Did he really think there was anything to worry about? Like any other guy had ever come even close to comparing to him? I leaned my head against his shoulder. "Yeah, Alec. I'll be your girlfriend." Raising my head to peek at him in the darkness, I said, "Now what? Do I wear your letterman jacket or something?"

He lifted my hand to his lips, kissing my knuckles in what I decided was the sweetest thing anyone had ever done. And he'd done it twice now. If I was the swooning type, I'd have crumpled at his feet long ago. "I might have to dig it out of storage."

Today had been heaven. But we weren't in high school. Who entered into an exclusive relationship after such a short amount of time? I mean, in high school, yeah. All the time. I'd agreed to be Alec's girlfriend when I'd spoken to him maybe three times.

He was watching me with those hooded eyes. ""You look worried."

"It's just a little fast. That's all," I finally whispered.

He nodded, dragging in a deep, deep breath. "Yeah. I forget—I'm sorry. I forget it's only been two days. It feels like more."

Struggling to lighten the very intense atmosphere in the truck, I said, "Wait... if time flies when you're having fun and two days feels like enough to talk about being exclusive, what are you saying about time with me?" I regarded him suspiciously. "Are you calling me boring?"

He laughed, pulling me against him to kiss my temple. "Not a chance in hell, Angel."

Alec dropped me off at the intersection and I could only brush my lips against his before I jumped out. I barely had time to feel the heat shoot all the way to my toes before I turned to see what waited for me… and I realized I'd left heaven behind and walked right into hell.

"QUICKLY, NAVI. SING TO them. We don't have much time." Elizabeth was the only ghost there, standing on the outside of Devil's Gate, pacing back and forth and tripping over her own skirts—which she rarely did and which I'd never been able to figure out. How did a ghost trip over something ghostly?

I glanced at Elizabeth and nodded. The asuwangs were already clawing their way up the beach and some were even climbing the walls of Devil's Gate. If they reached the row of houses, they'd be hard to track with too many places to hide. If I lost even one of them, they could shift and turn themselves into anyone when the sun came up. I'd never find them.

Well, not until they started killing people.

And eating them.

Then I'd find them pretty quickly.

But, if it was at all possible, I'd like for no one to die first. That seemed like a way better option. So I opened my mouth, letting the ancient words flow off my tongue. The asuwangs, realizing what it meant, screeched and tried to claw faster, but they were still struggling to make their flippers work like legs. Give them five minutes, and they'd be freakishly fast.

My voice was familiar—the same tone as when I sang on stage, but at the same time hauntingly different, even though I'd used it to call my ghosts a thousand times, it still sent shivers of foreboding up and down my spine. I had no idea what the words meant, only that they were ancient and super powerful.

My ghosts appeared, rising from their cells on the outskirts of hell. Elizabeth alone was free to roam our world—she'd been given the chance to move on, and had refused. She wanted to stay and fight with me, for some inexplicable reason. The rest, they lived in holding cells, only allowed freedom at night to watch for incoming demons and fight.

Luckily for me, Elizabeth acted as our first response, alerting me and freeing my ghosts. Otherwise, my life would be way more complicated.

Elizabeth ran down the beach alone, swords blazing in the moonlight. One by one as the rest of my army arrived; they went after her, diving furiously into battle.

Jesse, however, lagged behind. I rolled my eyes and unsheathed my swords. "I saw some make it further down the beach. Go stop them—take someone with you," I yelled as I ran by her. She muttered but I didn't have time to listen.

I sprinted down the beach, already swinging Kali through the air. I sliced through the claw dug deep into Don's soul, one of my newer ghosts. The asuwang screamed and jerked back as I whirled, gaining momentum. I came around and lopped its ugly half-human head right off. "Are you okay?" I panted, dancing away from the head as it rolled down the beach.

Don nodded, holding a transparent hand to his wounded soul. Without a word, he raised his sword with his other hand and dashed back into the fight, swinging it like a club. I hid a smile. Very brave of him. I'd have to mention this to Death when I saw him next.

But more of my ghosts were in trouble. I followed Don, wading through destruction, trying to save them. Yes, they were ghosts. Yes, they had all done things to land them on the brink of eternal fire and brimstone. But they were here. They'd chosen to fight for their redemption.

That meant a lot to me and I wasn't going to give up on them.

Humans can't hurt ghosts. But demons? Demons can. I heard Elizabeth scream and swung around to see an asuwang holding her by the throat, its claws slowly digging into her soul, cutting off the life force. The thing about dying by the hand of a demon is if they take your soul, you don't get to go straight to the afterlife. Best scenario is they wear you like a shield against the sun. Next best case was you get taken to their sea-witch, and she uses you to make a giant, impenetrable shell for herself, and if we're fast enough, we can cut you free before the sun hits you and melts you into an impenetrable shield—but not until she decides to leave her lair and attack the surface. Worst case is you're kept in a cage until the sea witch wanted to invade land and kill everything, and then you're worn as a shell on her back until the sun melts you into an impenetrable shield. It isn't until *she* dies that you finally get to go to hell. No more chances at redemption. And for Elizabeth, who had been offered redemption but turned it down to stay and fight for something she believed in—that just wasn't fair.

Hell didn't look so bad compared to that.

I leaped over the crumbling, bloody body before me, jamming my sword into its back and jerking the blade out as I landed hard on the other side. I used my swords as scissors on the next demon blocking my way, slicing through its neck. But I didn't have time to watch it fall. I spun around it like a football running back and fought my way closer to Elizabeth. The demons seemed determined to keep me away, blocking my path every step of the way. I screamed, the sound reverberating through the deserted beach. The asuwangs trembled and collapsed, writhing on the ground. My throat was hoarse, so much that it felt like it was on fire. I only had one scream like that in every moon cycle, so I tried to save them for emergencies.

Elizabeth was in trouble. This was an emergency.

I whirled through the collapsed bodies as my ghosts fell on them with their swords, tearing them to bits. I got to Elizabeth and chopped at the hand still somehow tangled in her throat until the arm fell away alone. Sheathing my swords, I dug the claws out of her neck, wincing at the rubbery scaliness of them.

Ick. Ick. Ick.

She gasped as I finally pulled them free, like she was gasping for air but I knew she didn't breathe. Behind me, the asuwangs were pulling themselves to their feet, moving in stunned slowness. I jerked back toward her. "Are you okay? Should I call Death?"

Her eyes widened and she shook her head vehemently. "I am fine, Navi."

I scanned her wounds, but I could hear the asuwangs howling. There wasn't time to baby her. "Okay. Just stay away from them, okay? Heal first." Thankfully, when the moon was up, they healed as fast as I did.

"Navi!" One of my army yelled and I spun on my heel, already unsheathing Kali and Golly as I turned. I thrust them out and into the face of a demon just rising from its crouch. The moon was setting. If they have a soul to shield them, they could shift into other forms when the moon set.

And my ghosts would get sent back to their cages when the moon set.

And I would lose my powers when the moon set.

"Hurry!" I cried. I spied Elizabeth running down the beach, so at least she was out of harm's way. My ghosts redoubled their efforts, racing against the moon. I swung my blades down, felt them slice through the rubbery skin, and jerked them free before spinning on the next demon threatening to impale me with its claws.

Because if that happened, it would eat me.

That would be unpleasant.

Faster. I had to move faster. I flew through the motions, dancing out of danger, whirling back in, jabbing, thrusting. Trying to save the souls in danger. It would be so awesome if someone could figure out how to make our blades start on fire. Then we could blaze right through these stupid monsters. But my mom didn't know how to do anything like that and I'd never met another Agent besides her. Someone should start a chat room for Agents. That would be super helpful.

"Navi!"

Crap. I'd gone too far into my own head, and the asuwang knocked me flying, pouncing on top of me as I hit the sand on my back. I squealed as its teeth reached for my face, hot drool scalding my skin.

And then it screamed and arched away enough that I could get my blades up and into its skin. I could see Robert, one of my ghosts, over its shoulder, jerking his own swords free.

The thing collapsed on me, its last breath rattling in its chest. "Get off, get off, get off!" I screeched, shoving it hard until I could wriggle out from under it.

The rest of the demons were dead, except for two that wouldn't last more than a couple of seconds, given that my entire army had focused their attention on them.

"That was close. I guess they wanted to remind us that this isn't supposed to be so easy," I panted.

Robert nodded solemnly, watching the fight. "If this keeps up, we're going to need a bigger army. We lost three tonight."

"Oh no," I murmured. "Who?"

"Don. Serena. Christopher."

The last two I could understand. They weren't my most

enthusiastic fighters. But Don had been. My heart ached.

"Navi!" Elizabeth screamed, racing down the beach, nothing more than a white blur. "They've made it through. They're past the city streets and already shifting!"

"Oh no, indeed," Robert said. He took off toward Elizabeth. I risked a glanced at the moon, already fading in the early morning light. I had only a few minutes with my powers before they were gone, too. If we could keep the escaped demons from making it back to their sea witch, we could kill them and save the souls.

"Don't let them past!" I yelled to my army. Not a problem, since the remaining demons *they* were fighting were already dead. Pulling off my heels, I left them in the sand and sprinted after Robert.

CHAPTER ELEVEN

Alec

I DIDN'T HAVE TO WORK THE next day. Which was good because I'd spent the night staring at my ceiling, re-living every single second of the day before. Every kiss. Every word. Navi was mine again.

All was right with the world.

I heard Bryson come in, stumble around, crash into things, and maybe fall over a few times. Drunk, again. Although this time, I didn't blame him. I'd be drunk, too, if I'd just lost Navi.

I'd fallen hard and fast. It was terrifying—so terrifying—but nothing in me seemed to care. I would gladly face that fear. Josh would tell me I was stupid. He'd tell me we didn't know each other and he'd tell me I couldn't possibly fall in love with her after one day.

And then I'd tell him I could if I'd never fallen *out* of love with her.

And he would tell me it wasn't possible. He'd tell me we had hated each other in high school. He'd tell me I'd hated her after high school. He'd tell me I'd dated thirty different girls since her. But he didn't know about my trip to Alaska. He didn't know about Navi's picture in my nightstand drawer. He didn't know she was only one thought away, day or night, always.

And he never would. Because I was a guy, and guys don't think like that. Or at least, we aren't supposed to.

It didn't stop me, though.

I wasn't sleeping anyway, so I rolled over and grabbed my phone. *"Text me when you're home, k?"*

She didn't respond, so I lay there worrying for the next couple of hours. I was finally drifting off to sleep when my phone beeped. *"I'm home. This better not wake you up or I'll feel bad."*

Maybe a little, but I wasn't gonna tell her that. *"Not asleep. Need you here."*

My heart pounded. She'd say no. I knew she would. Or she just wouldn't respond, like the night before. But then she did respond. *"I'm exhausted. And messy. Sleep is calling me."*

I swallowed. If sleep was all she wanted, I could do that. If it meant having her head on my chest again, I'd take it. *"Come here. We'll just sleep. I promise."*

The way my palms were sweating, you'd think I was asking for a lot more than her lying next to me all night. I had to attempt to breathe about fifteen times before I actually succeeded. And she still didn't respond.

I gave up, hating the acid of disappointment in my stomach. I wanted her here. I wanted her with me. I dropped my phone on the table and rolled onto my back to resume staring at the ceiling. She must have fallen asleep.

There was a knock at the door.

It was timid and so quiet I barely heard it. Bryson snorted from the other room. It couldn't be her, could it? She'd just barely told me she was home, and I hadn't heard a car pull up.

But who else would be here at four-thirty in the morning? I leaped out of bed and pulled on a pair of shorts, nearly killed myself in my rush out of my room, and tripped over an unconscious roommate in the middle of the hallway. "Dammit, Bryson!" I muttered as I hopped to the door and swung it open.

"Hi." She waved and bit her lip. Her hair was a tangled mess, like she'd been fighting with the wind. Her cheeks were bright pink and her clothes were covered in sand. I didn't care.

I pulled her inside and shut the door behind her. "Hi." I tugged her closer to me, sliding one hand up her neck as I lowered my mouth to hers. Heat seared me as our lips met and I could feel my entire body react instantly. She sucked in a breath, her hands clutching into fists against my chest. "Alec," she whispered.

"What the hell, Alec? I didn't think you were a big enough ass to rub it in my face," Bryson mumbled from the floor. I must have woke him up when I tripped over him.

Navi's eyes widened and she stumbled backward away from me, smacking into the door. "I didn't realize you were er… up…" Her voice trailed off as she stared at him lying on the floor.

"I wasn't," he said.

"Let's get you to bed, should we?" She brushed past me, scooping to help Bryson up.

"I don't want help. I want to lay here and make you miserable."

She smiled brightly and hauled him to his feet. For such a little thing, she was surprisingly strong. "No you don't. You want a nice soft bed to sleep off the nasty hangover you're going to have tomorrow."

I watched, more than a little jealous, as she looped his arm around her neck and led him to his room. I thought I caught a glimpse of bruising along one side of her jaw and the back of her neck, but it was hard to see as she moved away. She disappeared inside and I heard the bed creak. I didn't trust him at all—it would be just like him to attack her again. He'd probably pulled her down on top of him. Growling under my breath, I followed them in, but she was standing above him, pulling the comforter up to his chin.

"Just in time. The sun's about to rise," she murmured as she pulled his curtains shut.

"And you've been up all night." I came in and took her hand. "You need to sleep. With me."

Her eyes shot open and I chuckled, leading her out and into my room. "Just sleep, Angel. With your head on my chest."

"Okay," she whispered. Before she could chicken out, I slid under the covers and held out my hand, motioning her with my fingers. She hesitated, biting her lip, and then toed off her shoes. "You can't sleep in that." I raised an eyebrow and she looked down at her dirty, ragged outfit.

"Oh."

"There's a shirt hanging on the closet door. You can sleep in that if you want." I couldn't even put into words how much I wanted to see her in my shirt.

She picked it up and looked at me, so freaking adorable in her nervousness that I was on the verge of losing whatever was left of my heart. "Yeah, that one."

She nodded quickly and disappeared into the bathroom. Less than a minute later she reappeared, hurried to the light switch and snapped it off before I could even get more than a glimpse of her long, tan legs. I could barely see her through the shadows as she scurried over to the bed. "I'm nervous."

"I promise, I won't even touch you if you don't want me to." Although it would take a herculean effort to keep my hands off her all night.

"That's not what I want," she said quietly as the bed

sagged lightly under her weight. I pulled the blankets up over her, every molecule in my body hyper-aware that she was in my bed and lying very close to me.

And then she snuggled closer.

It was possible I was about to go into cardiac arrest as her leg slid over my thigh and she curled herself around me. And finally, *finally*, she laid her head on my chest.

So she could hear my heart.

I'm sure she was very impressed with my coolness.

"Sleep, Angel." I kissed the top of her head and slowly trailed my hand up and down her spine, drawing pictures on her back until her breath evened, and each breath she took drew delicious shivers across my bare skin.

At least one of us was going to get some sleep.

THE SMELL OF BACON woke me. I had no idea what time it was, but judging by the way the light was trying to blind me through the window, it was late afternoon. I went to roll over so I could see the clock, and remembered Navi.

She was curled on her side with her back to me, still sound asleep. The bruising I thought I'd seen the night before was gone, so it must have been a trick of the light. I remembered her being a fast healer, but even Navi couldn't recover that fast.

I finally leaned around her to see the clock. Two p.m. We'd slept for seven hours straight… and some crazy person was making breakfast in my kitchen at lunch time. Navi, though, was still sound asleep, making scared little noises while she dreamed. So I wasn't the only one who had nightmares… although last night, with her in my arms, the nightmares hadn't come. Lying back down on the pillow, I slid my arm around her waist and settled closer to her. Bacon be damned. I wasn't getting out of this bed.

Pounding on my door seemed to insist otherwise. "What, Bryson?" I growled. Navi groaned and stretched and rolled over to bury her face in my chest. I tightened my arms around her.

"Breakfast is ready," Bryson yelled back, way too loud for my small apartment.

"Then eat it," I snapped.

Navi smiled, eyes still closed. "Be nice," she murmured. Seconds later, she was back to sleep, breathing against my chest in my shirt, her legs tangled with mine.

I leaned on my elbow and watched her sleep, finally giving in and letting myself trace the curves of her face with my fingertip. Her eyelashes fluttered and finally opened, those dark, dark brown eyes hitting me before she smiled sleepily. "Hey."

"Hey." I leaned forward and kissed her nose. "Did you sleep well?"

She nodded and smothered a yawn. "You?"

"Yep." I smoothed a stray curl away from her face. "You're beautiful in the morning."

She twisted to see behind her to the clock. "It isn't morning." With a teasing grin, she rolled back to me.

I caught her before she could bury her face again. I kissed her the way I'd dreamed all night of kissing her, slowly lowering her back against the pillows. She moaned as I parted her lips with my tongue and delved inside. I wanted more. A hell of a lot more, but I couldn't ask for it. Not yet.

This had to last. I couldn't go back to the way things were without her. Which meant I had to be very, very careful.

But the fear of scaring her away didn't make me a saint, and when she slid her arms around my neck, I shifted so more of my weight was against her. Her heart hammered against her rib cage, so loud I could hear it.

Oh wait. That was my heart I could hear.

Or was it Bryson, banging on my door?

Navi jerked away from me as the door swung open and Bryson came in. "What the hell, Bryson?" I growled. Lately, he made me want to growl a lot.

"Breakfast is ready." The look he gave me was so blasted innocent, it had to be fake.

"And you're in here because...?"

Navi sighed and curled closer, burying her head against me and closing her eyes.

"I didn't want your breakfast to get cold." He held his hands out like he could possibly placate me right now. "It's a peace offering. For last night."

"That was very sweet of you, Bryson. We'll be right out." Navi's voice was muffled, and I was hoping I'd misheard her. But Bryson left and she threw the covers off, rolling out of bed.

Apparently I'd heard correctly.

"I have to get home anyway. I have a paper to write today." She looked as crushed as I felt with those ten or so words. I grabbed her tattooed wrist and pulled her back to the bed. She smiled, kneeling on the edge.

"Stay here with me. I'll write your paper for you."

She arched one perfect eyebrow. "Somehow, that doesn't seem like the best idea. Or the most ethical."

Her hair was a wild mess of tangled curls around her face, and she had no makeup on. Wearing only my shirt. And I swear in that second she was the most beautiful thing I'd ever seen in my life. "Stay with me today," I said again. When she looked like she might object, I added, "I have blueprints I need to go over. I can do that while you write." And then I gave her my best puppy dog eyes.

She laughed, leaning forward on her hands and knees to kiss me. "Fine. But—" she hesitated, looking up like she could see through the wall. I ran my fingers through the silky curls falling around us. "We need to go to my house. It's too hard on him having us here."

Bryson. Of course. "Okay. I'll follow you over."

"Actually… Can I have a ride?" She looked away, biting the inside of her cheek. I frowned. I knew that look. She'd always been a terrible liar. "I had a friend drop me off last night. My car is at home."

Something was up, but I couldn't see how it mattered. Maybe she'd wrecked her car the night before and was embarrassed to tell me. That would explain the disheveled clothes and hair and the bruises.

Except there was definitely no bruising today.

"Of course I can take you home," I said slowly. Shaking it off, I sat up. "After breakfast?"

"I hope you guys are hungry." Bryson was way too chipper. If he was going to act like this every time Navi was here, we were going to have to do some serious rearranging.

"Starving." Navi gave him a bright smile as she came out of my room, fully dressed in her clothes from the night before. "It looks great, Bryson."

"My grandma was one of the best cooks in Tennessee. She taught me everything she knew. And for the record, Alec can't cook at all." Bryson glared at me.

"Okay, stop it. Both of you. No more meanness. Be polite or I'm walking home." Navi planted her hands on her hips and scowled, like we didn't both tower over her and outweigh her by at least sixty pounds.

And both of us backed down immediately.

"Sorry, Angel. I'll be nice." I planted a kiss on the top of her head and gave her a gentle push toward the bar stool.

"Sorry, Navi. That was childish." Bryson nodded, sad eyes watching us.

Call me slow, but it was just barely dawning on me that he really did like her. She wasn't one of the many he'd brought home before. This, us, was really hurting him. I could only imagine how hard it would have been to watch him with Navi.

Yeah, I was a jerk.

Navi and Bryson kept up an enthusiastic conversation about cooking, of which apparently no one in their apartment could do. Bryson gave her tips and offered to come teach them all, and she took him up on it.

I tried not to wallow in self-despair.

"I'm gonna go jump in the shower and then we can go. Sound good?" I asked because if she decided to like him better than me because he could cook, I might just rip his head off. I could cook. I was an excellent cook. It just didn't make any sense to cook for one person, so I usually ate out.

It was the fastest shower I ever took.

When I got out, Navi was sitting on my bed, feet tucked underneath her, typing on her phone. She looked up with a smile. "Konstanz thinks I died last night. I forgot to tell her where I was going."

"Hey, how about if I come over today and do some cooking lessons?" Bryson appeared in my doorway, fully dressed but not, judging by the lack of wet hair, showered. "I don't have anything going on, and I know Konstanz and Reese aren't working."

Navi's smile faltered, but she nodded. "Sure. That sounds good. I'll be working on a paper, but I think everyone else is free." She climbed to her feet, sliding on her shoes, and turned to me. "I have to work at dark, but I'm all yours for the rest of the day." She smiled, leaning up on her toes to kiss me as soon as Bryson left the room.

This idea, I liked.

CHAPTER TWELVE

Navi

"YOU SPENT THE NIGHT WITH ALEC?" Konstanz squeal-whispered as soon as I walked into my bedroom. She grabbed my hands and bounced around like when we were teenagers.

"Shhh!" I laughed, disentangling my fingers so I could dig through my dresser for a clean outfit. My clothes still smelled distinctly like demons, and I needed a shower. I'd never found the ones that escaped last night. Which meant they'd made it into society. They'd shifted. They could be anyone right now, and I wouldn't be able to find them until darkness fell and forced them back into their asuwang forms. Who knew what kind of damage they could do between now and then. I'd only quit looking this morning because the sun had risen. I was worthless when the sun was up.

Stupid sun.

I'd never found Jesse, either. She'd either been captured or she'd gone rogue. But Elizabeth had promised to look all day, taking time out of her busy ghost-schedule to search for shape-shifting demons.

"Details, woman! I want details!" Konstanz blocked the doorway, arms crossed over her chest, and raised an eyebrow. Her hair was tied back into two braids, so she looked about as threatening as my bunny slippers.

"Nothing happened. We slept. And had breakfast. That's all." And I was going to spend tonight fighting demons, which meant that was all for the entire weekend. And tomorrow, it was back to reality and work and school and…

The thought made my chest hurt. I liked spending every waking minute with Alec.

"Well that's disappointing." Konstanz flipped her braids over her shoulder. "How is Bryson handling it?" She flopped on her bed and watched me pull out the rest of my clean clothes.

I shook my head. "Not well, I don't think. He was plastered last night and super weird today. Which is why he's here"—I smashed on my most cheerful smile—"to teach you guys to cook. Pretend to have fun, okay?" I pushed her out the door toward the kitchen. "And don't let him and Alec rip each other's heads off."

A day spent on the couch, writing a paper on the meaning of Faulkner's works, with Alec next to me studying layouts and blue prints, and kitchen fires and screaming in the background was still a day that was better than all the days of the last month combined, except for yesterday, of course. And last night. And the night before. I tried to focus on my paper, I really did, but knowing the asuwangs were loose in the city was a tad distracting. I kept flipping through the local news sites on the Internet to see if there had been any attacks yet. And then I tried to figure out how to find them. So the paper… wasn't my best.

As the sun went down, I saw Elizabeth's form shimmer into the room, near the back door. It was time to go. My blood hummed, like it was excited for the fight. "I've gotta go to work. I'll see you guys all later?" I stood up and stretched. Sitting with a laptop propped on my legs for hours on end was not advisable.

"You sure you can't stay home tonight?" Alec's lips quirked in a teasing smile as he rose too, gathering his papers.

"I wish I could. I can think of nothing I'd like better." I slid my hands around his waist and peered up at him. He dropped the papers and swallowed hard.

"Alec, you should stay a while. Sometimes she comes back after an hour or two. And Bryson isn't done here." Konstanz barely looked up as she attempted to mix batter in a large cracked bowl. She was covered in flour, as were Reese and even Bryson.

Elizabeth paced. There wasn't much time. More of my ghosts' outlines were beginning to appear. "Yeah, you should stay." I nodded too enthusiastically, nearly knocking my neck out of place. "I'll probably be back soon."

It was an outright lie. But it couldn't be helped. I had to go. I tugged on my tennis shoes and nearly hopped out the door, pausing only for one long, scorching kiss. Someone cleared their throat in annoyance. I wasn't sure if it was Reese, Bryson, or one of my ghosts, but it was time to go.

"ANY SIGN OF JESSE at all?" I asked. We'd been prowling the city streets for hours while the rest of my ghosts were on full lookout at the beach, to make sure nothing else came through. I didn't like the city at night. It gave me the creeps—demons were scary but bad humans? They were worse. However, the fact that I was walking, seemingly by myself but constantly chattering, seemed to keep the bad guys away. Acting completely insane will do that, sometimes.

"She was not taken, Navi." Elizabeth was more than a

little disgusted. "I looked for her all day. She has joined those in limbo." She'd never liked Jesse, and I could tell it bothered her that brave ghosts were taken by the asuwangs back to their sea witch master while Jesse hid in the shadows and did nothing.

It bothered me, too. I needed to talk to Death.

"The sea witch seems to be attacking more frequently. Taking more souls. Many of the souls in limbo that haunt your city have been taken. They are all on lookout, as well. I suspect she may be planning an attempt to rise from her ocean lair. They've been testing our response time. And how quickly we leave when the fight is over." Elizabeth didn't look at me as she said it; her gray eyes instead roamed the city streets. As if she knew her words would rock me to the depths of my being.

See, sea witches were the masters of asuwangs. They survive on fear. Like, somehow, that's what they eat. Their asuwang pets eat human flesh, which is just as creepy. So they come, attack my ghosts, take their souls, and then escape into civilization to attack more souls and breed fear.

The sea witch can't leave the ocean. Not without a lot of souls. They make a sort of shell for her to live in. But once she's out, there's no stopping her. For one reason: She can live in the day—when I can't fight her. She takes all those souls she's captured, and she uses them to form a shell that, when the sun hits it, melts and becomes impenetrable. She'd be practically unstoppable.

That was how my grandmother was killed. She tried to fight a sea witch during the day. She was killed, but my mother and my aunt hid until the moon rose, and then they attacked and drove the creature back to the ocean.

Even so, hundreds lost their lives that day. The government blamed it on a tsunami. There were a few who claimed to have seen her, but they were laughed into hiding. The rest who *did* see her were taken.

Ironically, the only way to free souls the sea witch has captured is by waiting until she comes to land wearing them. Cut them from her shell and they can escape to limbo or the afterlife or my army, if they'd so choose.

Probably not though, given what they'd just been through. I'd suspect hell is nothing compared to her lair.

There were nine sea witches living all over the world at specific latitude and longitude points. And they're immortal. They can be killed, but only if they rise from the ocean, and as far as anyone knows, only one has ever actually died. Mostly they just go back to their lair and recover and plot and plan.

Seeing as how this one killed my grandmother, I'd really like a shot at her. Plus, she'd stolen my souls.

And I wanted them back.

"Look, there." Elizabeth pointed through the darkness. There, scrabbling through the cute little garden, was one of my missing asuwangs.

I nodded, eyeing the monster. "One down."

She smiled grimly. "One to go."

I unsheathed my swords and sprinted through the shadows. I leaped from the car to the house roof, skidding down loose shingles until I was right above it. It had captured one of my souls—Don, I was pretty sure, judging by the face it wore. But this was good, because I could kill it before it took Don back to the sea witch, and he would be free.

Raising my Golly, I jumped from the roof. I landed on its back and felt my blade slide through the thick neck. It wore the soul like armor, and now I could see it had another soul as well—not just one of mine. The thing screamed at me, bucking like a wild horse, and I wrapped my legs around its hairy body and jerked Kali out of my sheath. I jammed it down next to the other sword and threw my weight back, using them both like a lever.

The head popped off with an awful ripping sound, and

the demon collapsed to the ground. Don flew free, and the other soul, too. Before I could tell them to run or fight or anything, another scream tore through the air. I whirled around, but too late. The sharp claws of the last missing asuwang tore into my stomach.

I gasped at the pain and shoved away from it with my feet, falling hard on the ground. Elizabeth and Don attacked, but it had several souls wrapped around it and their swords could barely penetrate.

The thing reared back, coming after me again. I dove out of the way, spinning and slicing with Kali and Golly. I hit it in the head, but not hard enough. It screeched, half-shifted into a weird combination of dog, spider, and human, and took off through the silent neighborhood. I risked a glance at the sky. The sun would be up soon. I had to finish this tonight, or someone would die.

Wrapping one arm around the wound, praying it would heal completely before the moon set, I raced after the monster.

CHAPTER THIRTEEN

Alec

AFTER WAITING UNTIL AFTER MIDNIGHT FOR Navi to come back home, and after texting her several times and calling once, I finally went home only to drag my exhausted butt out of bed and go to work three hours later. I wished, in those three hours, that I could have dreamed about the day I'd had before, but it was the same nightmare as always—if anything even more vivid than usual. I was glad when my alarm jarred me out of it.

Until I realized that meant I actually had to get up.

I decided while I was stumbling toward the shower that I had to somehow convince Navi to quit her night job and sleep with me every night. To keep the demons away, of course. She seemed to be the only antidote. I liked the plan immensely.

I doubted very much that it was safe for me to be driving as I yawned and squinted and tried to navigate the mostly deserted streets in the early morning light. Three nights in a row of not enough sleep… wasn't my brightest move ever.

But it had been worth it.

The memory of Navi's soft lips opening for mine, the smell of lilacs and her soft, soft hair… yeah. It was definitely worth it.

I was in love with her. Two days. And she had my heart in her hand.

But really, it wasn't two days. In the last four years, not one single day went by that I didn't think of her at least a hundred times.

I yawned again, stretching, trying to get some blood moving through my back and arms as I slowed for a stop sign. It was still dark enough that long shadows fell across the street, and I fought to keep my eyes open.

Until one of the shadows moved.

Forgetting my exhaustion, my eyes flew open and I leaned forward. Navi, disheveled and filthy, sprinted across the road and disappeared down a side street.

She was in trouble.

Screw work. I spun the wheel and went after her, roaring around the side street just as she turned into a cul-de-sac. I followed, gunning the truck. I got there seconds after she did—but she was gone.

I jumped out and turned in a slow half-circle, but there was no sign of her. "Where'd ya go, Angel?" I murmured. A movement at one of the windows caught my eye, and I jogged over, my heart in my throat. This was too much like before. Early morning light, peering through windows, wondering what the hell I was doing.

Inside, Navi and a big guy were all over each other. Crashing against the wall, knocking over the couch. She had her arms around his neck; his hands were locked around her lower back, holding her against him.

She'd been with me a few hours ago.

Now she was with some other guy. And apparently they liked it a lot rougher than I did.

I squinted, hoping in a sadistic sort of way that maybe they were fighting. Maybe this was part of her job—to beat big guys into submission. But no. They were not fighting. She had her arms around his neck, for hell's sake. If they'd been fighting, she'd be trying to get away, tiny thing that she was. She wouldn't have been holding him so tight.

Disgusted, yeah, that's what this feeling was. My heart wasn't shattered into twenty-five thousand pieces and sinking into my stomach. I was disgusted. I spun on my heel and stalked back to the truck.

"Alec?" Her voice was breathless and panicked. "What are you doing here?"

I turned slowly, hating the way my body wanted to pull her close to me. Hating the way my shattered heart wanted to beg her to explain. "I thought you were in trouble. Clearly, I was wrong."

"Alec, wait—It isn't like that." Her face, already pale and strained, went absolutely white.

"Really, Navi? I think I saw exactly what it was like." *Tell me I'm wrong. Please tell me I'm wrong.*

"No, Alec." She took three cautious steps forward. "It isn't what you think."

I ran a hand through my hair, staring at the sky. Wishing against all common sense. "Really, Navi? Then what was it?"

Her face, hopeful for about two seconds before I spoke, fell. "I—I can't—"

I rolled my eyes. "This is insane. Like, high school all over again. If you wanted to be with other guys, you could have freakin' told me, Navi." I shoved away the memory of her saying she wanted to be with me, into somewhere dark and less painful.

"I don't!" she cried, stumbling closer. I think she was limping, which served her right. "I don't want to be with other guys! It's just work!"

"So what—are you a whore now?" The second I said it, I wanted to take it back. It was pain talking, not me. I wanted her to hurt as much as I did. As much as she'd hurt me now, as much as she'd hurt me then. But with those words, any chance I had of her giving me a logical explanation was gone. Even if she could have come up with one. I started to tell her I didn't mean it, but I didn't get the chance.

Her eyes widened as her mouth opened in a silent *O,* and her arms curled around her stomach like I'd punched her. "Go to hell, Alec," she whispered.

Ouch.

Pain spoke again, lashing out, trying to protect me. "Funny, somehow I hang out with you for a couple days and I wake up there." I spun on my heel and jerked the truck door open, climbing in and slamming it so hard the entire vehicle rocked. She was still standing in the same spot, arms still clutching her stomach. Silent tears streaked down her cheeks before she turned away, back toward the house. She didn't even have the decency to wait until I was gone before she went back to him.

The big truck roared as I stomped on the gas pedal, taking us away from that hellish place and the little demon who had the power to crush my soul.

CHAPTER FOURTEEN

Navi

"YOU'RE HURT, NAVI. YOU NEED TO go home." Elizabeth's voice somehow found its way through the darkness. I forced my eyes open and stared at her. The asuwang lay at my feet, slowly changing from its human form back to the demon dog-spider-icky thing as the sun rose on the horizon.

"I can't breathe," I whispered.

She nodded, watching me sadly. "You cannot tell him?"

I shook my head. "I took an oath. If I tell him, it will open his eyes. He'll see the demons, he'll see the ghosts. It's too dangerous. If I don't tell him, I keep him safe."

"Did he not already see the demon with you?"

"He saw it in human form. They won't open his eyes in that form."

"Ah." She nodded wisely. "Then he is a fool."

Yeah. He was a fool. But I couldn't blame him. Just like in high school—I knew how it must have looked as I tried to cut through the demon's neck with my swords. It was way harder when he had a soul shell. But Alec wouldn't know that.

Because I was keeping him safe.

"You are hurt, Navi," Elizabeth said again. I pulled my arms away from my stomach. My shirt was ruined. The skin underneath was ruined too, at least until the moon came up again to heal me. I'd lost a lot of blood, I could tell. Or else Alec had hurt me enough to make the entire room sway. Black splotches came and went in front of my eyes.

But the asuwangs who had made it past us were dead. That was all that mattered.

We hadn't been fast enough, though. One man lay lifeless in an alley three streets over.

"What happened to Jesse? Did they—"

Don shook his head. "I watched Jesse go back to her cell. She was on the beach last night and did not chase them."

Because of her, a man had lost his life.

"Why?" My voice was hoarse. I felt like I was split into two agonizing vials of pain—one for the battle I'd just been in, and one for the fight I'd just had with Alec. He'd called me a whore.

Even the first time, he hadn't stooped to that.

One vial for night, one for day. My soul was torn.

"She said she was afraid."

Well. Wasn't that ironic. Because of that, Death would take her to hell. Then she'd truly know terror.

"Navi. We can do nothing for the lost tonight. Nothing for Jesse. We must get you treated."

Yeah. I wasn't sure how to explain this kind of wound. Dog attack? Not feasible. Hit and run? No… I wished I had a doctor friend who could fix me and wouldn't ask questions.

Oh wait. I did.

"Konstanz?" I asked as soon as she picked up the phone.

"Navi?" Her voice was sleep-slow and froggish. "What's wrong?"

"I need your help."

"NAVI, I DON'T KNOW what you're involved in, but we need to go to the cops." Konstanz's hands shook as she dabbed at my stomach with already bloody rags.

"I can't, Konstanz. I'm sorry. This can't go beyond us." My voice sounded robotic in my head. I wasn't sure how it sounded to her.

"Whoever you're protecting, this isn't worth it, Navi. You could have died. You were unconscious in the middle of a cul-de-sac!"

"It is worth it, Konstanz. I promise."

She scowled at me, shoving her hair away from her face. "Why can't you just be a normal girl who goes to school and has a not-scary job and you can grow up and marry Alec…"

I squeaked in pain and she looked up at me. "What's wrong? I wasn't even touching you."

"Alec and I…" Hmm. How to explain it? We texted late into the night. Spent an entire day together. I was planning my life with him when he assumed I was already cheating again and called me a whore. "We aren't friends."

Her busy hands stilled. I couldn't see her face because she had her head bent, but I could imagine her expression. "Seriously? What happened last night?"

Lots. Lots happened.

I shook my head, feeling traitorous tears snaking their way down my cheeks.

"Oh, Navi. I'm so sorry." She rose from her crouch and awkwardly wrapped her arms around me, trying not to touch the gaping wound she'd been cleaning for a half hour. I tried to be strong. I tried not to cry.

I failed.

I leaned my forehead on her shoulder and sobbed. "He thinks I'm a horrible person. I was just—" I hiccupped, "I was just trying to keep him safe." So I could cry. Look at that.

She leaned back and studied my face. "Navi, I was there when he saw what he saw in high school. I couldn't believe it was you. It felt wrong. I don't know what's really going on, but I'm sorry I didn't stand by you then." She blushed, looking down. "I just—I've just felt like I needed to say that. For a long time now."

She picked up her thick pack of gauze while I gaped at her. "Konstanz, you've always been there. You've always been my friend."

"I should have argued with him. I should have stood up for you."

I shook my head, closing my eyes briefly. "You couldn't. I didn't give you anything to argue with."

"You gave me ten years of knowing what kind of person you are. That should have been enough. Stand up so I can wrap this around you."

I stood obediently, feeling a wave of dizziness wash over me. "I thought—I thought I was in love with him. After one day. How stupid am I?" Stupid. Very stupid. I hid my face in my hands. Apparently I'd decided my life was a chick flick. With a really crappy ending. Wasn't there a law or something that chick flicks ended happily ever after?

She shook her head. "You aren't stupid. Everyone at that party could see the connection between you two. It was unreal. Also, you are way easier to fix up than a 100 pound unconscious dog."

I snorted, giggling despite all the pain. "Thanks?"

"All done. Go lay down. I'll talk to your professors and get your notes today."

CHAPTER FIFTEEN

Alec

I STUMBLED INTO THE APARTMENT THROUGH a haze of pain pills and alcohol. "You sure you're okay if I go home?" Josh asked, trying to free my keys from the door. I thought about pointing out that he had to pull up, then sideways to free the key, but he'd figure it out eventually.

If not, it didn't matter.

"Are you drunk?" Bryson turned from the TV to stare stupidly. "Is he drunk?"

"Drunk and drugged, yes. Smashed his hand at work. Then decided alcohol is the best way to deal with pain, not a hospital." Josh shook his head, swearing at the keys. Bryson got up and jerked the keys out of the door while I stood and watched. He looked at me, mouth still hanging open, and I raised my broken hand and waved it.

"I thought you said Navi hates alcohol."

"To hell with Navi. Josh, get me a beer."

Josh shook his head, leaving the doorway to steer me toward my room. "You're gonna be hurtin' in the morning."

"I'm already hurtin'. She smashed my damn soul with her bare feet."

"What? What happened?" Did I hear hope in his voice? I tried to turn on him but the world spun and I toppled over, right into Josh's arms.

"You're a good friend." I patted him on the head and tried to stand up straight.

It didn't work.

"I've never seen him drunk before." Bryson's voice sounded like it was moving away, but he was standing right next to me. Although he did seem to be waving in and out of focus...

"He caught Navi with another guy this morning." Josh tried to keep his voice low but I was inches from his mouth. Like I couldn't hear him.

"Well... it's not like they're together. She didn't swear off all other guys for him in two days. What's the big deal?"

"What's the big deal?" Were my words slurring or was that my hearing? "She *did* swear off all the other stupid guys. She said she didn't want anyone but me. Then she leaves me in her apartment with you"— I jabbed my injured hand at his chest—"and goes off with some other guy. Or guys. And she told me it was work. And I called her a whore."

Josh groaned. Bryson, even weaving in and out of my field of vision like some kind of colorful ghost, looked like he wanted to punch me. Well let him try. I wouldn't feel a thing, not with these pain pills numbing everything.

Except my stupid heart.

"You need to sleep, bro. Come on." Josh pushed me forward, but I dug my heels in. Or at least I tried, but it didn't help.

"I don't wanna sleep. She's there when I sleep. She dies and she's beautiful and I can't save her. I don't wanna sleep."

"Dude. If I wasn't holding you up, you'd be on the floor

right now. Go to bed."

I tried to growl at him but it just came out as a moan. I already missed her. It would have been easier if she'd yelled and blamed me or thrown a tantrum that I was following her or anything that involved breaking stuff. But that quiet pleading, the desperation in her eyes… it killed me. What if I was wrong? What if there was an explanation and I'd just blown it with the one girl I'd ever loved? "I was gonna marry her."

Bryson snorted. Josh sighed. "You were together for two days, Alec."

"Doesn't matter. I knew it the second I saw her at that party."

My heart hurt. Maybe I was having a heart attack. Maybe it really was possible to break your heart, and then you just wandered around all broken and crushed and stuff because life with a broken heart was like that.

No. I glared at the floor and stood up straight. Or attempted to. I knew what I saw. Navi was either trying to kill that guy or she was *with* that guy. And since she's a tiny little thing with the sweetest disposition ever, I doubted very much that she was trying to kill him.

I'd like to, though.

In fact, maybe I'd go back and punch him a few times. That would definitely make me feel better. I turned toward the door, ready to go seek my vengeance, and fell flat on my face.

This day sucked.

I WOKE UP WITH a freight train running through my head. I groaned, pressing my fists to my eyes. What the hell had happened yesterday?

And then I remembered.

Navi. The guy. Alcohol, lots of alcohol. And… a hospital? I groaned again, fumbling for my phone through the blur of pain. "Josh?" I mumbled when he finally answered, four skull shattering rings later. "What…" I couldn't even think how to start the conversation.

"Hey bro. How's the hand?"

"Hand?" My words were all slurred. Slowly, I raised my other hand, just now noticing that it was throbbing in something resembling agony. "Oh hell."

"Yeah."

"I drank a lot."

"Well, your hand hurt. I guess that's understandable."

But that wasn't the reason I drank so much. My heart hurt. How Navi could break my heart into so many pieces after only two days together was beyond me. I'd never fallen like that before.

Or, re-fallen, as it were.

I hung up. I'm not sure if I said goodbye or not. Mustering all my courage, I sat up. The room spun and my hand throbbed and I just about lost everything I'd eaten in the last twenty-four hours. I cursed in all three languages that I'd ever learned, and then I got up to make coffee.

"Josh said to give you your pain pills as soon as you got up." Bryson left the TV and followed my stumbling progress to the kitchen, catching me twice when I tried to fall. I found the bottle and fought with the lid for several seconds, until Bryson snatched it out of my hand and shook a pill out. Without a word, he started coffee brewing as I downed the pill. *Work fast, pill. Work fast.* If only the pill erased memories, too. If only it eased a shattered heart.

Every time I closed my damn eyes, I saw her. Smiling at me, nibbling her lip, twining her fingers with mine. I saw her eyes falling shut as she leaned toward me, I felt her soft lips opening for mine, felt the stroke of her fingers against my chest.

And then I saw her standing in front of that house, tears running down her cheeks, arms wrapped around herself. What if I'd been wrong? What if...

I'd go over there. That's what I would do. As soon as I could see straight to drive, I would go over there and talk to her. No raging emotions this time. I'd give her a chance to explain.

And then I snorted. Of course there would be raging emotions. There were always raging emotions if Navi was involved.

It took me several seconds, but I finally realized that Bryson was angry at me. "What's wrong with you?" I asked, peering blurrily at him.

"What's wrong with me?" His eyebrows shot up and he spun away, jerking the coffee mug out of the cupboard. "What's wrong with me. That's awesome." He sloshed coffee into the mug, missing for the most part, and thrust it at me. "What's wrong with you? When she chose you over me, it hurt. Oh yeah, I felt totally betrayed, Alec. But I should have known—after what you'd said... and I thought, at least he'll take care of her. At least I'll still get to see her and she's happy. If I would have known you were going to hurt her like this, I—I would have fought harder! Or—or something. I would have tried to protect her."

I stared at him, trying not to spill my coffee with my shaking hands. "She was with another guy, Bryson. I didn't do anything wrong."

"Did you give her a chance to explain?" He crossed his arms and glared, as if daring me to answer him.

I closed my eyes and sighed. "No. No, I did not. She wouldn't even if I had, you know."

"No." Bryson shoved past me, stalking to the TV. "No, I don't know."

It took an entire pot of coffee and a long, long shower before I could function. It took another hour before I could move my head without throwing up. It was almost two p.m. when I finally got dressed—which was hard one-handed. "You can't drive when you're taking those Percocet, dude," Bryson, still watching TV, said when I emerged with my keys in my hand.

"I'm fine." I didn't look at him, partly because moving my eyes still made my head feel like it was splitting open down the center. How much alcohol had I *had* yesterday before Josh convinced me to go to the hospital?

Bryson got up and blocked the doorway. "I know where you're going. She doesn't want to talk to you."

I would have punched him, if I didn't think it would hurt my only good hand. Even then, I still considered it. "How do you know?"

"Because I was over there this morning. She's pissed, Alec. She never wants to see you again. Hell, Konstanz had to talk her out of packing up and going back to Alaska just to get away from you."

Pain shot from my heart down into my stomach, so fierce it almost brought me to my knees. "No. She wouldn't do that."

"She's done it before, Alec."

I shook my head. Big, huge mistake. Pressing my good hand against my skull like it could hold it in place, I said, "She just got back. She has school. And work."

Her voice slammed through my head. *It's just work! It's just work!* Sobbing, tear-soaked words. I had to talk to her.

I shoved Bryson out of the way. "Alec, I can't let you drive. What if you kill someone?"

I glared at him for thirty whole seconds. "I took the Percocet hours ago. I was supposed to take another one at twelve. I'm fine to drive."

His brow furrowed and he crossed his arms over his

chest. "You need to keep up on your pain pills or the pain will be unmanageable."

"The pain is already unmanageable, Bryson. And those damn pills aren't gonna touch it." I wrenched the door open and stalked out to my truck.

It was difficult driving when I had to shift with my injured, bulky hand. I killed the truck twice before I got the hang of it, and I swore more times than I could count. I blew through a red light once just so I wouldn't have to shift back down. And then I parked in Navi's apartment carport and sat there.

She hated me. She'd told me to go to hell. *You called her a whore.* Technically, no. I hadn't called her a whore. I'd *asked* if she was a whore. It was a simple question, right?

I hung my head. No, it wasn't.

I started the truck again and backed out, feeling like I left half my soul waiting there at her doorstep.

CHAPTER SIXTEEN

Navi

I STARED OUT THE WINDOW, PAIN lancing through my chest. The wound in my stomach had healed when the moon had risen the night before, thankfully. So all I had to deal with now was the broken heart.

Yeah. No problem.

Alec's truck roared out of our parking lot, disappearing in a cloud of smoke around the corner as he gunned it. Good. He needed to stay far, far away from me.

So what, are you a whore now?

"Hey." Konstanz stroked my hair and I smiled over at her. "Was that—?"

I nodded. She slid her arm around my shoulders and I laid my head on her chest. "I wasn't with another guy, K."

She nodded. "I know."

We stayed that way, watching the cars below, watching people go about their daily lives, completely unaware and ungrateful of the sacrifices Agents made to keep them safe. Alec, completely unaware and ungrateful. I didn't tell him—

all this time, all these accusations, and I didn't tell him because I wanted to keep him safe.

"Bastard."

Konstanz sucked in a breath because I never swore. Reese could put a sailor to shame, and no one batted an eye. But me, one time, and it stunned the entire apartment.

"You know what I do to get over a guy?" Terrie asked, reclining on the couch like Cleopatra. I raised my head from Konstanz's shoulder and looked back at Terrie, waiting for her to continue. Heaven knows she had enough experience in the subject. She smiled wickedly. "I do a new guy."

I cringed at her coarseness. Konstanz sighed. "Navi isn't that type, Terrie."

She shrugged. "Maybe not *that* type, but I bet finding her another fella will take her mind off Alec."

If only she knew of all the times I'd dated different guys just to do that exact thing. Four years worth of guys, and not one of them ever made me get over Alec. Not one made me forget him. Even for a second.

"That's true. Now that you're feeling better, we should go out." Konstanz rubbed her hand briskly up and down my arm like my dad used to do when he was trying to give me a pep talk.

"I've got homework. And a meeting tonight. I can't go out, and"—I nodded at Terrie—"I'm sure your plan is fabulous and works every time, but I kind of don't want anything to do with guys for a while."

She rolled her eyes. "That's why I never fall in love. Because it *hurts* when they inevitably break your heart. Men don't fall in love. They fall in lust."

"It was two days, Terrie. Navi wasn't in love with him. It was just a crush. Crushes are easy to get over." Reese nodded with finality. Because in this apartment, what Reese said, *goes.*

It wasn't a crush. With Alec, it was more of an obsession.

It had never been a crush. I had met him, and a week later we were inseparable. For three years, every waking second was spent wherever Alec was. I even rearranged my school schedule so we'd have classes together. That shop class I'd taken junior year had really come in handy.

And that obsession? It hadn't gone away.

But Reese was only trying to help, and I wasn't going to correct her. Besides, I suspected we all knew how wrong she was anyway.

A knock sent hope soaring through my heart that somehow Alec had come back and he would apologize and everything would be okay.

"Bryson. Hey. Come on in." Reese swung open the door and stepped out of the way. "Welcome to the house of mourning."

I hadn't seen him since almost forty-eight hours ago when he'd been teaching Reese how to cook and helping Konstanz put out kitchen fires. "Hey, honey. How are you?" He came straight to me, barely nodding at anyone else.

"I'm fine." I forced a smile and moved away from Konstanz, proving that I could, in fact, stand on my own.

"I heard what happened. Alec went out last night and got rip-roaring drunk. I figured something was up."

Ouch.

"Well, he's a free man." I was surprised at the flat indifference in my voice. Like I really didn't care at all. Like the pain wasn't searing through my chest and starting all my internal organs on fire.

I had a meeting with Death tonight. I should ask him if he'd somehow managed to bring hell to Earth.

Konstanz moved between us like her physical presence could somehow protect me from his words. "You know, Navi probably doesn't need to know that right now."

"Right. Sorry. What was I thinking? I'm awful at being a

comforter."

"You're doing fine, Bryson."

"Have you eaten yet?" he asked Konstanz, since I was still staring out the window like a lost dog.

"No. We're in mourning. We don't eat."

"My grandma always said food soothes the soul. Konstanz, can you help me in the kitchen? We're going to make this all better."

Konstanz hid a smirk and nodded, following him out of the living room.

"Then maybe we can all take a nice walk on the beach or something," he continued, rummaging through our pans.

I stiffened. I already had to go to the beach tonight. I didn't enjoy the beach. "How about not," I practically snarled.

He looked at me, startled. "Okay. Sorry. I'm just trying to help."

Konstanz patted him on the shoulder. "She doesn't like the beach," she said quietly.

"Okaaay..." he studied me with those ice blue eyes for several seconds. "How about the Astoria Column? I've never been there and I hear it's fantastic."

I gaped at him, like, literally. I'm pretty sure my mouth was hanging open in a very attractive fashion. He wanted me to go out and pretend nothing was wrong and the world was still turning? I could think of no response for several seconds, and then finally, "You've never been to the Astoria Column? How is that possible? Everyone has been to the Astoria Column."

He shrugged. "I work a lot. Everyone I hang out with has already seen it. Going alone never sounded very fun."

I had seen the Astoria Column, and I still loved to visit it again and again. "Well that's just sad." I didn't want to go out. I wanted to stay inside and cry and wail and... and Alec was probably out having the time of his life with a whole bunch of girls. "Okay, Bryson. Let's go see the Column."

His face lit up like a little kid. "Really?"

I nodded, hoping the smile reached my eyes. He seriously looked overjoyed at the prospect. What kind of friends did he have that they wouldn't take him to see the Column when he wanted to before?

"You guys wanna come?" Bryson asked.

Reese and Terrie both shook their heads. Sightseeing wasn't really their thing.

"Sure," Konstanz said. "I like the Column."

WHEN BRYSON SAID HE could cook, he wasn't lying. It didn't soothe my soul, but my stomach was quite pleased with life. "Ready to go?" I asked as I tugged on my shoes. I hadn't even looked in a mirror yet. I probably should run a comb through my hair or a toothbrush over my teeth.

But it didn't matter. It didn't matter what I looked like. Not anymore.

Wait. I mentally gritted my teeth and dug around my soul for a backbone. *Not right now.* It would matter again. Just not right now.

So then I probably should at least get out of my stained sweats. "You know, I'm gonna run change really quick. I'll be right back."

This could be fun. It would be nice to get out and take my mind off Alec. Go somewhere I wouldn't be able to watch for him, hoping he'd pull into my carport again. I took my phone out of my pocket and set it on the dresser with a little more force than was necessary. At least now I wouldn't be waiting for him to text me.

THE ASTORIA COLUMN WAS built to honor Astoria's part in the nation's history. Inside, murals from Astoria's past lined the walls along the winding staircase to the top. Lewis and Clark, the first Astorians, the arrival of the railroad, and several others. We wandered up the staircase as Konstanz told him the meanings behind each painting. He totally could have read them for himself but he seemed happier to let her tell him.

"My favorite part, though," I said as we reached the top and went out onto the observation deck, "is the view."

The view, indeed. We could see forever. The column was sitting atop a 600 foot hill. Add to that the 125 feet we'd just walked up, and we could pretty much see everything there was to see. In fact, I was pretty sure I could see Alec's apartment building from here.

"Wow." He leaned on the railing and stared out over the city. "This is gorgeous."

I nodded, trying to keep my eyes away from the apartment building that held my heart. Two days. Two days and I was dying inside. This was beyond ridiculous.

It will get better. It will get better. I'd made it through this before. I'd lost Alec before, and I had survived. It had hurt more than this the last time, and I had made it. I also remembered that it got easier as time passed. It would get easier again. Maybe this time, I would be able to forget him completely.

What happened between Alec and I was stupid. It should never have been so intense. If we'd just taken it slow, become friends...

Everything would have still ended up the same, only it would hurt worse. Because I was still an Agent, and he would eventually think I was cheating. We'd been together for three years before, and it hadn't stopped him from thinking the worst then.

"Navi, no offense, but I don't get it. It was two days. Why are you both so upset? I mean this in the most innocent way possible. I've had years-long relationships that I've been less upset about."

I sucked in a breath. How, exactly, does one respond to that? "Bryson… I…" I ran a hand through my hair. "I have this thing with Alec. You might as well know." I turned away, unable to face him, or the pity in his eyes. "I can't get over him. I've been trying for four years and I just can't. He haunts me." I fell silent and kept my eyes firmly staring out over the city.

"It's true. She couldn't." Konstanz sighed, leaning against the railing. "But this time will be different. Me and Bryson, we got your back. Alec won't even be a memory soon."

Bryson nodded, sliding an arm over both our shoulders. "Yep. We got this."

WE WALKED ALONG THE edge of the river. Bryson and Konstanz kept up a string of conversation, and I ate my ice cream and stared at the setting sun, feeling my blood wake and hum with the rising moon. Death would be waiting for me. I had to report in and arrange to meet with potential new recruits. Hopefully, he had a lot of them for me. I had this overwhelming fear that something bad was coming. I needed an army ready to meet it.

"You're gonna get over him, you know." Bryson totally misread my silence as brooding over Alec, when in fact it was the first time that I hadn't been thinking of him. Well, not counting the times I was fighting for my life against demons set on eating our city.

As if conjured by that thought, Elizabeth appeared in

front of me, sliding backward through the air, not walking, not moving her feet at all. It was seriously creepy, despite her beautiful face. I bit my lip and peeked at Bryson, but he had fallen back into conversation with Konstanz about our Astoria's early history.

Even still, I couldn't exactly ask her what was up.

Luckily, she knew this. "Death waits, Navi." Her eyes, always so full of sadness, went to Bryson and Konstanz and then back to me.

"Guys, this has been a good day. Really, it has, and I appreciate it so much. But I have to go to work now. The moon…"

Holy crap.

I was too tired. Too distracted. Had I really been about to tell him the moon was rising and I had to go to work? Bryson frowned, glancing at the sky and the setting sun. I wracked my brain trying to come up with anything, anything at all. "The full moon makes people crazy. I have to go in tonight. I have a meeting." I was rambling. *Get it together, Navi.* His frown deepened, utter confusion on his face. "I have to go in early so I can make sure all my parolees are okay before my meeting." Voila. I'd somehow managed to make up an excuse that made sense.

"Right, I remember you saying you had a meeting tonight. I'll take you home."

"Thank you." I turned around and started walking toward his car—a little sports thing that barely fit all three of us and would be worthless in a big rain storm.

He didn't follow, pointing out something to Konstanz.

I looked at Elizabeth, panicked, but she only shrugged. It looked completely out of place in her colonial dress, but there it was. She wasn't going to help me at all.

"How about you let me make you breakfast tomorrow?" I heard him say, and then he raised his voice so I was included.

"Both of you."

"Oh. I have school in the morning. I have to be there at seven."

He planted his feet and crossed his arms. I started to fidget. Death did not like to wait. Not one bit. "You have school at seven when you work all night long?"

I nodded. It was true.

"Okay then. Lunch. Let me make you lunch."

I was getting desperate. "I have class until two. We can do lunch then."

He grinned, a big triumphant smile that lit up his ice blue eyes so they didn't look so cold. "Two it is. Konstanz? Does that work for you?"

She nodded. "I can take a late lunch."

"Perfect. Two o'clock. My place."

"Oh. No, Bryson. That's not a good idea." Go back to Alec's apartment? Was he insane? I couldn't see Alec again. I didn't know if I'd throw myself at his feet or claw his eyes out. It changed hourly.

"Alec works until six or seven. He won't be there, I promise."

Elizabeth smirked, tapping her foot. I got the idea that this simultaneously entertained her and annoyed her all at once. "Okay. Okay, Bryson. I'll be there at two. But please don't let Alec be home."

CHAPTER SEVENTEEN

Alec

I SHOULD HAVE KNOWN THE SECOND Bryson walked in that something was up. He was whistling. *Whistling,* for hell's sake. Who whistles? But I didn't want to talk to him. I didn't want to talk to anyone. I'd thrown my phone in the hamper so my mom or Josh or anyone else couldn't call me and raise my stupid hopes that it was Navi. Now I was watching violent movies and relishing every time someone died a horrible death.

Yeah. I was evil.

I don't care.

"Have you been here all day?" he asked, dropping his keys on the coffee table and settling himself in the armchair. Awesome. Apparently he thought we were going to be spending quality time together.

"Nope."

He leaned his elbows on his knees and studied me, an annoying grin on his face, like a Cheshire cat just waiting for me to ask him what he'd gotten into. I didn't want to. After several seconds of ignoring him, he said, "What'd you do?"

I stared harder at the TV. "It's a Tuesday, Bryson. I went to work."

He sat back, arms behind his head. "You went to work, really? How do you get anything done with that?" He motioned with his foot toward the huge cast on my right hand.

I'd been put on light duty, which meant talking to people and running errands. It sucked. But I wasn't going to tell him that. "I managed."

Several more seconds of that obnoxious grin. "Seriously, Bryson, what do you want?" I finally paused the movie and turned on him. Anything to get him to go away.

"Nothing. Just wondering how you are. Oh," He got up and went to the kitchen, making some weird herbal tea that made our whole house smell like a tanning salon. "I saw Navi today."

I felt like I'd been hit with a wrecking ball. My entire body tensed, the blood freezing in my veins. At the mention of her name.

I was a mess.

"How was she?" I asked, feigning disinterest while I hung on his every word. I didn't know what I hoped he would say. That she was as miserable as me? But there was a better man inside me that hoped she was okay. That she wasn't hurting. That she would talk to me and we could work this out.

"She's okay. Hasn't broken anything yet, so I guess she's better than you…" His voice trailed off, chuckling.

I take it back. I didn't want her to be happy. The better man inside died right then and all I wanted was for her to be as miserable as I was.

"We went to see the Column. It was beautiful."

"You've been there before." My tone was distinctly accusing, although I wasn't entirely sure why. "I went with you when you first moved here, remember?"

"That was a year ago, Alec." He leaned against the counter and frowned at me like I was an annoying child. "I can't remember that far back and besides, she took the time to explain each mural. You didn't." He gave me a lopsided smile.

I paced toward him, enjoying that he was only 5'10" and I was 6'2.

He raised his hands. "Chill out, Alec. Konstanz was there, too. It was completely platonic. Then we were going to go to the beach, but… "

The one thing saving me in the lifetime of nightmares I'd had of Navi dying in front of me was that she was on a beach, and Navi did not go near the ocean. Not for anything. Especially not for Bryson. "Navi hates the beach."

"Yeah. I was going to say that. So we got ice cream and then I took them home. See? Nothing to worry about, Alec. I'm just… you have Josh and your alcohol. You don't need me, but maybe she does."

No, I didn't need him. But why would she? She had a houseful of girls to help her cope. I grabbed my keys off the table and stormed out. This time, when I drove my truck to her house, I wasn't going to leave until I talked to her.

"WHAT ARE YOU DOING here?" Konstanz eyed me like I'd just crawled out of the sewer, the door opened only wide enough that she could peek out and snarl at me.

"I need to talk to Navi, K."

"Don't 'K' me, Alec. We're done being friends."

Ah, so Navi had told them everything. "Okay. Sorry. Konstanz, I need to talk to her. Please."

She must have heard the desperation in my voice, despite my best efforts to hide it. She sighed and opened the door wider. "You don't get to talk to her, Alec. Not again. Not ever."

"Konstanz, I just need to hear her—" *voice* "—explanation. I didn't give her a chance. It was wrong."

"You called her a whore."

"I didn't mean to. I was hurt. Please, Konstanz. Just let me talk to her."

"Why, Alec? You wouldn't give her a chance to explain before. Why do you think you deserve her time now?" She crossed her arms over her chest and glared at me, her normally friendly eyes shooting daggers laced with poison and followed by big, teethy fish.

"I don't. But I need it. I need to talk to her." My voice cracked. Holy hell, could I get any more pathetic?

"Alec, if you felt for her even half what she feels for you, you wouldn't be jumping to the most horrible conclusion every chance you get. I stood by and did nothing before. I failed her because I believed you. I'm not going to let you hurt her again."

I ran a hand over my face, peering over her shoulder, hoping to see Navi in the background. But the apartment was dark except for a light coming from the hallway. If Navi was here, she wasn't coming out. "I already hurt her, Konstanz. I'm trying to make it better."

"Just leave her alone, Alec. That's how you can make it better."

I hung my head, my good hand clenching and unclenching helplessly at my side. "I can't leave her alone."

I could feel her staring at me, but I didn't know what else to say to convince her.

"What happened to your hand?"

I blinked and looked up. Was that concern I heard in her voice? "I smashed it at work yesterday. Then I got really drunk. Then Josh dragged me to the hospital. It was a great day."

Her sea-green eyes narrowed at me. "You—you went to the hospital last night?"

"Yeah." This wasn't the conversation I was expecting at all, and I had no idea where she was going with it. "Want to see my doctors orders or whatever they're called?"

Slowly, she shook her head. I wasn't sure what I'd said that changed her, but the anger dimmed just a bit. "Navi isn't here. She's working. *Not* being a whore."

I closed my eyes against the pain. "I know, Konstanz."

"She won't be back until morning. She had an important meeting tonight, and they usually take hours."

Defeated, I felt every ounce of energy desert me. "Okay," I mumbled. I turned and started for my truck.

"Alec?" She sounded hesitant, like she really didn't want to say what she was about to say.

Which meant I really didn't want to hear it. But I looked back over my shoulder anyway. She was right behind me. She laid a gentle hand on my arm and bit her lip. "I know it's hard." She nodded. "I know how bad it hurts. But she's been through enough. Please, if you can find the strength, stay away from her. Or if you can't do that, if you can't stay away from her, then be her friend. But this," she waved her hand through the air like it explained what *this* was, "this will kill you both."

THE SECOND TIME I got drunk in two days, I made sure not to mix it with pain pills. "Dude, slow down. You're gonna end up in the hospital again." Josh attempted to steer me away from the bar, but I shoved him out of the way.

"I don't care." I wanted pain. I wanted the oblivion that alcohol could bring. *Get her outta my head. Get her out of my heart.* I knew I'd hurt her. But I honestly hadn't thought it was over. Not really. I didn't even believe she'd been cheating, if you could call it cheating when we'd only been together for two days. The look in her eyes when I walked away haunted me, and it told me everything I needed to know.

I just wish I would have realized it sooner.

But Konstanz was right. The relationship between Navi and I was too intense. It was either head over heels or absolute hate. It could destroy us both. I was okay with it destroying me. But I wasn't okay with it destroying her.

"I gotta move outta the state." My words were already slurred.

"Your mom won't let that happen. Neither will Jack."

Jack. He'd be real proud of his big brother right now, wouldn't he? I laid my head on the bar counter and groaned. It was hard and sticky and cool. "How much has he had?" the bartender asked. Same girl as last night.

"Too much. I'm taking him home."

"Is he okay?"

"No. Broke his hand. Broke his heart." I could picture Josh shrugging, but I wasn't raising my head to see it play out for real.

"Oh," she cooed. "How could anyone break his heart when it's attached to a body like that?"

I scowled, which was hard with my eyebrows pushed against the dirty bar. Was she hitting on me?

"She's an ice queen. You wanna take him home and put his heart back together for him?"

What the hell was going on? I forced myself up, rubbing my forehead and glaring at them both.

She smiled, red painted lips splitting into a seductive smirk. She was hot, with black pin-up curls and a low-cut tank top that left absolutely nothing to the imagination.

And she wasn't Navi.

"No thanks." I stood up, nearly toppling my bar stool. Her smile faded, replaced by hurt. Crap. Now I was going to have to find a new bar, and I planned on spending a lot of time in one for the next while. Until I forgot that demon angel for good. "It's not you. I can't do this anymore." I tried to give her an apologetic smile, but it didn't turn out so well.

"You know where to find me." She wiped the counter and left to get someone else's drink.

"You're an idiot," Josh said as he heaved me to my feet. "I hand you a hot girl who wants to take you home—"

"I don't want it, Josh. I'm done." I shook my head, which was a mistake. The room spun and my stomach heaved. "Shit."

"Okay." Josh pushed me forward, out the door and into the fresh air. "Time to get you home. No more alcohol for you."

My stomach, as I lost everything in it all over the parking lot, agreed with him.

CHAPTER EIGHTEEN

Navi

MEETING DEATH WASN'T AN EASY TASK. For one thing, dude is scary. He's got the glowing red eyes, the long skeletal hands emerging from the folds of his robes, and… nothing else. Well, he had a skeletal face, but I only got to see that when he pulled his hood back. That, however, was nothing compared to actually getting to him. It's *hard* getting through the gates of hell. Only an Agent can do it and return, unless she escorts someone out. So I went in with Elizabeth. The rest of my army kept watch on the shores.

So the asuwangs emerge from the ocean through a rocky gate that was almost impossible to scale unless you had super powers. (And I totally have super powers. As long as the moon is up.) Well, on the other side of that gate is a cave. And at the back of the cave is what looks like a plain, ordinary wall, but when I raise Kali and Golly and push their blades into the soft rock, the wall shimmers and crumbles, and the gate to hell is opened.

It wasn't hot, as one might expect, although the screams

of the damned could be heard in the distance. It was dark, with eternal flames lighting torches every twenty-five feet or so. Elizabeth trembled beside me, as she always did, because this path did not bring back happy memories for her. Usually we walked in silence, but this time, Elizabeth had something on her mind. I could tell because she fidgeted, and Elizabeth never fidgets.

"What's up, Buttercup?" I asked as we navigated our way over the petrified lava. Really, I could see the beauty of this place. Black, roiling waves of stone with hidden pockets, fragile and jagged and dangerous all at once. To fall here would mean stitches at the very least. Elizabeth looked at me and then away, biting her translucent lip. "Elizabeth?"

Sudden fear hit me. What if she was ready to move on? It was her right—she'd earned it. But she'd been with me so long I wasn't sure how to exist without her. Besides that, she was my friend. She might not know it, but she was. I'd adopted her as my own and I wasn't sure if I could handle the pain of her leaving.

Especially not right now. I wasn't particularly my strongest at that exact moment in time.

"You've never asked why I was on my way to eternal damnation."

I froze mid-step, nearly falling over. That wasn't what I'd been expecting at all. "No. I haven't." A very eloquent response.

"Why not?" She wouldn't look at me. I could feel the hairs standing up on the back of my neck and a fear I'd never had with Elizabeth rose from my stomach.

"It's your choice to tell me." I wasn't afraid of her. How could I be afraid of her—she's my Elizabeth in the colonial dress with the neat bun and the fierce battle ax. But still… being this close to hell can do crazy things to a person.

Er, ghost.

"I choose to tell you now."

I looked wildly around the cavern. We were maybe four minutes from Death's door. Not a lot of time to have a heart to heart. But this seemed important to her. "Okay. Shoot."

"In life, I loved two men."

I waited for her to continue, but she didn't. So then I spent several seconds listening to my soft leather boots make padding noises across the lava and pondered her words. "Umm. Elizabeth, most people love more than one person in their life."

She passed a ghostly hand over my arm. "You don't understand. I was married to one man. I loved him. Very much. But I also loved another man at the same time."

"*Oh.* So you—you had an affair?" This was an incredibly awkward conversation. Plus, I hadn't thought having an affair was a damnable sin, but I wasn't all that up-to-date on what constituted a trip to hell.

"No. I did not." Her voice was soft, sad. "I've seen the way you love Alec, Navi. That was the way I loved Wyatt. But I married someone else. And no matter how much I loved him, I could never love him enough to forget Wyatt."

I paused, turning my full attention on her. "So you're saying that if I don't find a way to get over Alec, I'll go to hell?"

She shook her head. "If you don't find a way to forget your Alec, you're already in hell. Or, you could tell him the truth and give your heart peace."

It was true. His constant presence in my head over the years, in my heart, was agonizing. Having him there but never being able to touch him or talk to him or even see him. There were even times over the last four years that I imagined he was a myth. Not real. Not real.

"I can't tell him the truth, Elizabeth. It will open his eyes. The demons will target him. I can't fight them and keep the city safe if they're constantly sending hunters after him. I love him enough to give him that. Besides, I also hate him. Right now, I hate him a lot."

She smiled gently. I bet, when she'd died, she'd been in her early thirties. She was still beautiful, despite the sadness in her gray eyes. "Hate is passionate. Sometimes it is easier to hate the things we love. I took my own life because of my guilt, and I was not allowed into heaven. I spent a lifetime not being true to my own heart and soul—not letting go of one of them and fully loving the other. Perhaps that is the worst sin of all."

And with that, we arrived at Death's door.

His house, ironically, was an adorable cottage with pretty flowers and wind chimes out front. I got the impression that perhaps, it *might* just be possible, that Death didn't really enjoy all the darkness and gloom that came with being Death.

I knocked, waiting to hear footfalls from the other side, even though I *knew* Death didn't walk. It was habit. Old habits die hard, you know.

The door swung open and Death's red, glowing eyes greeted me. I swallowed my customary shriek, because asuwangs had red, glowing eyes and wanting to shriek was pure reflex. But Death was a nice guy, despite his terrifying appearance. "Navi. You are prompt, as usual."

"Hi. Do you want my report first, or shall we meet the new recruits?"

"You can sheath Golly and Kali now." I imagined him raising an eyebrow at me, but then, I couldn't remember him having eyebrows. Hurriedly, I put them away, immediately missing the comfort of my swords in my hands.

"Let's have your reports first. I will have my pets round up the recruits." He whistled, an ear-splitting, skull-shattering *ouch* that brought the hounds of hell bounding out of the manicured back lawns. They were gigantic black dogs with flames dripping from their jaws, but they leaped around like puppies.

"Down! Down boy!" I yelled when one, whose name I could never remember, leaped toward me, spiked tail wagging in excitement. I danced out of the way, facing eminent death at the mouth of an overly enthusiastic dog.

Never mind that he was all fire and spikes and poison.

"Garmr. Down," Death snapped. Garmr, yes. That was it. Garmr dropped back, head down. I would have petted him if his fur wouldn't have sent waves of toxins through my blood. Instead I just murmured, "Poor puppy."

Death gave me an exasperated glare before he turned to Garmr and his sister—who also had a name I couldn't remember. "Bring me the lost souls."

The dogs bounded off, racing through a haze of smoke and fire, and disappeared behind a wave of lava. "Shall we?" Death stepped back politely and waved us inside.

His house was something out of a painting. Lots of pastels, lots of flowers. Lots of tea settings and comfortable furniture. "What have you to report?"

I sat on the couch. Elizabeth stood silently by the door, watching us, but she kept her distance from the man who'd held her soul in his skeletal hand.

"Jesse has failed the program. I'm recommending she be returned to your possession effective immediately."

"Oh? I thought she was very eager to join your program."

I nodded, picking up one of the little tea biscuits Death had set out. I nibbled on a corner, resisting the urge to moan in ecstasy. Death could bake. Well. "She was very eager to join my program. But since then, I have continually had to reprimand her for lackluster performance, and just the other night I sent her after two escaped asuwangs before they made it into society. They escaped and took four of my souls with them, but Jesse hasn't been seen since."

"And she wasn't taken by the sea witch?" Death's skeletal fingers steepled under his chin and the red eyes watched me.

"We don't believe so, no. My souls have said they can still feel her nearby."

"If you revoke her access to the program and she refuses to come back, she will join limbo. You realize this, correct?"

Limbo was the space between our world and the afterlife. Souls in limbo can't move on. They're trapped in a certain area. Basically, the ghosts that people see haunting buildings and terrorizing the general population? Those aren't my ghosts. Those are limbo souls. They can't communicate unless they're super powerful. They can't eat, they can't feel. All they can do is wander in their area for eternity. And yet, many souls choose that path because they're too afraid of the other side to move on, or they're too tied to something here to let go. It's a very sad thing, and I wouldn't wish it on anyone.

Even Jesse.

I glanced at Elizabeth. She nodded once and disappeared, fading in and out of the Death's domain as easily as she did my own.

"Any other reports to make?"

I nodded, eager for this one. "Yes. A good one. Don was critically injured in battle. I freed him from the demon, and he raced right back in to fight. He was then taken by the asuwangs when Jesse failed to stop them, and when I freed him from its shell, he helped kill it. He is always one of the first to arrive and the last to leave. I believe when his period of probation is up, he should be allowed to move on to the other side." I nodded toward the light over Death's shoulder. His home stood in the crossroads of the gates of hell and the stairway to heaven.

Death's eyes brightened. He liked it when souls were saved. It didn't please him at all to send people to an eternity of suffering. I wouldn't mind our meetings at all if it wasn't for the screaming in the background and the stiff formality I had to take on when I talked to Death. He took his Soul Agents very seriously.

Elizabeth returned just as the dogs did. I could feel the little cottage shaking with each giant step. "Navi," Elizabeth murmured as I went to follow Death outside. "Jesse has not been taken, but she refuses to come in."

Death paused, looking over his shoulder at her. This close, I could see the skull hidden in the folds of his robe. It was clean and bright white. "She knows the consequences of her actions?"

I felt Elizabeth tremble beside me, the air quivering around her. But she raised her chin, my brave warrior. "Yes."

He nodded sadly. "I will send the hounds. If she refuses them, I have no choice but to remove her access to the otherworlds."

The hounds would be busy today.

My potential new recruits waited outside, some standing nervously, hopefully at attention, watching me with eager eyes. Some lounged about, and some glared at me with an inexplicable fury. Ghosts can't hide their emotions. Especially not here. They don't have enough energy. "You, you, you, and you. You may leave. Enjoy your stay in hell." I dismissed all the angry ones right away. They were a waste of my time, and I could feel that the sun would be rising soon.

After they left, I faced the remaining souls. Probably about thirty of them, which would really help my flailing army. But I knew not all of them would work for my program. It was a sad thing.

"My first question for you: Who here is interested in my program? Please show me by raise of hands."

All of them but two raised their hands. I nodded. "You two may go." I watched as they turned and wandered off, lost souls in every sense of the word as they tried to follow the big hound leading them back to their cells. "For the rest of you. I will explain what your probationary period will entail. Then I will explain what is possible if you do well versus what will happen if you do not do well. At that time, I will take any questions you may have and then offer the position to those of you who I feel are right for the program."

I pushed my hair over my shoulder and faced them. One of the men who had been lingering near the back spoke up. "You're awful young and small and"—his eyes roved up and down my body—"pretty to be leading an army. Why don't you leave that to the men?"

I sighed. There was always one. "I've been doing this for over ten years. I have never lost a battle. Furthermore, it is not left to the men because men can't *see* demons unless someone opens their eyes for them. If we waited for that to happen, we would all be dead. On top of that," I growled, "if I left this up to the men, we would never win this battle. Only women can wield the swords of the soul and sing the call. I will thank you to keep your questions until the end."

He snorted. I looked over at Death and shook my head. Sad, I was losing too many recruits and I hadn't even told them the scary part yet. Death motioned to his hounds, who nudged the man away. No one argued with the giant hell hounds, especially when they had the power to tear a soul to shreds.

Because souls were already dead. So they couldn't die again, they would just endure the pain. For eternity.

"Okay, Basically my program works like this. We are assaulted on a regular basis by demons known as asuwangs. They're controlled by a sea witch who has taken the lives of many, many humans and not a few Agents. My army of souls fight off the demons before they can make it through the gate and into town. If a soul is taken by the asuwangs, he or she is kept by the sea witch until the time she uses the soul as a shield to come to shore and attempt to make her home in the sun to feed off the flesh of the innocent. Before the sun rises, the souls can be rescued, but once the sun hits them, they form a nearly impenetrable shield and are unable to be freed at that time."

I met each of their eyes. Yep, I'd scared them all quite a bit. I brought out my big, innocent puppy dog eyes. "However, with a strong enough team, the chance of getting taken is slim, and if a soul performs well during the probationary period of three months, he or she will be released to move on. No more fire, no more brimstone."

Indecision warred on each and every face. And this is when I brought in my secret weapon. "This is Elizabeth. She has been fighting by my side for many, many years. She was given her freedom after her three month probationary period for outstanding service, but she chose to remain here and fight alongside us."

Now they gaped. If the situation wasn't so tense, if I didn't need them so much, it would have been amusing to see all the translucent mouths hanging open. "And I would choose this path again," she said quietly, but loud enough that they all heard her.

"Any questions?" I asked brightly.

An hour later, I escorted twenty-seven souls back to the surface to meet the rest of my team.

I stood on the beach and stared down at the water. "Sea witch," I murmured, "I'm waiting for you."

"WHERE ARE YOU GOING all..." Terrie gave me a once over. Reese, from her spot at the computer, rolled her eyes and went back to work. "Dressed up?" Terrie finally finished.

I was exhausted. The meeting with Death had taken all

night long, and after that I hadn't slept well.

Stupid Alec.

But. I reminded myself there was a *but*. I had done this before. I had missed sleep and had nightmares and cried. And I had gotten thought it. I would do it again.

So, yes. I was tired and I looked like crap. These things couldn't be helped. "Has—has anyone called or—or anything?" I asked, feeling my cheeks redden. Obviously, we all knew who *anyone* was.

"No, Navi. And honestly, if you look like that, I don't know why you'd expect them to." Terrie didn't even try to soften the blow with a smile or anything.

Well. Ouch.

Reese sighed. "Konstanz was talking to someone for a few minutes last night but I didn't see who. Seriously, Navi, where are you going in sweats that don't even have cute words across your butt?"

I abhorred sweats that had cute words across my butt. They made me uncomfortable. "I'm having lunch with Bryson," I called over my shoulder as I practically scampered down the hall to my room. Konstanz was lying on her bed, neatly made while mine, across from hers, was still a disastrous mound of tangled blankets.

"Hey. Did…" My voice failed me, so I cleared my throat and tried again. "Did Alec stop by last night?"

Konstanz didn't look up from her tablet. "No, honey. I'm sorry."

My shoulders fell. I hadn't even realized I was so tense until she didn't give me the answer I was hoping for. I let a breath out in a strangled whoosh. "Okay. I just wondered… Reese said someone stopped by."

"Oh. Yeah, it was the delivery guy but he had the wrong house. I had to argue with him about it for, like, ten minutes."

I heard the knock on the door and caught sight of Reese

leaping over the coffee table to answer it. "Okay. Ready for lunch with Bryson?"

She rolled and shoved herself to her feet. "Yep. Aren't you going to get dressed?"

"I am dressed."

Her eyebrows both shot up and a faint pink tint colored her cheeks. "Oh. I—I didn't even look."

Right.

Bryson's sports car was small, and every time we hit a pothole the bottom scraped, and he had to slow way down for little teeny bumps. I wasn't a sports car girl. I was a truck girl. Or, ya know, a jeep girl, since that's what I drove.

"How was your meeting last night?" he asked, steering carefully over the gravel on the road.

I tried not to wince. "It was good. Lots of new recruits. Exhausting though. I'm not sure I'll be very good company."

"It's okay." Konstanz patted me on the head from her cramped space in the back. "That's what I'm here for."

Bryson smiled at her in the rearview mirror.

"So I guess you stayed home from school, huh?" He glanced at my sweats that didn't have cute words across the butt. I tugged self-consciously on my sweat shirt and shook my head.

"No. No, I went. I haven't been to bed yet." And holy snowballs, bed sounded so good.

"Wow. You must be tired." His face lit up. "Don't worry. I made something amazing for lunch. It'll wake you right up and then we'll go have some fun."

"Don't you work?" I asked without meaning to. Apparently when I was this exhausted, I had no filter.

"Yeah. I took today off."

Of course he did. And I didn't know why. He seemed fine with the whole friend-zone thing, but why on earth would he take the day off to spend it with me and Konstanz?

Boys. They're so confusing.

"I just think I'm going to swear off all men for the rest of eternity," I accidentally muttered out loud.

Umm. Awkward much?

Bryson didn't miss a beat. "I know you think that now." He lowered his voice like he didn't want Konstanz to hear, but she was *right there* with nowhere to go. "But how am I going to change your mind if I don't spend time with you?"

Well, he had a point there, didn't he? "It's just that I don't feel like this is fair to you at all. You know I'm in lo—that I'm having a hard time getting over him. I just think—"

"Navi." He stopped at a red light and turned to face me. "I know. I know how you feel about Alec. I know how you feel about me. I don't care. I'm here to change your mind."

CHAPTER NINETEEN

Alec

I WALKED INTO THE APARTMENT AND was immediately assaulted by lilacs. Or, the scent of them, anyway. There was a vase full of them on the table that we never used. And that smell…

"Was Navi here?" I asked, hating the way hope made my voice shake. *Please say she was here. Please say she was here.*

"What? Why?" Bryson asked, focusing really hard on the dishes he was washing so he didn't have to look at me.

The way he'd answered was suspicious. Like maybe I should stop hoping so desperately that she'd been there recently. "I smell her lotion." Yeah, I was pathetic. I recognized the smell of her lotion the second I walked in the room.

"Oh. Right. Yeah, we had lunch together. I made fettuccine."

"You—you had lunch together?" My stomach twisted and the dryness in my mouth made it hard to swallow. "Why?"

He didn't look at me. "She's hurting, Alec. Konstanz and I are trying to get her through this. It wasn't a big deal."

I ran a hand over my face and stared at his back through my fingers. "What are you saying, Bryson? That's two days in a row. Are you guys, like—" I couldn't even say it. Three days after she and I had that fight, and she was dating my roommate? She said she hadn't been able to get over me in the four years we'd been apart, but three days later and she forgot I existed and dated my roommate.

The world did not make sense.

Bryson finally emptied the sink and turned to face me. "No. We're not together. It's really hard to date a girl when her best friend won't let her out of her sight. I'm just trying to be a friend. That's all."

I dropped my keys on the table and shrugged out of my jacket, fighting to get the sleeve over my cast. "Fine. Fine, so you're bosom buddies now. That's awesome. Why in the hell are you bringing her here when you know how I feel about her?"

Bryson frowned, coming around the kitchen counter. "You called her a whore, Alec. You said she was a demon. I figured you were pretty much done with her."

"I didn't mean any of those things!" I yelled. I stared at the ceiling for several long seconds before I could force myself to look back at him. "We are done. Navi and I won't ever be together. But that doesn't mean you need to bring her back here." *That doesn't mean I'll ever get over her.*

"Okay. Sorry. I didn't know it would bother you. We'll hang out at her place. Hey, have you eaten yet?"

I glared at him, trying to comprehend what had just happened. There were future plans? I didn't want him to have future plans with her.

"It's just awkward at her place, you know? We have no privacy. She doesn't even have her own bedroom. Did you know that?" Those words nearly sent me to my knees. I fought to stay on my feet as the room spun. I did know that. I didn't want to know how he knew that, though.

He continued without waiting for me to answer. "And again, I ask. Are you hungry?" How could he be kind and considerate after he just blew a hole through my chest?

I jerked away from him. "I'm gonna go take a shower."

"Wait!" Bryson called as I stormed across the room. "I have leftover fettuccine!"

"No thanks," I muttered as I shut the bathroom door behind me.

AFTER THAT, I SAW very little of Bryson. He spent every waking moment with Navi and Konstanz. He came home late and left early. Normally, that would thrill me—less time with the roommate who seemed to live to torture me? Hell yeah. But when I knew he was gone because he was with her, it drove me absolutely insane. Not seeing her, only hearing bits of conversation between them or smelling her lotion when I walked in, and I still felt the same agonizing pain I had the first day I'd lost her. I was instantly sick—like a migraine and the stomach flu and maybe a couple knife wounds all rolled into one. It wasn't getting any easier. In fact, it was worse every single day. So I threw myself into work. I didn't know what else to do.

"Alec, you back here again?" My boss looked over his desk as I strapped on my tool belt.

"Yep. Just stopped for dinner." If I kept this up, I would make so much money I wouldn't even need a roommate. I'd be able to move out of my apartment and buy a house.

"You worked over eighty hours each the last three weeks. Did you know that?" Did I know that. Of course I knew that. I knew it because the week before, I'd gone home at night, and Bryson was gone, and I knew where he was. Then I'd come home the next night and had just walked out of the shower, and Navi was at the door, telling Bryson she would wait for him in the car. Another day, I'd happened to walk past the window to see her jeep in the parking lot below. This was *after* the week of trying to drown my sorrows in alcohol—and been arrested for being drunk in public. I'd also thrown up in Josh's car, so he wasn't very fond of me. Finally, I'd just decided to stay at work. It was easier here. The weekend was coming, though. I wasn't sure what to do with that.

My phone buzzed. I glanced down, praying it would be her, knowing it wouldn't be. "Hey Mom," I said, putting the phone to my ear.

"Hi Alec. We haven't seen you for a while. Thought I'd better check on you."

"I'm good, Mom. Just working a lot. How are things there?"

There was a couple seconds of silence—enough that I knew she was dissecting my words and tone to see if there was anything to worry about. "Fine, fine. We're just busy. Dad is trying to coach Jack's little league team, but between you and me, he's not much of a sports man." She chuckled and even I couldn't help but smile. "And Jack has his first baseball game this week. Do you want to come?" If my mom had been closer, I would have kissed her.

"Of course. Hey, maybe Dad needs an assistant coach?" I could hear the hope trembling in my own voice, so I knew she picked up on it. Mother's intuition and all that.

"Or maybe he needs to be the assistant. Hey Jack, how would you feel if Alec coached your team?"

I heard him whoop in the background. For the first time in several weeks, I could feel a smile trying to crack its way through. "I'll be there Friday night, as soon as I get off work."

Suddenly, the weekend couldn't come fast enough.

CHAPTER TWENTY

Navi

ALEC'S TRUCK WAS, AS USUAL, NOT there when I pulled in, and as usual my dumb heart was both relieved and devastated. "Heart, I think you've got issues," I muttered as I pulled into a parking space. Right then, I'd give my left arm for a chance to see Alec—even knowing that I would probably end up eaten by asuwangs with only one arm for fighting.

Yes, I was that desperate.

"It will get easier," Elizabeth said, sitting rigidly in the passenger seat next to me. I wasn't sure if she just sensed my desperate need to keep her near, or if she was worried I might do something completely insane if she left me, but Elizabeth had become my constant companion, unless Bryson and Konstanz were around. And they were around a lot. Maybe a little more than I wanted, because a part of me needed time to mope and cry and heal, and I couldn't do that with cheerleaders constantly at my side.

Thank goodness for Elizabeth, who let me cry and ghost-patted my head and gave up everything she usually did during the day to hang out with me. I leaned my forehead against the steering wheel and peeked at her out of the corner of my eye. "What would you be doing right now if you weren't stuck with me?"

A ghost of a smile crossed her face (a ghost of... see what I did there?) "When I first regained my freedom from Death, I explored the world and saw all the things I didn't get to while I was alive. I went to Egypt and Africa and Spain...all these beautiful places I'd always dreamed of. But it got old. I tried to make friends with the souls in limbo, but they, as you might imagine, aren't the friendliest. They're prone to violence and possession and screaming and wailing." She frowned. "Not enjoyable at all."

"I'm sorry." I hadn't realized how lonely her afterlife must be, and I felt guilty wanting her to stay with me to fight. Guilt is not my favorite thing to feel.

She shrugged. "Now I watch the waves, waiting for demons. I make grand plots to defeat the asuwangs and their sea witch. I visit your parents, because they can see me—you're supposed to call your mother, by the way."

I smiled. "Yes ma'am." We sat in silence until I spoke again. "They're planning something."

"Your parents?" She tapped her translucent chin.

I half-heartedly giggled. "No, Elizabeth. The demons. Something is up."

She nodded. "I agree. But we're doing everything we can. When they make their move, we will be ready."

I swallowed hard. I sure hoped we would. My grandmother had thought she was ready. She'd had a larger army than I did—because back then, more people were willing to fight for their salvation. And she'd still lost.

"Are you planning on staying here tonight?" She quirked an eyebrow, a very modern movement to go with her old-style clothing.

"Oh. Right. No." Since Alec wasn't here, it was safe to go up. I slowly slid out of my jeep before I turned to Elizabeth. "See you in a bit?"

"Always." She shimmered and was gone and I felt like she'd taken all my strength with her. I trudged up the stairs to Alec's—er, Bryson's—apartment and knocked listlessly on the door.

He swung it open so fast, I had just a touch of a suspicion that he'd been watching me. Well… that didn't make me look crazy at all, did it? Sitting in my jeep, talking to myself. And I wasn't a calm talker, either. I liked to throw my arms around a lot. I cringed.

"Hey Navi. How are you today?" He tipped his head to the side.

Konstanz appeared behind him. I'd been watching for Alec's truck and completely missed her little car parked nearby.

I waved and I smiled, like a friendly person would do. "I'm fine, Bryson. Ready to go to the museum?" He had made it his mission to reacquaint us with all the historic destinations in Astoria. I didn't mind—they were beautiful, and I loved history. Even though I was sacrificing sleep for these little outings.

Hmm. Maybe I did mind.

He was answering me and I'd completely zoned out. "Yep. I haven't had dinner yet. Wanna grab something on the way?" He snatched his keys off the cute little table by the door and locked up. I pitifully tried to see any trace of Alec behind him, and kept one eye on the parking lot, praying Alec would show up and then praying he wouldn't.

I was a very confused girl.

"Yeah. But I have to work tonight, so we have to be fast."

He raised an eyebrow as he brushed past me to lead the way down the stairs. "Again? That's like the fifteenth night in a row. Don't you ever get a day off?"

I wish. Fighting demons every freaking night was exhausting. Didn't they realize I needed to sleep? They'd upped their attack frequency by about a thousand percent, and the sea witch was sending a whole lot more at once, too. This, of course, kept me fighting all night every night, and I was so stressed about it that I didn't really sleep during the day, either.

It was *awesome.*

"Not lately. Things are intense." I yawned, nearly falling down the stairs while I wasn't looking.

Bryson caught me, studying my zombie-like face. "You need to sleep."

"Right?" Konstanz nodded. "Tell that to our roommates. Reese is like a walking bull horn. Terrie sings like a strangled goose."

I snorted, very unladylike. "For some reason, they like to be awake during the day, which is all well and good for them. For me? Not so much."

We were stopped in the middle of the stairwell, and I was still praying Alec would show up. I just wanted to see him. Would that be so bad? Realizing belatedly *again* that Bryson was talking, I struggled to focus. Because that's what good friends do, right? They listen when the other one talks. "You know, Alec and I work during the day. Our apartment is empty and silent. You could sleep here."

I shook my head, dodging around him and heading to my jeep. "Alec would throw a fit. He doesn't want me anywhere near him."

Bryson shrugged, climbing in the passenger side. "I can ask him. The worst he can say is no. And you can sleep here all weekend, too. He goes… away… on the weekends."

"Away?" I asked, wincing at how my heart started to pound just talking at him. Hopeful and frightened, all at once.

"Yeah. I think… never mind." He looked out the window, refusing to meet my gaze, but I pounced on his words like an overly enthusiastic cat—and news of Alec was my red laser dot.

"What, Bryson?"

He turned toward me, pity in his eyes. "I didn't want to tell you." He made a face, like he'd eaten something icky. "I think… I think he sort of has a new girlfriend. He stays at her house on the weekends." Seeing the distress his words caused, he rushed to continue, "But I'm sure you're way prettier than she is."

"Oh," I said weakly. "Thanks."

"Hey." Bryson grabbed my chin and turned my head so I was facing him—a risky little move since I was driving us through traffic. "So he's an idiot. But there are a billion guys who would give their right arm to be with you." His eyes darkened. "Trust me on that."

"If they gave their right arms, they couldn't hug me." I pulled my chin away so I could focus on driving. And on not crying, but mostly the driving.

"I'd still find a way," he said quietly. I squirmed. It made me massively uncomfortable when he talked about feelings. Because while I enjoyed his company *as a friend,* and I appreciated the distraction he gave me *as a friend,* the more time I spent with him, the more I knew I'd never feel "that way" about him. When I tried to tell him that, he said he'd find a way. The boy was an unending well of determination, that's for sure. "I'll tell you what. I'll even clean out a drawer, just for your stuff. Let's go buy you some extra toiletries right now!" He sounded way excited about it—and who said the word toiletries anymore?

"What about the museum?" I asked dumbly.

He shrugged. "I've been to the museum lots of times. Let's get you all set up at my place. We don't want you collapsing from exhaustion or something."

I frowned. "You told me yesterday you'd never been." I distinctly recalled the conversation, because I'd been trying to escape to the beach with Elizabeth and he'd kept up a constant chatter—like he knew I was trying to leave and thought he could stop me by not letting me get a word in.

He patted my cheek, reminding me of my aging aunt when I went to visit. "You're so tired. I said I hadn't been recently."

"Oh." I swear I could remember… but then again, he was right. I was so tired after all the fighting that I couldn't think straight. I wasn't even sure why I kept agreeing to Bryson's outings when I knew with a ninety-eight percent certainty that I'd be fighting again that night. I guess… I guess I just needed the distraction, from Alec and from my Agent life. I needed something to remind me the world was okay, that things were still moving forward even when I felt like I was banging my head against a metaphorical brick wall.

Bryson was very caring and always around, which made me wonder if Bryson actually had a job. He was only gone a few hours a day. But he always had money and he took work calls all the time, so I guess he must have a job somewhere.

He insisted on buying me an extra toothbrush and a comb. He said I was free to sleep in his t-shirt, but that felt too intimate. So I grabbed some pajamas that covered me from feet to chin—to hide battle wounds, of course. The fact that it also hid me from Bryson's ice blue eyes was just a bonus. And then, of course, I felt guilty for not being madly in love with him when he was so considerate and patient with me.

We grabbed muffins and went back to his house. "I've gotta run by work," Konstanz said, digging her keys out of her purse. "I'll be back in a bit."

That left me and Bryson alone. I panicked, like a trapped rabbit, but there was no polite way out of it. She smiled and waved and disappeared and I wanted to smile and strangle her.

"You're sure Alec won't be here?" I asked Bryson, not sure whether I wanted to be wrong or right.

"No, he's at work. And he never comes home before eight. You'll be long gone by then." He sank on the couch with a frown. "I wish, just one night, I got to wake up with you." He looked up at me, blue eyes pleading. "Is that too much to ask?"

My heart hurt for him. "I'm sorry, Bryson. I can't miss work. Things are too stressful right now. And then I have school..." School. Crap. I had a project due the next day. I ran a hand through my hair and glared at my muffin. I felt like I was juggling all these things, trying to keep all the balls in the air, and soon one would fall. Or they all would fall. Maybe they'd turn into giant boulders and crush me when they came down. Maybe they already were giant boulders and they were already coming down.

When I woke up, the sky was dark outside and Elizabeth was trying to shake me. "Oh crap!" I sat up so fast I toppled off the couch. Bryson was nowhere to be seen, but Elizabeth was pacing, back and forth so fast I could feel an icy breeze.

"I've been trying to wake you for almost an hour. The asuwangs have risen, and some have already made it into the city."

"Oh my gosh. Oh my gosh!! How could I sleep so long?" I was going to strangle Bryson. He knew how badly I needed to be at work and he'd let me sleep anyway. Because he thought he was helping. "Arrgh!" I growled, tugging on my tennis shoes and shoving my tangled hair out of my face. I followed Elizabeth out the door, leaping down the stairs three at a time. I hit the landing and took off running as the world blurred around me. I saw Alec's truck out of the corner of my eye, just pulling in. The mere sight of him hit me so hard I stumbled and fell, skidding on my hands and knees. And let me tell you, when you're moving that fast and fall, it's more than a little asphalt burn. I felt the skin tear, then the muscle, and then I felt it clawing away at my bones.

I forced myself to my feet and tried to ignore the pain as I jogged after Elizabeth. Thankfully, by the time I caught up, I was almost completely healed. I risked one last glance over my shoulder, just catching a glimpse of him as he slowly climbed the stairs up to his door. I felt tears burning the backs of my eyes, but I refused to let them fall. Elizabeth had a point—I couldn't spend my whole life in love with him. I had to let him go so that I could give my whole heart to someone else and escape this hell I'd been living in the last four years. I needed to free my soul before I died and ended up fighting in someone else's army.

I just wish letting him go was as easy as, say, cutting off an asuwang's head. *That,* I could do with no problem.

"Do you feel them? They are near." Elizabeth stopped—since she merely floated and had no momentum to push her forward, she could stop instantly. Me, I went skidding past, arms cartwheeling and trying not to fall again.

I grabbed Golly and Kali and spun just as the asuwang flung itself off the roof of the shed we were standing near. I raised my swords just in time, cringing as black blood sprayed my face as it impaled itself. It screamed, but I mercilessly pushed my foot against its face and jerked my blades free. Its lifeless body fell to the ground as three more asuwangs barreled around the corner. "Holy crap. How many escaped?" I panted, swinging my swords up to fend off the claws. "And what time is it? How long until the sun rises?"

"It is past midnight. I do not know how many escaped. We have to"— Elizabeth brought her battle ax down with startling speed, neatly detaching the head of the demon—"find the rest of your army."

I scissored my swords to take off the other one's head, dancing away from the blood that sought to ruin my shoes. I dove after the third one, which had finally realized what I was and decided to escape. I landed on its back, cringing at its scaly, furry, slimy back. I wasn't even sure how it could have so many icky things at once, but somehow it managed. I plunged my swords into its sides, seeking the heart, riding it like a very fat horse. It screamed and bucked, throwing me in the air, but I held tight to Golly and Kali. They twisted and dragged upward and the demon finally collapsed, sawed almost in half.

I rolled away, coming up on my feet. "It will be a long night." Elizabeth was staring down toward the beach, toward battle, toward hell. More demons waited for us there, I knew. I wiped my blades on the grass and sheathed them.

Closing my eyes, praying for strength, I nodded. "It always is."

CHAPTER TWENTY-ONE

Alec

WEEKENDS AT MY PARENTS' ARE WHAT saved me. Without them, I would have worked myself to death. Instead, I ate my mom's cooking. I helped my dad build a deck. I coached Jack's baseball team and played football on the lawn with all the neighbor kids. I exhausted myself to the point that when I fell asleep, I was too tired to dream about anything but Navi's death.

Over and over and over.

I was so tired, that sometimes when I'd come home late at night from work, I'd think I could see her. She was like a ghost, barely more than a blur, but I'd catch a just a whiff of her lilac lotion in the air and I'd look up, praying she'd be there. She never was. There was nothing but my desperate desire to see her again slowly driving me absolutely insane.

"Hey." Josh nudged me. I wasn't even sure when he'd shown up, I was so tired. "You're still alive, right?"

I blinked at him and waved my newly-freed-from-the-cast hand around. "I'm peachy."

"It's for the best, anyway."

I did not want to have this conversation again. So I ignored him.

"I mean, Navi... she would have tied you down. You're only twenty-two, bro. You don't want a girlfriend who—"

"Knock it off, Josh." I hadn't had a reason to growl at anyone for a while, with Bryson gone all the time. It was somewhat refreshing.

"I'm serious. I mean, yeah, she's hot, right? But what else? She's got zero personality."

No personality? Was he serious? She had more personality in her pinky than most girls did in an entire clique. I stood up abruptly, glaring at him. "Knock. It. Off."

He held up his hands, "I'm just saying"—he stuttered for a second before he regained his footing —"she's not worth this, Alec."

"You don't know a damn thing, Josh. Shut the hell up."

"I'm just trying to help."

You can't help me. She was the only one who could. And that wasn't going to happen.

CHAPTER TWENTY-TWO

Navi

"IT'S BEEN TWO MONTHS, ELIZABETH. I'VE done everything humanly possible to forget him. I've been so busy fighting demons that I barely have enough energy to brush my teeth, but I always have plenty of energy to miss him." I flopped back into the soft grass, my feet still dangling in the river, and stared at the rising sun. "I can't love anyone else."

She nodded sadly, her eyes telling me she completely understood.

"So… maybe I'll become a nun. Nuns don't go to hell. I've never had a nun in my army. If I can't get over Alec, maybe I'll just be in love him from a convent, and never hurt another guy with my traitorous heart."

She rolled her eyes, which was both alarming and slightly amusing from a ghost with translucent skin. "I think quitting school was unwise. It provided a much needed distraction. Perhaps enough that you wouldn't have had to spend time with Bryson to find relief."

I cocked my head to the side to see her. There was still the outline of tears in her soul from the battle the night before, or the night before that… we'd been fighting every single night for so long that I couldn't keep track anymore. "You're probably right. But I can't keep up. I was failing two classes and mid-terms were coming up. There was no way I could study for them."

"When the sea witch rises, we will kill her and then you can finish school." Elizabeth nodded like she was so positive that's what would happen.

"She's killing off all my army. I'm not going to have one to fight with by the time she rises." I traced a dandelion, wondering why I was here at the river where I'd come with Alec so often instead of home sleeping. "That's probably her plan, huh?"

Elizabeth nodded slowly, her ghostly fingers trailing in the water as she lay on her stomach, one hand propped under her chin. "She's sending her demons every night to diminish our forces, and when she's confident she can overtake us, she will rise."

"Well that's just awesome. I wonder if Death will let me scour hell for some more recruits." Rumors of our constant battles had spread, and finding more souls willing to fight with us was getting difficult. Death himself was trying to bargain with them, offering rides on his hell hounds or tea and biscuits at night when they returned to their cells. So far, it wasn't helping much, but I held out hope.

"I wish we could contact some of the other Agents. I'd like to see if they're having the same problem we are." I sat up so fast my head spun, and I had to try to hold my brain in my skull with both hands. "Ouch. Maybe we could ask Death if he would consider creating another Agent."

Elizabeth looked up sharply. "Are you going to quit?"

I shook my head, but gently this time. "No. No way. But if there was another Agent, with my strength and power, we'd have a much better chance of killing the sea witch."

"Your mother and aunt were both Agents and they did not succeed." Elizabeth relaxed back onto her fist as the sun's rays shone through her, sparkling against her soul. It almost hurt my eyes to look at her, she was so bright.

I slumped back onto the grass. "Yeah, I guess. Maybe we could convince the souls in limbo to join us. But I can't offer them freedom."

"They might join just for protection. Her demons are snatching up any of the souls they see—whether they're yours or just trapped ghosts."

The sun felt like it was frying my eyes. I slowly rolled over and shoved myself to my feet. "I'll get started early tonight. We'll see if we can find some souls to recruit before the sun goes down and we have to fight."

Her eyes widened. "Your shoulder is wounded, Navi. You should have taken care of that as soon as the demons sank into the sea."

I glanced down. "Oh. Yeah, so it is. It will heal tonight. I won't die from blood loss before then." I started slowly walking down the dirt road, swinging my shoes. "What are you going to do today?" I asked as she floated beside me.

"I will search for recruits. Maybe I could go to the other Agents. Gather information."

"That will take you clear across the world. You won't be able to come back quickly if something were to happen. Unless you went through Death's chambers."

She shook her head vehemently. "No, no. I'll stay here. In case you have need of me."

I gave her a sympathetic smile. She was so brave. But facing Death alone, no matter how adorable he seemed to me, was something she just couldn't do. And I didn't blame her. "Maybe one day we will find someone to travel with you."

CHAPTER TWENTY-THREE

Alec

THE WEIRDEST SOUND WOKE ME—LIKE a moan, but not a moan. I sat up, rubbing my eyes with my finally cast-free hand. The fingers were weak and sore and misshapen, but I didn't care. I had my damn hand back.

Another moan echoed through my room. "What the hell?" I swung my legs over the side of the bed and stood up, staggering into the living room. "Bryson?" I called. If he was in there with Navi while I was right through the wall, I'd kill him. A guy only had so much willpower, and I had reached my limits.

I pounded on his door but there was no response, and then the weird moan thing slithered through the living room, coming not from Bryson's room, but mine. Just to be sure, I pushed his door open and stuck my head inside. It was empty. No Bryson, no Navi.

"Alec."

I spun, but there was no one there. Without a doubt, though, it was Bryson's voice. Weak and barely audible, but definitely Bryson's. "Dude, you're not funny. Where the hell are you?"

"I'm right here, bro. I need your help."

I could hear him like he was standing in front of me, but I couldn't see him. Maybe my phone... I stalked back to my bedroom and grabbed it, checking to see if he was somehow on the other end, but it was off. I'd long since gone to turning it off at night so I'd stop waiting for Navi to text me and tell me Konstanz was wrong.

Because she never did.

"Alec, I'm right here. I need your help."

I spun in a circle, checked under the bed, and then went back to the living room and looked in every hidden space in the blasted apartment. He wasn't there. And as far as I could see, there were no wires or speakers. "This isn't funny, Bryson. I'm going back to bed. I have to work in two hours."

I went back to my room and snapped off the light. And suddenly, there in front of me, stood my roommate.

Except it wasn't my roommate. The Bryson that stood in front of me wasn't standing at all, he was hovering, and he was translucent. Like a... "Ghost?" I stumbled back, bellowing like a mad bull, and slammed into my door. "Bryson, what the f—?"

"I know! I know, Alec, but calm down. I need your help."

"You're a freaking ghost, Bryson!"

"I know." His head hung in defeat as he wafted two feet away. I tried to rationalize my way through this. I knew it wasn't a dream because I'd just impaled myself on my doorknob and it *hurt.* And I know I should have suspected tricks or... or something, but he was right in front of me and there was no damn way any tricks were involved.

My roommate was a ghost.

"Look, I need you to get Navi for me. She'll know what to do."

I stared stupidly. "What do you mean, she'll know what to do? You're dead!"

"No! I'm not dead!" He held his hands up toward me, completely see-through hands. "I'm still alive. My body is on the beach, and if you get me to a hospital, Navi will know how to fix me. But there's not much time. Hurry, Alec!"

I stared stupidly some more.

"Alec!" He rushed toward me, a blast of cold air preceding him and freezing my exposed skin.

"Dude!" I screeched. Like a girl. I'm not proud. "Back off!"

"Get your keys. We have to get my body. I feel it fading."

I swore. I hadn't even had time to process this, but I was shoving my feet into shoes and pulling on a shirt. Before I realized it, I was in my truck, driving like a madman down the freeway to the beach. And Bryson appeared on the seat next to me. "Explain. Now. Before I go check myself into a psychiatric hospital." It was official. Navi had finally caused me to lose my mind. Maybe I'd killed Bryson in a jealous rage and I just didn't remember? Was this guilt that made me completely lose all sense of anything?

He started talking really fast, like he realized I was about to drive myself straight to the psych ward. "Okay so Navi has been working a lot at night, right? And Konstanz was really worried, because she's always gone and Konstanz can't sleep when she's gone. Navi kept saying work was really insane, that her parolees were losing these fights they were in and something big was coming. It… it wasn't believable at all." I risked a glance over at him. Yeah, I'd been there. I knew how bad it hurt when she started going out every single night.

"She was really edgy. Really nervous. She freaking dropped out of school, Alec."

I was having a conversation with a ghost and all I could think about was Navi. "What? Why? What kind of trouble is she in?"

"Something you can't even comprehend."

That sounded awful and ominous. "What do you mean?"

"There. Turn up there."

"You can't even get to the beach from there, dude."

"There's a rock formation. My body is by the base."

I followed his instructions as far as the truck would go and jumped out. He was already racing down the beach, his translucent form catching the moonlight and shimmering like a rainbow. If the situation wasn't so bizarre and terrifying, I would laugh at how completely unmanly he looked right then. I might have even tried to take a picture for Navi. *Real tough boyfriend you've got there—he's all shimmers and rainbows!* Yeah, the fact that I was having this conversation with myself clearly showed how out of touch with reality I was.

But he stopped by the base of Devil's gate, a huge rock formation that faded out into the ocean. He paced around and threw up his hands and then dove onto the sand, and before I made it very far I could see Bryson's body laying motionless in the darkness. I slid to a stop next to him and fell on my knees. With one shaking hand I dialed 911 while the other one took his pulse. "What happened, Bryson?" I asked hoarsely.

"Well, I followed her to see who she was seeing—"

The emergency dispatch answered right then and I jerked a hand up to silence him. "I need help. My friend is unconscious. He's still breathing, but his pulse is really slow."

"Where is your friend, sir? Can you tell me what happened?"

"I'm by the Devil's Gate. I think he must have fallen or—or something? I don't know. I was looking for him and I found him and he needs help—"

"We'll send someone right away, sir."

I dropped the phone. "They're on their way. Talk fast."

Bryson was watching his body with such a horrified

expression that I finally had the sense to feel sorry for him. The whole experience must have been terrifying. "I followed her." His voice was numb now. "She's not what you think she is, Alec."

"So—so what? You caught her with some guy and he attacked you?"

"No." He shook his head slowly, almost like he was suddenly in some kind of trance. "No. She fights sea monsters, Alec. With a bunch of ghosts. Ghosts like me. She fights sea monsters and a sea monster came out of the water and attacked me and she didn't see me but she chased it and killed it. With an army of ghosts. She fights sea monsters."

I fell backward like I'd been punched. Or maybe whacked in the head with a two by four. Everything spun and nothing made sense. "What?"

Seriously. What else could I say?

"I tried to go to her house. To get her to help me. But her ghosts won't let me through. They said I was in limbo and that I was haunting her and they wouldn't let me through." His head suddenly snapped up, trance gone, and his milky eyes focused with a terrifying intensity on my face. "You have to help me, Alec. You have to tell Navi to fix this."

I could hear sirens in the distance, coming fast. "Why can't you just, like, hop back in your body and wake up? That's how it works on TV."

"This isn't TV, Alec! My girlfriend's roommate is a sea monster fighter with an army of ghosts and I'm almost dead!" Bryson screamed. The air around him shook—like I could literally see it shattering away from him in waves. "Navi is the only one who can help me."

Funny. I'd had that same thought yesterday.

My mind wanted to grasp at something else he said in that sentence, but the flashing lights distracted me.

The ambulance roared past my truck and right up the

beach, skidding to a stop in the sand not far from where I knelt. The next hour was a blur of red and blue lights and a thousand questions I couldn't answer and racing ambulances. And then wires and doctors and questions *they* couldn't answer—like why he wouldn't wake up and what had caused the weird injuries that looked like he'd been attacked by giant claws and then I was standing in a hospital room at six a.m., watching my roommate struggling to breathe while his ghost stood next to me, sobbing quietly.

"Please, Alec. Navi is the only one who can help me."

I ran a hand through my hair, noting absently that I needed a haircut. "Okay. I'll go talk to her. Just—just don't die, okay?"

"I'm coming with you."

"If you come with me, how will you not die?" I asked, exasperated. A nurse walked in to hear that last little bit and looked at me sympathetically with big brown eyes through black-rimmed glasses. Her black hair waved away from her face, and her badge said *Jasmyn Stamper.*

"He'll be okay, honey. We'll figure this out. Probably head trauma is all." She patted me on the arm as she passed by to check his vitals, her hands moving easily through a routine she'd obviously done at least thousand times.

Bryson stopped sobbing to watch her. "She's good. Tell them I don't want any other nurses. Just her."

I sank down in a chair and watched, wondering how, exactly, to do that. "Have you notified his next of kin?" she asked, glancing at me over her shoulder.

"Uh. No. I'll—I'll call his mom. I didn't think—" Holy crap what would I tell his mom?

"No! No, you will not call my mom. She'll have a heart attack." Bryson crossed his arms over his chest and stared me down, which was somewhat not effective when it had the substance of milk. I ignored him until she patted his hand (the physical hand, not the ghost hand) and left, telling me very sweetly to get some rest.

"Bryson," I said, my head in my hands, speaking through my fingers. "I don't even know how to process this."

"Well at least you have someone telling you what's going on. I watched it all while I tried not to die. It was crazy, Alec. She was there alone, and then she wasn't there, and then this thing came out of the water and right at me, and then she *was* there, but it was too late, and she had these swords and there were all these ghosts… and then I tried to go to her house, but the ghosts won't let me through."

"So you're telling me that Navi fights demons. My tiny, sweet little Navi."

She's not yours anymore.

It was true. She wasn't. If she fought demons and had this whole secret life, maybe she never had been.

"Dude," Bryson said as he hovered right in front of me, face desperate and only half-there, "I need you to go to Navi's house. She'll know what to do." He spoke very slowly, like I might not be completely comprehending his words when he spoke at a normal speed.

He was right.

I called my boss on my way out to my truck because clearly I wasn't going to work today, and then I thought about calling Navi to give her a heads up. But I knew she wouldn't answer if she saw my name on screen and my brain was beyond able to function, so I just drove over to her apartment in a confused haze of disbelief and prayed she'd let me through the door.

I thought—stupidly—that seeing Bryson's ghost standing over his unconscious, barely-breathing body would be the weirdest thing I'd see in probably this whole life time. But as I pulled into her apartment building, I finally realized what Bryson meant when he said her ghosts were keeping him out.

Because her entire apartment building was surrounded by ghosts wielding very large, very dangerous weapons. Swords and axes and knives. I froze in my truck, staring in horror. This was pretty much every nightmare I'd had as a kid come to life.

"What am I supposed to do now?" I asked Bryson, who sat silent in my passenger seat.

"They won't hurt you. You're not a demon. Or a ghost in limbo. Just walk through them."

I glared at him, horrified. "You're kidding, right?"

He shook his head.

"I can't just walk through them—can you see their weapons?" This morning was pretty damn freaky and I'd had about as much as I could handle.

Reese strode briskly out the door, digging through her purse, looking for her keys in the twilight. The sun would be up soon, and I wanted to jump out of the truck and beg it to hurry. But Reese didn't even see them. She walked right through them, and they parted like a river around a rock to let her through. "Those are Navi's ghosts?" My voice sounded strangled. And scared. I sounded scared, even to my own ears. Not gonna lie.

"Yeah. They fight the monsters with her."

Holy Hell.

I took the longest breath ever and shoved my door open. "If they attack me, I'm coming after you."

Then I turned my back on my ghost roommate and walked toward the sea of nightmares.

CHAPTER TWENTY-FOUR

Navi

I WAS JUST GETTING OUT OF the shower when I heard the pounding. Thinking Reese had forgotten her keys or something, I wrapped my towel around me and padded into the living room, dripping on the carpet. Reese might kill me, but she was already late for work. She'd have to kill me later.

But Konstanz beat me to the door. She gave me an odd look as she passed, and I realized my entire shoulder was a bloody, bruised mess. The moon had sunk too far in the sky to heal me, and I could already feel my ghosts outside fading.

Except for Elizabeth. She was almost always there, but outside so she didn't accidentally open my roommates' eyes. Because *that* would be the epitome of awful.

The fights last night had been brutal, which might have explained why I'd had to hang out at the river for a while to chill. We'd lost a lot of our new recruits, and some of my older members. Several asuwangs had gotten past us and made it to the other side of the rock, but we'd caught all of them but two before they made it to the city streets. Still, it was going to take me a while to recover from that one.

Thank goodness I didn't have school.

Konstanz had spent a good amount of time lately fixing my random wounds. I couldn't go to a doctor, because I couldn't explain them, and even though Konstanz had hinted once or twice, when I told her I couldn't tell her what happened, she'd quit asking.

The girl was a saint.

And possibly the only thing that was a balm to the open wound Alec had left on my heart.

"Alec." Her voice was absolute ice. "What are you doing here?"

I froze, standing there beyond the doorway in my towel. I was absolutely exhausted. Maybe I'd misheard her? Maybe I'd imagined the whole thing? But suddenly Elizabeth appeared just beyond the door.

Clearly, it wasn't Reese coming to retrieve lost keys.

"I need to see Navi." His voice sounded desperate and, if I wasn't hearing things, terrified.

Konstanz, unaware that she was surrounded by unearthly beings, crossed her arms over her chest and dug in her heels. "I told you no, Alec."

"Konstanz, this isn't the time, and it's not personal. I need to talk to her now, and if you don't get out of my way, I'll move you. You have no idea what kind of freaky crap I've seen tonight."

That was my second clue that something was very, very wrong.

Forgetting that I was standing in a towel, only knowing that he was so close I could touch him and that I could hear fear in his voice, I left my soaked spot and came around the door. "What's wrong?"

His eyes widened. Oh, right. *Then* I remembered the towel. "Navi, I need to talk to you. Like, now."

"She doesn't want to talk to you, Alec." Konstanz narrowed her eyes until they were slits of anger.

Well, that wasn't exactly true, but I wasn't going to argue. It wasn't about what I wanted. It was about keeping him at arm's length for the rest of forever. I couldn't get over him if he kept up this permanent residence in my head.

"I don't care, Konstanz. This isn't about Navi. Or you." He looked up at me again, his eyes scanning my face with an intense desperation that made my skin flush and my heart pound.

"It's okay, Konstanz." I smiled reassuringly. She glared at him once more for good measure and then backed out of the way, letting him in. He edged around Elizabeth and shut the door behind him.

Wait.

He edged around Elizabeth.

"You can see her," I whispered in shock.

"Yeah. It's been quite a night. I need your help." I wanted to memorize every feature, every tight muscle against his t-shirt. I wanted to throw myself into his arms and sob because I'd missed him so much.

But that would only hurt worse. I had to hate him. I had to not let him hurt me. Because I couldn't survive this again.

"What happened to your shoulder?"

I twisted my head to see it. Yeah, it looked pretty awful. "Work. What do you want?"

Elizabeth gave me a pointed look. "Perhaps you should dress yourself, Navi. I feel this may not be a conversation to be had in a towel."

"They talk to you." His face was absolutely white. He shook like a small dog in a hurricane. My big, tough Alec was scared out of his mind. Which meant only one thing—he could *see*. Someone had opened his eyes and he could see my ghosts. And if he could see my ghosts, the demons would hunt him.

I swore. Several times. "Stay here. I'll be right back. Do. Not. Move."

I raced into the bedroom and threw on one of Bryson's sweatshirts he always left at my house. He had a bigger clothing budget than I did, and his clothes were softer than mine. Soft on my wounded shoulder would be fabulous. "Wait, at least let me wrap it. You'll get Bryson's clothes all bloody and you know how he hates that." Konstanz already had her kit in her hands, biting her lip as she watched me try to settle the fabric over the wound.

"I haven't, technically, gotten his clothes bloody before. Just dirty." The look she gave me said she was less than impressed. "Okay, just… let me get dressed. I can't—Alec is out there—they might—" I swore again under my breath. There was too much she didn't know. Too much I couldn't say or I'd open her eyes and she'd be in just as much trouble as Alec. And the sun, the blasted sun, had still not risen.

I pulled on shorts, pulled *off* the sweatshirt, and put on a sports bra, then hurried back out to the living room, Konstanz on my heels with her first aid kit. "One sec. Sit." I pointed to the seat across from me where I could keep an eye on him. Everything I'd gone through, everything I'd done for the last ten years, was all for nothing. He was a target now. It was my worst nightmare come true.

He sat, his elbows on his knees and his face in his hands. "Can you tell them to let him in?" he mumbled through his fingers.

"What? What do you mean?"

"Bryson. Your friends won't let him in."

Konstanz's fingers stilled in her poking and prodding of my wound. "Have you lost your mind by any chance? Of course we'll let Bryson in. He's always here."

"Not you." He looked pointedly at me and then at Elizabeth.

"Alec." My throat was attempting to close in horror. "What do you mean they won't let Bryson in?"

He threw up his hands and now looked at Konstanz. This had to be the most frustrating conversation I'd ever had. "Bryson was in an *accident* down by Devil's Gate. He's in a coma with unexplainable injuries."

"What?" Konstanz asked, horror making her voice harsh.

But she wasn't as horrified as me. Because I suddenly realized exactly what Alec was saying. Somehow, the asuwangs had gotten Bryson—but not his soul. Not if he was here.

I looked at Elizabeth. She was watching me silently, her eyes wide and worried. Without a word, she turned and disappeared through the door.

Konstanz finished wrapping and I slid Bryson's sweatshirt over my head. "I'll call in sick to work. I'll be at the hospital," she said quietly. Now she was shaking as hard as Alec. This was a disaster. The first guy Konstanz had seriously dated in *ages,* and this happens.

But that didn't matter. Right now, I had to protect Alec and keep Konstanz's eyes closed to the demons in the world.

Please, for the love of all that is holy, go, Konstanz. " If—if Bryson is—isn't okay, call me."

She nodded and practically sprinted out the door, still in her pajamas. The second she was gone, I turned on Alec. "Tell me what happened."

Elizabeth appeared through the wall. Bryson followed close behind. And he was a *ghost.* My hands shook and my stomach roiled dangerously as splotches appeared before my eyes. "Bryson! What happened?" Whirling on Alec, I cried, "I thought you said he was in a coma!"

"Is she going to be okay?" Bryson's eyes followed Konstanz's disappearing form.

I could only blink at him like he'd lost his mind.

Adrenalin had kicked in, forcing my sluggish brain to function, but it didn't seem to be catching up with the conversation. "You are a ghost, Bryson. And you're worried about Konstanz?"

"I love her, Navi. You know that."

Alec's head jerked his elbows slid off his knees, nearly plummeting him to the floor. "What?"

"Konstanz and I sorta... sorta fell for each other while I was trying to woo Navi. But Navi doesn't mind," he finished in a rush.

"Not at all." And then I shook my head because really, this is what we were choosing to talk about right now?

"What happened, Bryson?"

"I followed you."

"You what? Why would you do that?" I screeched. Like a harpy eagle. Not my most beautiful moment.

"You lied to me! After everything we've been through!"

"Navi, your shoulder is bleeding," Alec murmured.

"Bryson, this is insane. Will you please just calm down and focus on the problem at hand?"

"Navi, you need to ice your shoulder." Alec nodded toward my wound, which I could feel swelling as the moon set and the sun rose and my magic faded.

Bryson ignored him. "You told us you're a probation officer."

"I am." I twisted my fingers. "Bryson, you're dead. My job is not what we need to be focused on. Tell me what happened." I think, I *think* this was the third time I'd asked him, and I still hadn't gotten any answers. Have you ever tried to mourn a loss when the person you're mourning is standing in front of you, accusing you of lying? It's difficult. Little bit.

"We were just trying to protect you. And you lied to us the entire time." Bryson shook his ghostly head and paced.

"Can I grieve, at least? Or do I not get to do that, either?"

I snapped, because he was dead and in my living room and I wanted to cry and not have this conversation right now.

"He's not dead." Alec got up and went into the kitchen to dig through my freezer.

"You're not dead? Then how are you here?" I asked Bryson, relief sweeping through my blood like ice thrown on panicked fire.

"Why don't you tell me why you lied, first?" He crossed his arms and tried to look tough. Throwing up the hand that wasn't attached to my wounded shoulder, I turned my back on him to focus on Alec, who seemed terrified and more than a little shaken up, but he was rational, at least. He handed me an ice pack and pushed me down onto the couch. That brief contact sent heat flaring through my recently cooled blood, so fast and so fierce that my knees gave out and I sank obediently into the soft suede.

"Alec." My voice shook and I cleared my throat, trying to steady it. "Do you know what happened?"

Alec sat across from me again, close enough that our knees almost touched, staring at the floor. "They thought you were into some sort of trouble. They didn't believe the work story you were feeding them—"

"I thought you were with some bad guys—"

"Bad guys? Are you serious? I know what Alec thinks I am, but you—?" I glared at Bryson, forgetting for just a second that he was dead. Or not, as the case may be.

"Well you're gone all the time and you were moody and you had absolutely no interest in —"

"Navi, I don't think that, and can we please focus here? Bryson is in a coma." Alec sounded exhausted, and there was zero emotion in his voice as he stared at the carpet. Bryson, too, refused to look at me. "He followed you last night to the beach. Now that we're past the part where you look as idiotic as I did, would you like to tell the story, Bryson?"

My heart pounded. Alec thought what he'd done was idiotic. Bryson was dead but not dead. I couldn't process any of this information.

"I followed you to the beach. To Devil's Gate. And then you just—just disappeared, and I was trying to find you… and then this sea monster came out of the water and attacked me." I could hear genuine fear in his voice as his eyes widened and his entire countenance shook. I got up and crossed the room to him, standing so close that part of his hand swirled and disappeared in mine.

"Hey. It's okay. It's over and we'll fix this. But I have to know what happened."

He nodded, swallowing hard, although technically he didn't need to swallow at all.

"Then suddenly you were there again and you followed it. The monster. You followed it and it ran and you ran after it and then there were more of them, and there were ghosts everywhere and they wanted to kill me—"

"We did no such thing," Elizabeth interrupted. I'd almost forgotten she was there, but now she stood next to Bryson. "We thought he was in limbo. We forced him to leave." Elizabeth shook her head. "We didn't recognize him in this form."

I'd heard that ghosts looked different to each other than they did to us, so that made sense, although it didn't make things any easier on Bryson.

"I could see you talking to the ghosts, telling them what to do. I knew you'd be able to help me so I followed you home. But they wouldn't let me in."

Of course not. Because ghosts in limbo were dangerous. They possessed things and threw things and attacked things. "They were protecting me," I said softly.

He ran a trembling hand through his ghostly hair. "I couldn't get to you so I went and got Alec. He found my—my body— and called 911."

"He's stable, but in a coma." Alec spoke for the first time in several minutes. I glanced at him over my shoulder, but he still stared at the floor.

"Did you try going back in? If you touch your body, it should just absorb your soul."

"This is the most surreal conversation I've ever heard," Alec mumbled. "Like you're giving him computer advice, except for bodies."

This had to be hard on him, too. I'd assumed he'd be with his new girlfriend this weekend. Probably not the way he'd planned to spend his Monday morning.

And he was talking. I shook my head, trying to focus. "Yeah, I did. But nothing happened."

I looked to Elizabeth. She was a ghost. Maybe she had answers. She shook her head, as lost as I was. "Okay. I have to talk to Death. He'll know what's going on."

Alec and Bryson both choked. "Death?" Alec gasped.

"Yeah. He's my boss." I ran a hand through my tangled, wet hair and moved away from Bryson. "You both have to know—I didn't tell you because I was trying to keep you safe. If I'd told you what I was, it would have opened your—like your soul's eyes, and you would be able to see the demons and the ghosts."

"Would that be so bad?" Bryson asked, his voice shaking as much as the rest of him.

Alec stared at me, dark blue eyes so intense and confused that it sent chills up and down my spine. How on earth he could have this effect on me in such an awful situation was just ridiculous. It was taking everything I had not to bury my head against his chest and beg him to understand. But I couldn't. I couldn't survive this pain again. I couldn't survive him again. "What do you mean you were protecting us?"

"If you'd opened my soul eyes or whatever, I would have

seen the monster before it got right on top of me and I could have run away." It was the angriest at me I'd ever seen Bryson. Usually, he let me get away with everything—all my whining, crying, pouting, snapping, exhaustion, insanity. It was new territory we were in, and I wasn't sure how to proceed.

"You can't run from them. And you saw it because you became a target. If I'd opened your eyes, they would have sent hunters after you. Like, immediately. Humans do not survive well when they can *see*."

"All this time?" Alec's voice was barely above a whisper as he met my eyes. I was shocked at the pain there. Bryson might be the one fighting for his life, but Alec was definitely the most hurt.

I left Bryson's side to kneel in front of Alec. He swallowed hard, his hands twitching where they rested on his knees. "Yes, Alec. All this time. I was protecting you. I—I couldn't put you in danger. Please, *please* don't be hurt. I loved you so much I would have done anything to keep you safe."

His pain-filled eyes widened and I realized what I'd said. But it wasn't exactly a surprise, was it? It was pretty obvious to everyone and their ghost how head over heels I was for him.

He cleared his throat. "But I can see them now."

I nodded. "Bryson opened your eyes when he came to you. Living in close proximity, in Bryson's home, it made it very easy. But now you're in a lot of danger, Alec. They'll hunt you, and you can't fight them."

"Will they come for me, too?" Bryson's eyes were big, dark pits of terror against his translucent white face. "What about Konstanz? We have to keep her safe."

I rose, away from Alec, away from his pain. My body protested. It wanted to be near him, despite everything. Despite every painful thing he'd done for the last two months.

"I'll talk to Death, but I can't until the moon rises. We'll have to wait until then. Bryson, Elizabeth can show you the ropes, if you'd like. She's been doing the ghost thing for quite a while." I offered my best encouraging smile.

"I'm not leaving you. You're the only one who can save me."

"Navi is the only one who can save any of us," Elizabeth said. "We don't have to be in her constant presence for her to do it."

"Please, Navi, don't make me go. I—I don't feel safe without you." I wanted to point out that just two minutes ago he'd been mad that I'd lied to him. But he was scared and confused. His mood swings were understandable.

"It's okay," I said when Elizabeth moved toward him. "It's fine. Of course you can stay with me. I just thought it might give you something to distract yourself. Why don't we go up to the hospital and see what's going on. Maybe I can figure something out from there."

Alec dug his keys out of his pocket. "I'm going home if you don't need me anymore."

Panic, sharp and overwhelming, shot through me. "No!"

He froze at the door. Elizabeth appeared in front of him, blocking the way. He could have walked right through her, but he wouldn't. I'd seen the way he'd edged around her before. "You don't still need me here, Navi. You can take care of Bryson. I have stuff to do."

I left Bryson to go to Alec, starting to feel like a ping pong ball between them. "You can't go anywhere without me, Alec. If they attack—"

"I'll run." He shrugged. "Or I'll keep my gun loaded all the time. It's fine, Navi."

I closed my eyes, grasping his wrist in case he tried to escape while I prayed for strength.

"You don't understand. You can't fight the demons. Only

Navi or those in her employ can." Elizabeth peered around him as I opened my eyes. "But the asuwangs cannot come out in the day. He should be safe until the moon rises."

"Yeah, but we had three get away from us last night. I only caught one. That means the other two have shifted to a human form and they'll come after him as soon as they catch his scent." I turned to Alec. "You have to stay with me."

He looked, if anything, more tortured. "I'd rather take my chances with them."

Wow. Was I really that awful? A part of me wanted to stomp my foot and pout and tell him to go, to lash out because he'd hurt me. But this was my job, my destiny. I protected people from the monsters. And Alec, more than anyone, I would not fail. "Alec." I forced myself to meet his gaze, no matter how beautiful it was, no matter how much it seared my soul. "Please?"

I could see the indecision warring across his face. "Navi, I'm like a foot taller than you and I outweigh you by a hundred pounds. I'll be fine."

"You can't kill them. Soul blades are the only thing that can kill them, and only an Agent and her army can wield them." If Elizabeth's face was any indication, she was completely annoyed at his argument.

It was part of the reason I adored her.

Alec's eyebrows raised—they didn't shoot up, like he was too exhausted to show adequate surprise. I moved in for the kill. "Please, Alec? Please stay with me." It was a risky little move, pulling that line. If he refused, it would cause me a lot of pain I wasn't sure I could handle. He had a girlfriend, he'd forgotten all about me, but hopefully *that* would bring back at least one good memory that would keep him here.

Where I could protect him and watch the pieces of my shattered heart slowly crumble away.

His face paled and he sucked in a breath, those gorgeous

eyes searching my face for an answer I couldn't give him unless he asked. And then he nodded. "Okay. Fine, I'll stay. Thank you."

"We need a plan. Something proactive," Bryson mumbled and paced my small living room, walking right through the coffee table. "I'm dead. I don't know how to be dead."

"You aren't dead, Bryson. And we'll fix you." I tipped my head to the side, considering him. "Actually, of all of us, you're the safest. Death can't take you while you're in limbo, although your body could die if we don't take care of it." His mouth dropped open and I rushed to continue, my hand out and placating. "But we are! So it's okay. And the asuwangs won't hunt you like they will Alec. They'll only attack if you get in their way." I gave him my very brightest smile, which was difficult given the tenseness of the situation. "See? You're all set."

"Navi," he growled. Bryson rarely growled. In the two months that I had seen him every single day in every free moment Konstanz had, he'd only been angry once. It was when I'd missed Konstanz's birthday party because of a war on the beach. They'd invited guys from his work that I might be interested in. In my defense, it was better that I hadn't gone because even now, all this time later, I had no desire to touch anyone or kiss anyone or be involved with anyone at all.

Except the guy with the dark blue eyes watching me with a quiet intensity that made my knees weak.

"Are you okay driving to the hospital?" I asked Alec because he stood there with his keys in his hand, looking like he couldn't decide whether to make a break for it or humor the little girl who couldn't possibly be tough enough to defend him. "I'll call my mom and see if she's ever encountered this before."

"Holy hell." Alec groaned, shaking his head. "Your mom. She's the same thing you are. There's no probation officer.

That's why she couldn't ever talk about it."

"Now wait." I grabbed my jacket and my purse, sliding my feet into shoes. In all the times I'd hoped to run into Alec, I'd always looked really good, so he'd see me and think about how stupid he was for letting me go, and I would, of course, be prettier than his new girlfriend. It was disappointing that he saw me now, wet and tangled and battered and bruised in Bryson's sweat shirt and yoga pants. But it was a little late and not really appropriate to yell, "Wait! I need to put makeup on!"

So instead I followed him outside. "We are probation officers. Just... probation officers for lost souls. We give them a chance at redemption if they fight alongside us." I paused in the doorway, looking for Elizabeth. Ghost Bryson stayed so close I could feel the coldness emanating from him. He loomed nervously, watching every movement like an overly observant hawk. I didn't blame him, though.

I, also, watched every movement like an overly observant hawk. It was my job, but I'm ashamed to say that I was only watching *Alec's* movements. I was hyper aware of everything he did, and my heart felt like it was trying to leap through my chest to him.

But I had one secret weapon. Pain. I hurt so much and I'd cried so much that going anywhere near Alec was too painful to even consider. It was like chocolate. If you ate so much that it made you sick every time you had a bite, you eventually stayed away from it—no matter how much you loved it.

"Where is your army?" Alec asked, inching out the door, looking around warily. "And their weapons?"

"They're only released from their cells when the moon rises. My powers and my soul blades also appear when the moon rises."

"Then how do you fight demons during the day?"

I snuck glances at him through my eyelashes while he

wasn't looking, so desperate to memorize every detail before he was gone again that I'd resorted to ninja-like tactics. I was pathetic.

And he was so beautiful.

His black t-shirt hugged his biceps and his chest. He had a hat on, pulled low over his eyes like it could protect him, but it didn't. I could still see that being with me hurt him as much as it hurt me.

"Navi?" he asked, and I realized belatedly that he had asked me a question.

"Oh. Yeah, demons can't come out during the day, either. The sea witch can, but only if she's taken enough souls to make a shell for herself. And her doorway only opens by moonlight."

"Sea witch?" Alec sounded slightly strangled.

I nodded gravely as he opened the door to his truck for me and I tried not to remember the last time he'd opened the door to his truck for me. "She's bad. She killed my grandmother."

"I have so many questions," he murmured as he slammed the door and went to his side. Bryson appeared, mostly sitting on top of me, but I couldn't feel anything but cold.

"If the ghosts go away during the day, how is Bryson here? Or the one inside?"

"Bryson is in limbo. He doesn't belong to Death, so he can come and go as he pleases, except that he's tied to a certain area. That's why places are haunted, you know? Like cemeteries or homes or hotels."

"Well he showed up at his home. So…"

"Oh." Bryson looked up as I frowned. "We thought you were out of town this weekend." I hurried to change the subject because thinking of Alec with his new girlfriend sent shards of pain through my stomach. "Elizabeth was a lost soul. She fought with me and earned her freedom, but she chose to stay instead of moving on. So she can come and go as she pleases like Bryson can, but she isn't tied to anywhere."

Alec shook his head, but I didn't miss the glare he threw at Bryson. And I wasn't exactly in a position to ask about it. What fun.

But of everything, Bryson's lies were the least of my worries. I rolled down the window as Alec backed out of the parking stall. "Elizabeth. Be wary. We have twelve hours before the sun goes down. If the asuwangs show up… we'll just have to be ready to run.

CHAPTER TWENTY-FIVE

Alec

I WANTED TO KNOW WHERE THEY thought I went every weekend. The look they'd shared… surprised, maybe hopeful, on Navi's part. Or I could be reading in the hopeful thing. I don't know, and it wasn't something I could ask about now. We were sort of in a crisis, and besides that, she was on the phone. So I glared at Bryson until he looked away, and then I focused on the road.

"Hey mama. I need your help."

Navi's voice slid over my senses, soothing and tearing all at once. I was still in love with her. All this time, all the work, all the alcohol, all my mama's cooking—everything I'd done to get over her. And I was still in love with her.

There was hope, though. She wasn't with Bryson like I'd assumed.

Wow, Konstanz and Bryson. Crazy.

Oh, and back at her apartment, I'd seen the look on her face when she'd realized I was in trouble. She might not want to, but she still cared. And she was stuck with me for who knew how long. Maybe she would forgive me.

But I remembered what Konstanz said. We were too intense. I caused her too much pain, even when I was trying to love her. And I didn't want to hurt her anymore. *Stay away from her, Alec.*

"No, he's not dead but his soul—" she paused, listening. Bryson leaned closer, his head almost against hers, and she twisted toward him, just a bit, so he could hear better. And it killed me.

"No, I haven't ever seen something like this." She sat quietly. I could hear her mom's voice, this woman who I thought was a tiny probation officer her entire life and she was really a demon hunter who recruited ghosts to help her. But I couldn't make out any words.

"I killed it. But two got away." She bit her lip, drawing my eyes to that mouth I'd been dreaming about every waking moment for two months, "No, or it would have freed him." She nodded. "Is that possible?"

She tipped the phone away from her ear. "Did they take any part of your soul?"

Bryson's eyes widened in horror. "I don't know. How do I tell?"

"Because you feel like part of you is missing. Like—like when you lose someone you love."

And her eyes landed on me.

She flushed and looked away. "It feels like that."

"Oh." Bryson examined his arms and chest. "I don't see anything missing. I don't—I don't think I feel anything wrong. Besides the fact that I'm, ya know, a freaking ghost."

Navi's eyes that had the power to scald my very blood with just one glance my way, now went up and down Bryson's body, taking in every inch. And I had the sudden, overwhelming desire to shove him out of my truck. If I could figure out how. Was it even possible to shove a ghost?

All in all, I think I was taking the sudden knowledge that not only do ghosts exist, but also that my roommate was one, rather well.

She went back to her phone. "I don't think I see anything missing but it's hard to see… Okay. I just thought I'd check with you. Umm, no. Alec? He's here right now. Yeah, Bryson opened his eyes." She glanced at me again, worry creasing her forehead. "Yeah, I'll protect him."

Awesome. She was half my size and pretending she hated me—and she was supposed to protect me from demonic hunters.

I'd feel better if she didn't look so resigned about the whole thing.

BRYSON'S BODY LOOKED EXACTLY the same as it did when I left a lifetime ago. Still alive. Still unconscious. Konstanz sat by his bed, holding his hand and barely glanced at us when we came in. She looked worried sick.

"Oh, hello again," Jasmyn the nurse said as she breezed out just as we came in. "We haven't had a change in condition, but we're bringing in a specialist in the morning." She looked at Navi, standing close behind me. "Are you his sister?"

I wasn't sure which "his" she was referring to, but I spoke before she could. "This is his girlfriend's roommate." The words felt like heaven leaping from my lips.

"Ask her why I can't wake up," Bryson said, hovering over his body like any stereotypical ghost might do.

"She won't know," Navi hissed under her breath.

Jasmyn gave her an odd look before patting her cheek. "Don't worry, hon. I'm sure he'll be fine. We've got some of the greatest minds in the world collaborating on this."

Navi turned wide eyes on me, as if playing along hadn't

even occurred to her. I came to the rescue, because I'm cool like that. "I'm sure you do. We appreciate it."

"You are such a sweet friends to be here for him right now." Jasmyn motioned between Navi and I with that same sympathetic sparkle in her eye. Turning to Konstanz, she said, "And what a supportive little girlfriend. This must be so hard on you."

I shrugged, because I wouldn't be here at all if it wasn't for Navi. "He's my roommate."

The nurse smiled. "Of course." And then she was gone, bustling out, shoving notes in her pocket.

"While you're here I'm gonna run grab a drink. I'll be right back." Konstanz edged past us, her eyes red-rimmed.

"Bryson," Navi moved closer to his body, away from me like I didn't have ten thousand questions suddenly berating my brain. "Put your hand here. See if the strength of your heart will pull you in." She leaned low over him, so close I could imagine the heat of her body against his. This, this being with her constantly while she was with him, it hurt. A lot.

Bryson's hand past through her shoulder to his heart, and I held my breath. But nothing happened. Bryson didn't get sucked back in or whatever I'd been expecting. His ghost face fell in defeat. "I really thought you'd be able to save me," he said quietly.

Navi watched him. "I'm sorry, Bryson. But I'm not giving up. We'll figure out how to save you." There wasn't much hope in Bryson's eyes. Navi swallowed hard, like maybe she was fighting tears. "Hey. On the bright side, you're very powerful for a new spirit. It took Elizabeth months before she could manipulate air currents. And you're still here in the daylight. That takes strength, too."

Awesome. Not only did he get to spend all his alive time with her, but he was impressive when he was mostly dead, too. Any hope I had of changing her mind about me was slipping through my fingers. *No. No, we're staying away from her, remember? We can't hurt her again.* And... I seemed to be talking to my heart. Perfect.

"There's nothing left for us to do here. I need to get some rest so I can go see Death tonight. Can you take us back to your house?" She finally looked at me. I'd noticed she didn't unless she absolutely had to.

"Should we try again? Maybe try something else? I don't want to just leave me here. Or maybe we should go to your house? Isn't it safer there?" Bryson paced around his body, sometimes walking, sometimes floating. It was creepy, really. Navi, however, didn't seem to notice. Maybe because she hung out with ghosts on a regular basis. "What about Konstanz?"

"You can't be at my house, Bryson, or stay here. We run the risk of you opening Konstanz's eyes, and I will not make anyone else a target. We'll have to stay at your house until we get this figured out." Navi slung her purse over her shoulder and marched out. Apparently I didn't have a say in the matter. Not that I'd protest. Navi in my house for an indefinite amount of time?

Yeah, no complaints here.

I did wish I could get rid of Bryson so I could talk to her, though. I had some things I wanted clarification on. And, if it was as I suspected, I had some serious apologizing to do.

"I won't open their eyes. I'll stay in your room."

"I share that room with Konstanz, Bryson." Navi hurried down the hall, eyes constantly scanning everything around us. I stayed close by so she didn't look like she was talking to herself. "You know that."

Damn. I hated it when she reminded him that he'd been in her room. I wondered what exactly had happened between them before Bryson realized it was actually her roommate he was in love with.

The wondering hurt.

"Anyway, if you're in the house, they'll sense you. And I doubt very much you'd be happy hanging around outside with Elizabeth."

Bryson scowled. Without another word, he faded away.

"Where'd he go?" I asked, turning in a circle without slowing because Navi didn't even pause.

"He's upset. It's a lot to deal with. He'll be back."

"Okay well while he's gone, I have questions." Suddenly my palms were sweaty and my throat convulsed. I felt like when we were freshman and I'd been trying to work up the courage to ask her out.

"Of course you do." She sighed and glanced over at me, slowing her pace. "This is a lot to take in for you, too. I'm so sorry it's been thrust on you like this. I tried—I tried to protect you."

I nodded, overeager, like a puppy. How pathetic was I? "I know. I know you did. I just need to know." I grabbed her wrist and pulled her to a stop. She slid closer to me, almost as if her body had a will of its own. Then her chin came up and she pulled away. "Those times I thought you were with someone else—?" I didn't know how to finish that sentence.

Luckily, she didn't make me. "I was killing demons." Jerking her wrist free, she spun on her heel and stalked away. I watched her go, feeling like I'd just been shattered under the weight of my own stupidity.

CHAPTER TWENTY-SIX

Navi

BEING SO CLOSE TO HIM WAS going to kill me. It absolutely, positively was going to kill me dead. My nerves were frayed. I couldn't think straight. Every single cell of my body screamed to be closer to him, and sometimes my brain lost control and let them. He'd hurt me.

Remember, heart? Remember how we've been completely demolished the past two months without him? Remember how we tried for four freaking years to forget him and failed? Remember how after two days he had the power to crush us?

Yes, let's remember that.

But he was in a ton of danger and no matter how much it hurt me *and* my heart, I had to protect him. Because losing him completely would hurt me so much more. At least now, I couldn't have him but he was still *here*. In this world. And the world wasn't quite so dark because he was in it.

But dang it! I was tired of hurting! I wanted the pain in my chest to stop for a while. Was that really too much to ask? Couldn't someone just invent a potion so I could forget he ever existed?

Well no. No, that wouldn't work. If I forgot he existed, I'd probably fail at keeping him alive, wouldn't I?

As we got in the truck, Bryson settled on my lap, I tried for a conversational tone—at least as conversational as one could get when discussing demons coming after one's soul. "So, you're in more danger today than you would be most days."

Bad start, clearly, by the way Alec's face whitened and his eyes widened in horror. I thought I should probably drive, given his current mental state. "No, listen, it's okay. See, the asuwangs—the demons that will hunt you—they only come out at night. That's when I have, like, super powers and big tough swords and an army and I can kill them." I nodded, trying to look encouraging.

He didn't buy it. "Then why am I in trouble today?"

I bit my lip, twisting my fingers in my hands. "Well... they've been super aggressive lately, and last night three of them got away from me. Once they make it up the beach, they hide from me until daylight, when they shift into human form or animal form or, ya know, something normal. Which, of course, makes them even harder to find, until the moon rises and they're forced back into their natural form."

"So there are three of these things out there that are after me?" He glanced at me as he drove, somewhat erratically, through the streets to his apartment.

"No, only two. One—the one I'm thinking got Bryson" —I glanced apologetically at the ghost on my lap—"I caught that one and killed it just as it was shifting. And I'll catch the other two tonight." Unless there was another attack. I couldn't be in two places at once and my army was stretched thin. Even with my new recruits, we were going down fast.

"YOU CAN SLEEP IN my bed," Bryson said, appearing in front of me as I followed Alec into the apartment.

I glanced uncomfortably at Alec. This might be awkward. "I have to sleep where he sleeps."

Alec stopped so suddenly I ran into the back of him. "What?" he gasped.

I stumbled backward and tried not to notice the way every inch of skin that had just touched him felt like it was on fire. "I can't—I can't protect you if they find you and I'm in Bryson's room. I probably wouldn't even hear them."

Alec turned slowly, running a hand over his face. He had stubble along his jaw and he looked rough and… dang it. He looked sexy. That was all there was to it. Especially as he peered at me through his fingers. "You have to sleep in the same room as me?"

"Are you sure that's a good idea, Navi? What about… everything?" Bryson whispered, as if Alec, who was standing right next to me, could somehow not hear him. "I don't think it's a good idea at all."

I ignored him. I had to. If I didn't, I'd be forced to admit he was right—me and Alec in that same room—it had memories. And intimacy. But I had to keep them safe.

"I'm sorry, Alec."

"Navi, no offense, but you're, like, half my size. You said you don't have super powers until the moon rises, so what, exactly, are you going to do to protect me?"

I crossed my arms over my chest and glared at him. "I might be half your size and weigh less than you do, but I've been fighting demons for over ten *freaking* years, Alec. If one attacks, I can fight it off, *super powers* or no."

I expected more arguing. Clearly the thought of spending the day stuck in a room with me—even sleeping—was not pleasant. If Bryson had a problem with it, I could understand why Alec would be hesitant. His girlfriend was going to love it.

And of course he would tell her. Because he didn't keep secrets like I did.

"I promise, I will stay on my side of the room," I said more gently.

"That's not what I'm worried about," he grumbled as he turned and sorta stumbled away. "You can sleep in my shirt again if you want."

I froze. That memory nearly demolished me. He froze, too, which told me he wasn't completely unaffected, either. Hastily, I cleared my throat, trying to keep the pain from climbing its way out. "It's okay. I have pajamas here."

"What?" he asked without turning. He was asking me that a lot lately.

"You're gone a lot." Bryson shrugged as he wafted past Alec. It sounded so much worse than it was. Bryson and I had never done a thing.

"I told you she couldn't be here, Bryson." Alec's voice was deadly in the quiet apartment. And it tore through my chest like one of those arrows that have the split, spread tips, leaving a horrible gaping wound that only I could see.

"It's not like that, Alec. I only—" I started but he shook his head, glaring at Bryson.

I was too tired for this. I went into Bryson's room and dug through the drawer he'd designated for me, pulling out my fluffy pajama pants and a tank top and thank the heavens, a toothbrush.

"Can I take a shower without you standing guard?" Alec asked when I emerged. He was leaning against the door frame, eyes dark and unreadable.

There were no windows in the bathroom, so I nodded without looking at him and went to wait on the couch. Bryson appeared next to me, looking forlorn. "Hey." I rolled my head to the side so I could watch him. "How ya holdin' up?"

"I've been better. Do you think she's safe at the hospital?"

"Yes. And Death will know what to do." I smiled encouragingly. "We'll get this all figured out in no time."

"Yeah. And while we're doing that, how about you remember that you swore him off? He's gonna hurt you again, Navi."

I sat up, blinking because I couldn't even think of a cohesive response to that. "What?" I finally asked. It was as good as I could come up with.

"I'm only saying this because I've been there while you tried to get over him. I've seen the worry in Konstanz's eyes, and the pain in yours." He eyed me. "And I mean this is in the most supportive way possible, but what can you really do? You're tiny."

Seriously. The big guys thinking I was a helpless little girl was getting old. *So* old. "Bryson, I understand that you are struggling right now with everything that has happened," I said through gritted teeth, "But trust me when I say I am doing the job I was born to do, despite how inefficient you both think me to be."

"I don't think anything, Navi. " I'd been so mad at Bryson I hadn't even heard Alec get out of the shower until his voice was right behind me. "Except that I'm tired, so you must be exhausted. Ready?"

I peeked over my shoulder. He was towel drying his hair, his basketball shorts resting low on his hips and he wasn't wearing a shirt.

Dear sweet heavens.

I closed my eyes and prayed for strength or a cold shower or a semblance of rational thought. None appeared, so I nodded meekly and followed him into his room. It hadn't changed at all since I'd been there last. The bed was unmade. That was about it.

"Bryson, can I borrow your comforter and pillow?" I

asked, but he didn't answer. I stuck my head back into the living room, but he wasn't there. "Awesome."

"You can sleep in my bed." Alec sounded like he was forcing the words past a lump the size of Mount Fiji in his throat. "I'll sleep on the floor."

Strength. Cold shower. Rational thought.

Nothing.

"No, no," I yelped. "No. Despite the fact that you don't think I can protect you, I need to stay between you and the window."

"I never said you couldn't protect me, Navi."

"Well then good. You won't argue with me."

He swallowed hard, looking from the bed to the floor to me and back again. "I'll sleep by the wall. You can sleep on the bed between me and the window."

By the wall. In the bed. In the bed next to me. "We can build a pillow fort if it'd make you more comfortable." I could swear I heard hope in his voice. Or vulnerability. Or maybe that was my hope or vulnerability and I was projecting it onto him.

I was so confused.

And tired.

And weak. So weak.

Because I nodded. "Okay," I whispered. "I'll sleep next to you."

I SHOULD HAVE KNOWN I wouldn't get any sleep. And not because Alec was lying next to me, as tense as that made everything. Not even because Bryson had figured out how to interact with objects and was making as much noise as ghostly possible in the other room.

No, I should have known because I know demons. And

when they hunted, they were fast and ruthless.

Alec's clock read 4:56 p.m. when I heard the scratching at the window. It sent chills of terror up my spine, but Alec was snoring lightly and didn't hear it. Praying I was wrong or paranoid or anything else, I slid out of bed, being careful not to wake Alec, and crossed the room to the window.

A face, distorted and discolored, stared back at me.

It was still struggling to figure out how to use its fingers, so it scrabbled at the window where it clung, two stories up. Swallowing my revulsion, I inched closer, my breath caught in my throat, so I could see around it. "Please be alone. Please be alone." My face was dangerously close to its face, only separated by the thick glass, and I could see into its very soul through the red, glowing eyes. Tearing my gaze away, I checked the ground below, wincing as it squealed right next to my head and bashed its face against the glass.

The other one I'd lost last night stood below it.

Awesome.

"Navi?" Bryson asked, appearing next to me.

And promptly started screaming. His screams woke Alec, who swore in three different languages as he sat up. "What the hell?" he finally sputtered.

"You need to go into the living room. Get your shoes on and your car keys and be ready to run." Despite the way my heart was pounding in my chest, I sounded perfectly calm. Go me.

"Holy shit!" Alec yelled. Ah, so he'd just now noticed the demons clawing at his window.

"Alec, go!" I yelled, abandoning all sense of calm. I heard him crash out of the bed and stumble around, probably trying to free himself from the blankets he'd been tangled in, but I couldn't look away to check. If I looked away, the asuwangs would make their move and I would miss it.

And we'd die.

"Navi, come on. We'll run."

"Alec, they'll chase us. If I fight them—"

He was having none of that. "No." He snarled behind me. "I'm not going to leave you here to face them." He grabbed me around the waist and hauled me out of the room, grabbing his keys off the table. "I'm gonna put you down and we're gonna run like hell to my truck. Do you understand me?" *His* voice didn't sound calm at all. He sounded scared out of his mind.

"Alec, I can fight them. It will give you enough time to run—"

"Dammit, Navi!" he yelled, cutting me off, somewhat impolitely. "I *know* you can fight them. But there's not enough willpower in the world to make me leave you so if you don't want me in there fighting with you, you're running with me."

The window broke.

Alec spun, grabbing my wrist, and we sprinted out the door. He leaped down six stairs, dragging me with him, half-turning to catch me when he realized my legs weren't nearly as long as his. I shoved him forward and he raced to his truck as the creatures crashed through the door above us.

Metal splinters rained down on my head. I skidded to a stop, searching desperately for anything that could be dangerous at all. Squealing when I heard the asuwangs on the stairs, I grabbed a metal shard that looked like it could be useful and smashed it on the ground twice, shattering the blunt end into sharp, lethal looking pieces. I whirled around, hurled it end over end at the first asuwang's face as it appeared on the stairwell. It screamed and clawed at the shard, but I'd blinded it, and it fell the rest of the way down the stairs, shoving the piece further in.

Right into its brain.

It wasn't dead. It could only be killed by soul blades, and I had none. But it was immobilized for who knew how long.

Unfortunately, the other one wasn't, and it didn't even

seem to notice that its friend was laying with a stick shoved into its head. The human form leaped over the twitching demon and ran straight at me, zombie-like in the unfamiliar shape, but still faster than I'd been expecting.

"Go. We'll take care of this one." Elizabeth was suddenly just there, Bryson already running toward the fallen demon, and I spun away and ran for all I was worth toward Alec's truck. He leaned across the driver's seat, swearing at me as he shoved open the door.

I leaped in like a hurdler and he slammed on the gas. The truck rocketed out of the parking lot while I struggled to pull the door shut behind me. Alec had a death grip on my wrist, like he thought I might get any crazy ideas about jumping out or something.

"You couldn't just run. You had to stay and fight. They almost had you, Navi!" he bellowed as he drove like a madman through rush hour traffic. Which, in Astoria, was thankfully very light.

I slumped against the seat, breathing hard. "I need some weapons. And maybe some shoes. Can you take me to my apartment?" I worried for my ghosts. Elizabeth could take down the one I'd hurt and keep it down until dusk when their weapons would allow them to kill it, but what if the other one stayed to fight? What if he took her soul? And Bryson wasn't trained at all, but he'd jumped right in after Elizabeth. I shouldn't have left them. But if I'd stayed, Alec would have been in even more danger.

Why had no one figured out how to clone me yet?

"I thought you said your sword things didn't come until nighttime?" He spun the wheel hard as we careened around a corner, watching the rear view mirror more than he was watching the road in front of us.

"They don't. But I have other weapons that can slow them down until I get my swords. Something a little better than broken door bits."

He stared at me like I'd grown two heads. And to him, I probably had. The sweet little girl he'd grown up with would never have played with weapons or decapitated demons.

But she wasn't me. Not really.

CHAPTER TWENTY-SEVEN

Alec

I'D JUST BEEN ATTACKED BY DEMONS. Demons that looked human but not quite. Like, zombie humans, maybe. Or someone with a really bad migraine. I don't know. I wasn't thinking clearly.

And I'd just seen Navi pick up a broken piece of door and throw it hard enough to impale that migraine-zombie-person-demon thing in the face. My Navi, the one so sweet she wouldn't even tell our high school math teacher his addition was wrong because she didn't want to hurt his feelings.

And now she was talking about weapons and fighting and shoes and I couldn't make her be the person in my mind she had been before. She was different.

Scary.

And I was still in love with her.

I pulled into her parking lot and checked the rear view mirror for the twenty-fifth thousandth time. "How fast do those things move?"

She looked over her shoulder, too. So I wasn't just being

paranoid. "They're fast, but not truck-fast. We have a bit."

"Okay. Get your shoes… and stuff. Then I have questions, Navi."

She nodded and slid out of the truck, padding barefoot and adorable up to her door. "Come on, Alec."

"If you can fight them off, why can't I?" I asked as I followed her in.

"Well… technically you *could.* You can't kill them, though. It's just really dangerous, Alec. It isn't worth it. One claw into you and…" Her face paled as she stared up at me, and for the first time in all this, Navi looked scared. "They'll take your soul, Alec."

I didn't want Navi to be scared. I wanted my brave Navi back. "Grab your stuff. Let's go."

"Hey there, Navi. I was wondering where—Alec?" Terrie dropped the magazine she was holding as she stared at me. "What are you still doing together?"

"Bryson got himself into some trouble." Navi didn't even hesitate as she breezed through the apartment. Her shoulder had started to bleed again through the bandages. I watched Terrie to see if she'd think it was weird that Navi had massive war injuries, but Terrie was too busy glaring at me to notice.

That, or this wasn't an unusual thing for them.

"I thought you agreed, Alec," she hissed as soon as Navi left the room. I seriously, *seriously* didn't have the energy to defend myself while waiting for something to come exploding through the door to kill me.

"So apparently you talked to Konstanz?" I asked, not taking my eyes from the window.

"Yes I did, and she said you agreed to stay away from her."

"I do agree, Terrie. I'm keeping my distance."

"Yeah." She glowered harder. "I can see how you're keeping your distance."

"What's that supposed to mean? I haven't touched her!"

She shook her head and tossed her magazine to the side, storming out of the room. I paced, alternating between worrying about Navi and watching the door.

Bryson appeared next to me.

"You're not supposed to be here." I kept my voice low so that Terrie wouldn't hear me. Heaven knows that's all Navi needed—someone else to protect if Bryson happened to open her eyes.

"I thought Navi would like to know that her ghosts are okay." He floated past me toward Navi's room.

"Bryson…" I growled, but he ignored me. Just like Navi ignored him when she came around the corner. She saw him—I know she did because her eyes narrowed just slightly and her shoulders tensed, but she walked right through him.

"Let's go, Alec." She called over her shoulder, "Terrie, I'll talk to you in a bit."

I led the way to my truck, eying her bag suspiciously, wondering what she kept in there. Bryson appeared as soon as she buckled her seat belt.

"I told you to stay out of there, Bryson." Her tone was colder than when she'd told me to go to hell. Did he really not realize how important her roommates were to Navi and how much danger he was putting her in?

"I was trying to help." Bryson threw his hands in the air, sort of going right through the truck's window. "I know how worried you are about Elizabeth!"

I focused on the road, because if I didn't know better, that *thing* was close. I swear I could feel it. I had no clear destination in mind. Just to drive. To escape. To run away from this nightmare that Navi dealt with on a daily basis.

Navi sighed. "I'm sorry, Bryson. I do appreciate knowing she's okay. I just can't afford to have someone else to protect. I'm already trying to be in three places at once." She twisted so she could see backward. She felt it too. The demon was coming.

"I'm just scared, Navi. I'm doing the best I can," Bryson said quietly. "I thought you'd want to know."

"I can feel Elizabeth. I can tell when she's in trouble. But thank you." She slid around in her seat, running a hand through her hair. I risked a glance before I went back to watching the road. Navi was completely exhausted. There were circles under her eyes.

She caught my look and smiled. "It's okay, Alec. I'll heal as soon as the moon rises."

I nodded. "Where am I going, Angel?"

I snapped my mouth shut. I hadn't meant to call her that. It had just happened and now I didn't dare look at her to see if she was furious or only hurt.

"Inland. The farther from the water they get, the slower they move." Her voice was so soft I could barely hear her.

"She's not your Angel anymore, Alec." Bryson appeared next to my ear. He was getting good at this popping up all over thing. I did not enjoy it.

"Shut up, Bryson."

I FINALLY HAD TO stop for gas a little before seven p.m. The sun was setting low in the sky. Navi was having an intense discussion with Elizabeth that I was pretty positive involved me, and Bryson watched it all while he floated back and forth through the gas pump. "What's going on?" I asked when she got back in the truck. It was the first time we'd spoken in hours. All my questions were not getting answered, not with Bryson there all the time, hissing in my ear.

"Well." She winced. I wasn't going to like what was coming, clearly. "See, I've been waiting for the moon because

I'd have power to kill the *one* asuwang chasing you, and somehow completely forgot that the sea witch will probably send a whole lot more of them after you as soon as it's dark. Especially if she realizes you're important to me."

I almost wrecked the truck.

Navi sighed. "I'm too tired to skate around this issue anymore. Alec always has and always will be very important to me. There, I said it. We all knew it anyway. Now we have to figure out—"

"I'm important to you?" I asked. My voice shook and I didn't dare look at her for fear she'd see the hope in my eyes. She'd just told me that a whole herd of demon things were about to be unleashed on me and all that mattered was that I was important to her.

"Yes, Alec. Obviously." Her voice was as quiet as mine in the silent cab, but it didn't shake. "So somehow we have to keep you safe while I meet with Death and try to figure out how to help Bryson."

"Why can't I just go with you to meet this—this Death?" I asked, although it was pretty much the last thing on earth I wanted to do. Ever.

"You can't. No mortal can look into the face of Death and survive. But, I think we have a plan." She nodded enthusiastically. "My mama."

"Your mom is our plan? I'm not sure—" Too slowly, I remembered that Navi's mom was the same thing she was—not just a regular probation officer like I'd always believed.

Navi watched realization dawn on my face and nodded. "Elizabeth went to her earlier. They're driving toward us now. We should meet them within the hour. Elizabeth will stay with you and my parents. This far inland, it will be hard for any escaped asuwangs to catch your scent, except the one that's still following us. Then Bryson and I will meet Death and my army will try to stop the demons when they come out of the sea witch's doorway." Navi took a deep breath. "Yeah. Easy peasy."

"Navi, nothing in that statement is easy."

Her face fell and I felt like I'd kicked a puppy. "But easy won't save my life, right? I'll be okay, Navi. Just try to figure out what's going on with your—your Death friend."

She snorted.

"We need to have a conversation, Alec. Because if you're hitting on Navi while you have a girlfriend—" Bryson started.

I cut him off. "I don't have a girlfriend."

Navi's eyes looked like big dark pits in her pale, tired face. " You—you haven't been spending weekends with your blond girlfriend?" This time it was *her* voice that shook.

I know there was a demon chasing us, but at that point in the conversation, I was unable to drive and talk. I slammed on the brakes and pulled the truck off the side of the road, turning in my seat so I faced her. "I don't have a girlfriend."

"You haven't always secretly hated brunettes?" she whispered, biting her lip and fingering the tears in her jeans. Pink stained her cheeks.

"Navi, look at me."

Slowly, she raised those gorgeous eyes to meet mine. And I was lost. "I haven't been able to function without you. I've been working eighty hours a week and spending the weekends with my little brother. There's no girlfriend. There's no getting over you. And given that I've had an obsession with your hair"—I reached out, tugging a strand free from her messy braid to slide through my fingers, something I thought I'd never get to do again—"since the day we met, I most definitely do not hate brunettes."

"But I—"

This. This thing I had to say might possibly be the scariest thing I'd ever said in my life. I knew what Konstanz said. I knew how intense and volatile Navi and I were. I knew how scary her life was. It didn't matter.

"Navi, I know you hate me, and you have every right to. I know I don't deserve another chance with you—not after I screwed it up twice. But I'm still in love with you and dammit, I'm going to fight for you. Until you take me back or I die trying."

Her mouth opened and closed like the most adorable fish on the planet. Her eyes filled with tears and she leaned back, blinking and rubbing with the long sleeve of her pink shirt. "But you—you hurt me, Alec. A lot." She was whispering again, which I was realizing she did when she was trying *not* to let her voice shake.

"I know, Angel. And I'm so, so sorry. I can't ever make that up to you. But I can promise I won't do it again. I can promise to beat the hell out of anyone who tries."

The barest hint of a smile broke as a tear traced its way down her cheek.

"Navi, he hurt you. Way more than you hurt him." Bryson glared at me and I wondered if, even though he was in love with her roommate, he might not still have a thing for her, too.

But she didn't seem to notice. Navi, the girl I'd realized was stronger than Hercules, looked up at me like a small, lost kitten. "Is—is that true?"

"No. It's not true and he knows it. He *lives* with me. He knows how much pain I've been in."

Bryson threw up his hands. "I was trying to protect both of you! How do you not see that? I could see how much you hurt each other. Hate is easier than pain, isn't it? I was trying to protect you both!"

I could only blink at him. In slow motion, I thought back to how he'd tried to hide Navi's presence from me, but how he was always asking if I was okay, if I was forgetting. How he'd picked me up from the bar when I'd get too slammed to drive home. I guess in some crazy ass way, what he said made sense. But that didn't mean it was right.

Elizabeth delicately cleared her throat from behind Navi, standing mostly in the door. "Your mother arrives, Navi. And darkness falls soon." She turned that milky blue gaze on me and smiled encouragingly, like there was something hidden she and Navi shared that I didn't know—something about me. And if she hadn't been a ghost, I would have hugged her. "Perhaps this conversation would best be continued when things are not so tense."

Navi sniffed, sucked in a breath, and nodded, pulling that bad-ass persona back on. "Okay. Okay, we'll revisit this in the morning. When we're all still alive."

A sleek black jaguar pulled up in front of us and her dad got out. He was a huge man, towering over my six foot frame. Now I understood why—he had to be to survive their line of work. One day I would ask Navi *how* he'd survived with his eyes open so that he was hunted 24/7. Because I intended to survive the same way.

If she'd have me.

"Hi Dad." Navi threw herself into his arms like a little girl, hugging him tight. By that time, her mom was there too—an older version of Navi. Slight build, barely over a hundred pounds, and yet I could see the bands of steel running through her veins. She was undefeatable. Just like her daughter.

"Alec." Joanna said as I approached them. "It's been a while. Welcome to our world."

I chuckled. "Thanks."

"Joanna hasn't fought for years, but she still trains. You've got nothing to worry about."

"Thank you." I handed my keys to Navi. "Be careful, Angel."

She glanced at her parents, blushing again, and grabbed my hand, leading me back to the truck. "Alec, I don't—I don't know what will happen. Tonight, tomorrow, with us, with the world. But in case I don't make it back, I need you to know. I never stopped loving you, either. Please stay safe." She leaned up on her toes and brushed the barest of kisses across my lips. It took everything I had to not pull her against me and keep her there.

Instead I had to stand back and watch as she drove off in my truck to face hell alone.

CHAPTER TWENTY-EIGHT

Navi

WHERE ELIZABETH WAS WISE AND COMFORTING on the path through the lava tunnels to meet Death, Bryson was scared and very talkative. "What if he tries to steal my soul?"

"He's not going to steal your soul," I said. "He doesn't want your soul."

Bryson hung his head. "Maybe he should want my soul. I have a good soul. Konstanz says so all the time."

I smiled half-heartedly at him as I stopped to ghost-pat his shoulder. "I know, Bryson. I share a room with her."

"It doesn't bother you, does it? I don't know if we ever asked—does it bother you that we're together?"

I nearly choked. "No, Bryson. It does not bother me." Quite the opposite, really. About as far opposite as one could get.

"It's not that I don't still have feelings for you—"

I started walking again, faster this time. "I don't have time for this."

At that exact moment, my ghosts were fighting. Without

me. I'd warned them—I couldn't be there. They wouldn't think I'd abandoned them. But there was no Elizabeth with them. No me. They were facing the demons alone and it *killed* me. I felt like my insides were all squiggly and messed up, being here while they were out there.

"Right. Sorry."

Thank the sweet heavens he fell silent then, and we walked through the paths to hell in peace.

"Navi. I didn't expect you." Death rose up in front of us like one of my ghosts, and I, in all my demon-hunter strength and courage, screamed like a little girl and danced around in a circle. His red eyes crinkled in amusement. "I take it you didn't expect to see me, either."

I put a hand over my rapidly beating heart, trying to keep it in my chest. "Well I *did,* but not right here." I motioned to Bryson with my other hand. "I need your help."

Bryson made a sound that was a cross between a scream and a whimper and floated backward so fast I thought he was going to escape clear out of the cave. *Right.* I forget that to people not used to seeing Death on a regular basis, he could be a little scary. Heck, even to people used to seeing him on a regular basis, he was scary. Evidenced by my little freak out. "Bryson! Bryson, come back. It's okay! He's friendly!"

"I serve tea," Death said helpfully.

I smiled over at him, but Bryson only stared in horror and refused to come closer. "Bryson," I started, trying not to be impatient because he was totally justified in his fear but I *so* didn't have time for his panic attack right now. "You knew we were coming to see him. It's not like he's here to take your soul."

"I'm not?" Death asked with a wicked gleam in his red eyes.

"You're not helping." I twitched my lips at him, trying to decide whether to laugh or scowl. "Bryson, I already told you,

Death can't take you if you're in limbo."

"He's in limbo? Then how is he here?" Death gave up trying to lure Bryson closer and instead turned to me. And then I heard the hell hounds coming.

"Oh dear." I shot Death with my best pleading eyes. "They'll scare Bryson to death—er—to... to I don't know."

Death sighed, raising two fingers to his mouth. An ear-splitting whistle nearly shattered my skull and the ground stopped shaking. As much as I adored those dogs, now was not the time.

"Thank you." I nodded, couldn't figure out why I was nodding, and quit abruptly. "So here's the thing. Bryson was attacked by an asuwang. There are no physical wounds on his body but he can't get back in. And he opened the eyes of my..." Alec. What to call him. The boy I loved and had left in danger? The boy who broke my heart repeatedly and I didn't seem to care? "My friend, who is now a target. We can't figure out how to get his soul back in his body."

Death lost all hint of friendliness, crooking a finger at Bryson and glaring when Bryson still didn't move. "Come here," he snapped, and against his will Bryson's ghost self slid forward to Death's hands. I held my breath, waiting to see what would happen. I knew Death wouldn't take Bryson if it wasn't his time, but maybe it had been his time and something had gone wrong?

"The asuwang—did you kill it after the attack?" Death asked, somewhat distracted as he spun Bryson in a slow circle, scrutinizing him like the world's most terrifying tailor.

I nodded, relieved to know why I was nodding this time. "I think so, yes."

Death straightened, eying me. "You think so?"

I winced and ran a hand through my tangled hair, working out knots instead of meeting his gaze. "Well, I didn't exactly see Bryson. He was pretty sure I killed it though."

Now it was poor Bryson's turn to be under that gaze. Again. "How sure are you?"

Bryson finally found his voice. "I'm pretty sure, but there was a lot going on."

I closed my eyes. "Holy crap." Three asuwangs had escaped me. I'd killed the one that had attacked Bryson—or so we thought. But what if the one that had attacked Bryson was really one of the other two? "Is there a piece of his soul missing?" I whispered.

"Yes." Death pointed, a low beam illuminating from his fingertip like a flash light. Well that was a handy little trick I hadn't even known Death possessed. There, lit up under the glow, was a torn piece of calf. It wasn't gory or icky—it was like a piece of paper when you tear a little bit off. Just a ragged edge against the smoothness of the rest of the soul. "If you'd killed the asuwang that took it, the piece would have been freed and he would have been allowed to go back into his body."

"But I killed one of them, and by now the second should be dead—and the other one was chasing Alec."

Death shook his head, dim red eyes lighting the rest of his face inside his hood. "If the piece isn't freed by their deaths, then there must have been another—another that took the piece straight back to their witch because they sensed that he was important to you. The only way to free your friend is to kill the witch." His eyes brightened. "Which is convenient, because she's on her way to land now."

"What?" I gasped, stumbling backward like he'd punched me. "I have to go. I have to get to my souls!" Blast it all, I *knew* something big was coming, what with the massive attacks and constant deluge of bad guys every night. I knew she was creating a shell to come to land. If she made it to daylight, we were all screwed. She'd devour the entire town and there wouldn't be a thing I could do about it.

I turned to run, but Garmr rose stoically out of the lava in front of me, just as Death had. There was no puppy playfulness in him or his sister this time. "Get on. They will take us to the surface." Suddenly in Death's hands appeared his scythe, glowing red hot and angry. "I will ride with you this time."

"Umm, yeah. I can't ride your dog. I'll die."

"Don't be ridiculous. Your Agent blood protects you." Death sounded utterly exasperated as he leapt astride Garmr's sister. "They're only lethal to humans."

I didn't need to be told twice. My souls were in trouble. The entire city—maybe the country if we didn't stop the sea witch—was in trouble. I clambered up Garmr's side and settled on his back, gripping the poisoned fur. "Bryson! Stay out of her reach!" I yelled as Garmr leaped forward, bounding through the lava tunnels so fast it blurred my vision, and all I could do was follow Death.

"Gwendolyn," he yelled over his shoulder.

Confused, I sat up and smacked my head on the jagged edge of petrified lava. "What?" I winced as the blood soaked down my temple, but I could already feel it healing. *Thank you, moon.*

"Her name," Death motioned easily to the giant, flaming dog he was riding. "Is Gwendolyn."

We burst from the cave. Bryson was already there, waiting anxiously just beyond the entrance. He backed away and pointed silently down the beach.

Toward Devil's Gate.

My army was there, fighting valiantly, holding the demons at bay. But more arose with each wave, crawling toward them. And the sea, where the gate dropped and I knew the doorway to be, bubbled and steamed and hissed.

I could barely speak around the horror in my throat. "She's rising."

CHAPTER TWENTY-NINE

Alec

"SO I HEAR YOU'VE BEEN GIVING Navi quite a bit of trouble lately." Joanna raised a perfectly arched eyebrow at me as I paced in front of the truck. There was nothing for as far as I could see but rolling hills and yellow grasses. And us. And our cars. And a lot of dark. No ghosts, no demons, no Navi.

"I have." I nodded, not about to piss off her mom. "I'm sorry."

She studied me with those wise, wise brown eyes—more wise than they should have been for as young as she was. And then she nodded. "I know."

I turned to Blair, Navi's dad, the one picking his fingernails with an overly large pocket knife. He'd scared the crap out of me in high school, and that was before I'd broken her heart.

Twice.

"Can—can I ask you something?"

He looked up from his knife. "Yep." He had black hair and light brown eyes, and they were kind eyes, so even though I worried a little that he would hurl that knife at my face, the rational side of me knew he wouldn't.

"How—how do you survive? You're a constant target, right? Since you can see them... how do you not die?"

He tipped his head to the side, considering me with the same wisdom Joanna had. He pursed his lips and set his knife aside, pushing away from the car. "If you really want to make a life with her, Alec, you have to realize something." His eyes were infinitely sad as he laid a hand on my shoulder. I wondered how he saw right through me so easily, how he knew I wanted her for forever with just that one question. "You will always be a target. You will never be safe. You'll move farther inland, which helps, but as long as the sea witch is out there, you'll be a target. They'll hunt you, even more so because the sea witch will realize that you are a tool to hurt the thing she hates most. The Soul's Agent."

I swallowed hard. "But—but you're still alive."

Joanna smiled gently, sliding an arm around my waist and leaning her head against my shoulder. "He traveled a great deal. To stay away from the ocean and out of her reach while I fought her from here. When I retired, we became less of a threat. I don't hunt them anymore, but they still hunt me." She nodded slowly, breathing deeply before she continued, "But remember this when considering your choices." Her voice was so similar to Navi's it made my heart ache. "Navi is ten times more powerful than I ever was. Each generation becomes stronger, and one day we will rid the ocean of the sea witches and we'll be free."

"And one more thing to consider." Elizabeth, who had faded away a while ago so that I thought she'd left us, appeared in front of me. "Navi is the only agent in the history of them all to have ghosts give up their freedom to fight beside her."

Her words, so quiet and so calm, nearly knocked my feet

out from under me. "The only one—ever?" She nodded. I knew Navi was sweet. I knew people loved her. I just hadn't, until that very moment, realized there were people out there that loved her as much as I did.

Joanna tensed and then left me, stalking over to the car and pulling swords and a rifle out of the trunk. Of a jaguar. My life had gotten so surreal over the past two days that it the insanity of it all barely fazed me. She handed the gun to Blair, and both of them studied the road leading west.

It was coming.

But it wasn't here yet. I could tell by the way her shoulders relaxed and she resumed pacing like a caged lion—sleek and deadly and beautiful. "Our weapons can't kill it. But we can weaken it and make it easier for Elizabeth."

Elizabeth waited a little in front of the rest of us, like she was eager for the fight. She wasn't much of a talker. I got the feeling she didn't like people much, except Navi. And for her, she seemed willing to protect us all.

"Can I ask you one more thing—one thing I should have asked years ago?" I approached cautiously.

Blair cut me off. "There's a baseball bat in the car."

"I'm really good with guns." I looked pointedly at the one in his hands. "And that wasn't my question."

"Sorry, kid. This one's mine. Hopefully we'll keep it away from you so the bat won't be necessary."

Joanna frowned at him before turning to me, but I could tell I only had half her attention. This was too important to wait until a better time, though. "Every night since I met her, in seventh grade—" I could see dread building in Joanna, by the way she curled in on herself like she knew what was coming. But I couldn't stop talking now. It was like a flood gate was opened and the horror came flooding out. "I have these nightmares where I watch Navi being killed and I can't stop it. I can't do anything about it. Every night, except when she's with me." I finished in a rush and prayed the pain in her eyes was because I'd endured a lifetime of watching the girl I loved die every night.

"I've never seen this in my own experience." She started carefully, like she was surrounding the discussion, trying to decide how best to attack it. "It's only been a rumor in our inner circles. Some say it is Fate, warning you so that when it happens, it doesn't hurt you so much."

I snorted. Right, because watching it over and over made it so much better.

A ghost of a smile graced her lips. "Others say it is Fate warning you—that you will be her downfall."

As I felt the blood drain from my face and my heart freeze in my chest, she rushed to continue, "But I believe, as do many others, that it is Fate giving you the information you need to stop it. Perhaps that's why things between you two have always been so very deep. You were meant to save her."

Or kill her. You know, whichever.

"Joanna." Elizabeth pointed into the darkness, where there was barely a rustle of movement through the long grasses. "It comes."

"Get that bat, boy." Blair motioned back to the car with his head before raising the rifle to his shoulder, sighting through the scope. Obediently, I hurried to the trunk, grinning when I saw what he called a baseball bat—an over sized club with spikes all the way around it. I pitied the ball that got hit with that thing. I hefted it in my hand to get the feel of it, watching as Joanna raised her swords. Elizabeth suddenly had a shimmering ax in her hands that seemed to draw power from the moonlight.

Those must be the soul blades they'd mentioned this morning.

The relief I felt at a weapon that could finally kill this thing was enough to knock me flat. And that relief made me pause. Maybe I wasn't strong enough to be in Navi's dangerous life. Maybe I wasn't brave enough.

Those eyes, her voice, flashed across my mind like she was there in front of me. My Angel. And I knew it didn't matter if I was a coward or weak. It didn't matter how scared I was—with Navi, I didn't have a choice. I had to be in her life. I had to have her in my arms.

That was it. Nothing else mattered.

The demon leaped out of the grass and onto the road with an inhuman scream that would haunt my every waking moment for the rest of my life. It was different now— it seemed to be a mix of a spider and a dog with a human-like face, and its red glowing eyes were focused with so much fury right on me.

Suddenly my spiked bat didn't seem so comforting.

It screamed again, crawling so fast it blurred, straight at us, like Joanna and Blair and their weapons didn't matter at all. And I thought maybe they didn't and I was going to die and I was glad that I had told Navi I loved her.

And then Blair fired the gun.

It hit the thing in the face and sent it hurtling backward into the grass. There was no way it could survive that. Even though I *knew* only the soul blades could kill the demons, it seemed impossible to come back from a hit in the face by a bullet.

But it did.

Shrieking, it rolled back on its feet, black blood gushing from the wound. But it only seemed angrier. Blair reloaded but Joanna was already in motion, flying through the air like an acrobat, swords glinting in the moonlight. They didn't glow, like Elizabeth's, but they moved so fast they sung in the darkness, chopping at the creature as it screeched and lunged with its claws. Elizabeth threw herself into the battle, and now I could see the real damage their blades could do.

But it wasn't enough.

It threw them off as Blair's gun exploded again, and the thing got hit again, but it was back on its feet and racing toward me faster than ever, bleeding from a thousand different wounds. It shrieked and lunged and I, suddenly grateful for twelve years of baseball practices, swung that bat for all I was worth. I felt it connect, felt the spikes run deep, felt the claw graze my chest, and then it flew backward.

Right into Joanna's battle ax.

Impaled and trapped, it fought to free itself. But it wasn't trying to attack Joanna or Elizabeth who walked right in front of it.

Me. Just me. It only wanted me.

Elizabeth raised her sword, long and delicate and so fitting for her ghostly frame, and swung it down across its neck. The scream coming from the broken, trapped demon was silenced as the head rolled away from the body.

A soul, one I hadn't even seen until now, shook itself free. It was a woman I'd seen around town. She sobbed and threw herself into Elizabeth's arms. Elizabeth patted her on the back and spoke low, soothing words and watched me over the woman's ghostly head. A brief smile lit her face and she nodded.

"It is done," she said.

Four of us against one demon and we'd barely survived. But Navi was ten times more powerful than her mother, and her blades would kill these things.

I prayed that my tough little Angel was strong enough to fight them all.

CHAPTER THIRTY

Navi

SUDDEN, PARALYZING FEAR FLOODED THROUGH ME and I found myself frozen to the spot. "Death, help me," I whispered.

"She's not going to wait for your bravery, Navi. And your souls need you now. Pull it together!" His scythe gleamed in the moonlight. Like my blades, given power by the moon. Like my blades.

My blades.

Kali and Golly.

I was free, my hands reaching almost without my brain telling them to, grabbing my swords. Their familiar weight gave me strength. "Let's go, Garmr!" I yelled. He barked, the sound sending waves across the beach, knocking my souls off their feet and sending the demons reeling backward into the water.

"Nice!" I raised my swords. "Let's do it again! Souls!" I screamed. "Give him some room!"

My souls fled backward, creating a tunnel straight to the demons. Garmr and Gwendolyn bounded forward, barking and snarling as flames leaped from their mouths and melted the sand, turning it into swirling molten glass.

The demons screeched, trying to go around. My army swarmed them, meeting them at the water's edge. I hurled myself from Garmr's back and landed in a crouch on the other side of the quickly cooling glass.

"Navi!" Bryson appeared next to me. "I know you're busy. I just—just be careful, okay? Konstanz can't lose us both." And then he was gone, just like that. Hopefully somewhere far away from this hellish place, where he was safe.

The sea witch rose out of the water in front of me. I'd heard rumors, but hadn't been prepared for her beauty. Long blond hair swirled around her, silver waves sliding through it. Wide, sea-green eyes stared at me with such a furious hatred my blood ran cold. She raised her hand with a shriek, and the water rose with her. "Garmr, run!" I screamed as she threw the waves over us all.

Because flaming dogs and water do not mix.

It dragged me out toward sea, toward her doorway. I coughed and choked as I fought my way back to the sand, kicking hard through the water. She was making her way up the beach by the time I got back on my feet. Thankfully, Garmr and Gwendolyn stood beyond her water's reach, barking and snarling, making each step she took as difficult as possible.

Death rose from Gwendolyn's back, scythe shooting flames of its own.

"This is not your fight to be involved in, Death." Her voice was like silk, pulling me toward her, lulling me into a comfortable trance. "You are not allowed to interfere."

"You attacked my dogs. I think that gives me the right." Death sounded almost conversational. I waded out of the water and hit the beach, leveling my swords. I could see the souls, hundreds of thousands, caught on her back, creating a protection against the rising sun. If we didn't force her back into the water, they'd all be lost.

Bryson would be lost.

I looked around wildly, but there was so much movement, so much flurrying and screaming and slicing. And then I caught sight of him, fighting with borrowed weapons, across the beach from me, near the northern wall of Devil's Gate's interior. I was so afraid for him that I nearly found myself paralyzed again, and without Elizabeth or Death to tell me to snap out of it.

Which means I had to tell myself. "Knock it off, Navi," I snarled. Bryson would be okay. He would fight and if he was taken, I would save him, just like I would any of my other souls. Leaping out of the water onto damp sand, I ran stealthily at the sea witch. She had the body of an octopus, with eight legs like in the Little Mermaid fairytale, and those legs protected her torso.

"Go back to your domain, Death." She sang sweetly, but it had no effect on him.

"No." He lowered his scythe, meeting my eyes and as the fire shot across the beach at her, I raced forward, slipping and sliding across the glass. The dogs barked, the ground shook, the sand melted and burned my feet and legs. And I ran. I threw myself at her just as Death's fire hit her, whirling Kali and Golly over my head and driving them down. She screamed and screamed as her legs flailed around her, beating at Death's flames, trying to lunge free of my swords.

One leg collapsed and withered into dry, dead seaweed. "Seven more," I panted. Souls that had been caught on the leg were freed and raced away, but some—some of them stayed, picking up fallen weapons. I watched them in shock, wondering how they found the courage. Which was stupid—you never watch souls in shock while you're within range of sea witch legs. Six more swung around and I didn't move fast enough—I threw myself back but slid on the half-cooled glass, and stumbled as three legs at once slammed into my body. Ribs cracked and snapped as I flew through the air, landing hard half in the water, half out. Demons swarmed me, their claws stabbing and pulling at my soul.

But my army would not let me go. They fell on the demons as I struggled to rise to my feet, bloody and broken but not beaten. I swung my swords up, chanting the ancient lyrics, and more ghosts rose from the ground around us as my swords hummed with me. I slashed my way free, feeling every hit, every soul freed. Whirling between claws and teeth, I scissored Kali and Golly through the demon's head. It gurgled and collapsed and I sprang on top of it, using it as a launching pad to throw myself onto the back of another demon. My blades rammed into its neck and I pulled them apart, slicing through the neck. The head rolled free.

I felt claws tearing at my skin, tugging on my soul, and I could feel the moon's power fading. I wasn't healing as fast or moving as fast. None of us were. The sun was rising and Death still fought the sea witch, Garmr and Gwendolyn keeping her away from the walls of Devil's Gate with their fierce, flame-ridden barks. She couldn't get around them, but unless we drove her back into the ocean, it wouldn't matter soon.

Ignoring the pain, ignoring the screams of my souls, I threw myself over the frenzied bodies and landed on the other side. The demons followed me, of course they followed me, but I ran faster than they did, around the glass to her side. I hurtled Kali through the air, watching in satisfaction as it shot past the legs and impaled itself into her side. "Kali, stay," I murmured when it shimmered and started to return to me. I needed it to stay there and cause more damage.

She screamed, her legs flailing, but I danced out of the way, using Golly to slice through the demons nearest me.

They fell under the onslaught. We were gaining the upper hand. Death's scythe leveled whole lines of demons at once, when he wasn't fighting the sea witch.

She jerked her hands up with a skull-shattering shriek, throwing more water at me. I gasped for air, fighting to stay on the sand as the waves tugged me out, toward the ocean, toward her lair. "You will not beat me," I growled under my breath as I fought my way back to her side.

"Hey you stupid monster!" My blood froze as a kitchen knife whizzed past my face, embedding itself into the witch's neck. "Leave her alone!"

Konstanz. Konstanz was here.

"Noooo," I moaned as she climbed over the rock into the interior.

"I told you," she yelled, as if it were possible to hear me over all the screaming, "I wouldn't abandon you again!" Somehow, despite how careful I was, we'd opened her eyes. And now she thought she could save me. My heart shattered in my chest—more painful than when Alec had broken it, more painful than anything, *ever.*

The demons saw her, their focus suddenly taken from me and my army, and they raced toward her, climbing the wall like possessed spiders. "Konstanz, run!" I screamed, leaving the sea witch to go after her pets. My army joined me, the ghosts leaping up the sides of rock to hover in the air—a nifty little trick that I couldn't do.

And Konstanz, my brave, sweet friend Konstanz, who had been by my side through so much, stood on the rock like a goddess and hurtled sharp kitchen utensils like a professional knife thrower.

Bryson appeared next to her, swinging his borrowed blades like he'd been born to it, bashing demon faces when they got too close. "We'll protect her, Navi!" Don yelled as he raced past me. "Kill the witch!"

Right, the witch. It took more will than I knew I possessed, but I spun and ran back across the beach. The sea witch was distracted by Death, throwing water and screaming and trying to lure him close enough that she could catch him, and she didn't see me coming.

Blood gushed from the wound in her neck, and from the wound in her side. I slid across the glass, using it to my advantage this time, skidding under her legs as I grabbed Kali and wrenched it free, causing as much damage as possible.

I felt the legs hit me, the suckers attach, the overwhelming pull of my soul. I could feel it breaking free from my body and I saw Konstanz fighting and Alec telling me he loved me and my mother training me and riding Garmr and all these memories.

But I wasn't done yet. She'd killed my grandmother and she could kill me too, but I was taking her down with me. Because if she lived, Konstanz, Alec, my dad—they were all in danger forever.

I couldn't let that happen.

I swung the blades sideways, hitting the legs that held my soul and twisted them apart, like separating a head of lettuce. She shrieked as a leg was wrenched away from her body. It writhed on the beach before withering away and the souls escaped. I closed my eyes and tugged my own soul back, feeling it settle as the first rays of the sun hit the top of the wall.

"Death! We're out of time!" I yelled. He nodded. Garmr roared forward, snapping and lunging, fangs bared. He caught a leg in his teeth and shook until it fell off. Gwendolyn followed and Death, now standing alone, hit the witch again and again with flames from his scythe.

I slid into the space left from the removed legs and attacked her body. I felt other legs hit me, break me, attach and fall off, tug at my soul, and give up, but I kept swinging and plunging, dancing out of the way when I could and taking the hits when I couldn't.

She started to move back. Back toward her water, trying to escape the dogs or trying to lure them into the waves—I wasn't sure which.

I stayed with her. She swung at me, trying to get me out of her weak spot. With every hit, I freed a soul. With every stab and every swing I freed more. She didn't have enough souls left to protect her from the sun, but she didn't seem to care. Her focus now was me—she wanted me dead. I was covered in her blood and in my blood, and I wasn't healing like I would have in the moonlight. I couldn't check on Konstanz or Bryson. I had to move as fast as she did, even knowing that once we reached the water, I had no way out.

I'd go down with her.

It didn't matter though. I was grateful I had told Alec I loved him. I was grateful I got to see my mom and dad one last time.

We hit the water. I felt her gathering it, ready to wash me into the doorway with her. She was giving up her chance at freedom to take my soul, and there was nothing I could do about it.

The waves washed over me. The doorway shimmered in the inky blackness below us, swirling like a whirlpool. She laughed as we were drawn toward it, lulling me into a trance even as it sent terror shooting down my spine.

Teeth chomped around my ankle, very hot teeth that burned my skin and shattered the bone. I screamed, water filling my lungs as I was dragged back, back toward the beach and the sun and life and away from her doorway.

She shrieked in fury, reaching for me, but she was too far away. Her claws swiped across my throat but not enough to reach my soul, and then she was gone and I was on the beach. The sun shone weakly through the clouds.

"At least for today. I won for today. And I freed souls. But not Bryson's." I struggled to sit up so I could see him. "I didn't free yours. So I'm not done yet."

Alec watched me, dark blue eyes so intense I could barely breathe. Or that might have been the broken ribs. "I love you, Navi. Whatever you choose, I will be by your side."

"I love you, too, Alec." Such strength in those few words. So much that I needed to tell him, to explain, to forgive. But that would have to come later.

With herculean effort, I turned away to glare at the ocean. "No. I'm not done. Next time she comes I'll be better prepared. I'll gather more forces. She won't escape back into the ocean again."

CHAPTER THIRTY-ONE

Alec

"ARE YOU SURE YOU'RE OKAY TO fight again tonight? You were pretty much dead this morning." Bryson floated backward in front of Navi as she stalked toward the door.

She pointed at the window, where the full moon gleamed across the glass. "I'm fine. The sea witch lost a lot of her forces, but that isn't going to stop her. They'll come tonight, and tomorrow, and the next day… and they'll hunt Alec and Konstanz. Unless I stop them."

In front of my eyes, her long, lethal swords shimmered to life against her back. "What can we do to help?" Konstanz asked, slowly waving her hand through Bryson's ghostly arm.

"Will you stop that?" He pulled his arm away, scowling. "It's weird."

"I'm a vet. I'm curious!"

"Stay here. Inside. If any of the demons get past my army, my mom will be able to hold them off until I get back here."

She glanced at me, a flush staining her pretty face. We hadn't had a chance to talk yet, since she'd been comatose for most of the day. Until the moon had risen, and her wounds had healed before my eyes, and she'd popped up like a watered flower. Ten minutes later, we were all trying to get her to go back to bed.

But my Angel, she wouldn't do it.

I crossed the room, aware of her parents both watching curiously, and Elizabeth swinging her sword through the air in impatient boredom. Bryson had weapons, too—apparently he thought he was a warrior now. I turned my back on all of them, tugging Navi against my chest. "You're going to start training me tomorrow, right?" I smiled down at her, my blood roaring in my ears as her big eyes landed on my mouth and stayed there.

"What?" she asked, leaning into me, until I could feel every curve of her, molding against me. I chuckled, although it took everything I had not to drag her back to her bedroom right then and show her how much I needed her. But we couldn't do that, and if I tried, her dad would probably skin me alive.

So instead, I tipped her chin up until her eyes found mine. "Training. Tomorrow?"

She nodded, her lips quirking just a bit. "Yes. Training. Tomorrow."

Unable to control myself any longer, I lowered my head, trying to devour her. She gasped against my mouth as her hands clenched and unclenched against my chest. She rose on her tiptoes and bit my bottom lip, not hard but enough that I wouldn't be able to think straight for the next year, at least. Then she dragged herself away from me, raising an eyebrow. "Get some rest tonight."

I shook my head, running a shaking hand through my hair. The girl made my knees weak. "I'll wait up. If you think I'm ever sleeping without you again, you're crazy, Angel."

She grinned, her entire face lighting up. Once more, she

kissed me—light and brief—and then whirled away and was gone, disappearing into the darkness like her ghosts. Bryson and Elizabeth went after her.

"Well. This has been interesting. I'm gonna go pick out my outfit for training tomorrow. I might need to buy some new shoes…" Konstanz disappeared down the hall and I wondered how on earth she could be concerned with shoes when there were demons trying to fight their way through a ghostly army to eat us alive.

Blair smacked me on the shoulder as he walked by. "Welcome to the family, kid. Break her heart again, and you'll wish the demons had got you."

I tried to swallow the terror sized lump in my throat. "No sir. I'm not going to break her heart. Not ever again."

ABOUT THE AUTHOR

WENDY KNIGHT was born and raised in Utah by a wonderful family who spoiled her rotten because she was the baby. Now she spends her time driving her husband crazy with her many eccentricities (no water after five, terror when faced with a live phone call…). She also enjoys chasing her three adorable kids, playing tennis, watching football, reading, and hiking. Camping is also big: her family is slowly working toward a goal of seeing all the National Parks in the U.S.

You can usually find her with at least one Pepsi nearby, wearing ridiculously high heels for whatever the occasion may be. And if everything works out just right, she will also be writing.

ALSO BY WENDY KNIGHT

Fate on Fire Series
Feudlings
Feudlings in Flames
Feudlings in Sight
Feudlings in Smoke
Spark of a Feudling

Riders of Paradesos Series
Warrior Beautiful
Warrior Everlasting

Gates of Atlantis Series
Banshee at the Gate

Stand-Alone
Shattered Assassin
Star-Crossed Hurricane
(also available in *Trouble Enough: A Collection*)
Rocker Boy

Coming Soon
Warrior Innocent
With These Wings

Wendy
KNIGHT
BOOKS

Made in the USA
Middletown, DE
25 November 2022

16029257R00151